SERAPHIM

SERAPHIM

JOSHUA PERRY

A NOVEL

MELVILLE HOUSE
BROOKLYN • LONDON

Seraphim

First published in 2024 by Melville House
Copyright © 2023 by Joshua Perry

First Melville House Printing: May 2024

Melville House Publishing
46 John Street
Brooklyn, NY 11201
and
Melville House UK
Suite 2000
16/18 Woodford Road
London E7 0HA

mhpbooks.com
@melvillehouse

ISBN: 978-1-68589-113-8
ISBN: 978-1-68589-114-5 (eBook)

Library of Congress Control Number: 2024932739

Designed by Kyle Kabel

Printed in the United States of America

1 3 5 7 9 10 8 6 4 2

A catalog record for this book is available from the Library of Congress

For Anna—

When you lost your voice one day in court, I stood with you at the podium, repeating out loud what you whispered in my ear:

How to be brave, not just talk tough; how to tell a hard truth; how to keep fighting when you're afraid. Justice and devotion.

I thought: *I want my girls to be like this.*

They are, our daughters. They sound just like you.

But how can that be?
Isn't it true—
Wherever there's judgment, there can be no justice.
And if there's justice, there can be no judgment.
—Talmud, Sanhedrin 6b

"This is how we wear our pants in my Section!"
—Orleans Parish Criminal District Court Judge

Apprehension

They used to put dogs on the boys. Maybe they still do. The prisoners would shuffle in—leg shackles, handcuffs, belly chains, by the dozen—and there would be some kid with arm or side or neck in bandages, dirty after just a few hours at the jail, stained red-brown with seeping blood. It smelled like the kid was already losing something, like rot had already set in.

Ben and Boris once went to a yard off Claiborne Avenue where a kid had gotten himself arrested. The police said he'd broken into a school to shoot basketballs in the dark gym. He ran when he heard the squad cars and hid under a filthy mattress in the summer-hot back bedroom of a shotgun, empty now for two years since the storm. The police cordoned off the block and sent dogs in. Afterward there was blood on the mattress and blood all over the ankle-deep trash and shit on the floor. At First Appearances the kid had staples in his cheek, ear, hand, leg.

Boris said:

"He needs to see a doctor."

The judge said:

"He was in good enough shape to run. Fifteen thousand dollar bond, cash or surety."

"It's a misdemeanor and he's eighteen, in school, he's not a flight risk—"

"Not anymore." Laughter from all the freemen assembled. "Fifteen thousand dollars, cash or surety."

The police, in their glory—the brave first responders, the ones who stayed. The city was theirs. So they kicked the boys and men until they broke, beat them up against the hoods of cars. The blank windows like nobody was watching, a city without the constraints of society. The only record of their depredations was in their reports, strange empty words in the shape of language but without any meaning: *We relocated to the sideyard whereupon Officer Bronco alerted and assisted in the apprehension of the Black male.* The dogs got names and the boys didn't.

It was always the boys who were dumb enough to run, through unsettled blocks, between abandoned garages, over broken fences, into vacant houses. There were hiding places everywhere. The joke was that the police didn't even need the dogs. They could have just waited. Boys only hide for a little while. Boys always run home in the end.

2

Perp Walk

Robert held the gun in his hand the whole way home. Nobody—at least nobody who would come to court—saw him running and no cameras caught it either. He didn't throw out his sweatshirt but slept in it that Saturday night and wore it the next day when the story was all over the news and was still wearing it Monday morning when the police came to get him at school. It was, after all, his only sweatshirt.

Ben would check, last thing every night and first thing every morning, for the passing of old clients and the advent of new ones. It started like this: *Black Male Shot on St. Bernard Avenue.* By the next news cycle: *Shooting Claims Life of 16-Year-Old.* That night they'd put the kid's name in the papers, but usually someone would already have called Ben. He'd go see the mo with an aluminum tray of wings or whatever he could buy at the closest corner. The front room of the house filled with relatives and neighbors and friends. He'd pick up some money on the way over because the family was always trying to figure out how to pay for the funeral. A couple days later, if he had the courage to swing back by, the family would still be sitting around the living room with the blinds closed, trying to dream up money.

That Monday morning after someone murdered Lillie Scott— *Recovery Leader Shot on Kerlerec*—Ben and Boris were up in their office catty-corner from the courthouse getting costumed up in their ties like grownups.

3

"You saw that woman. In the Marigny."

Ben, cleaning something white and flaky from his sleeve with saliva and a gray paper towel: "Maybe it was a boyfriend?"

Loop and through, with a red silk number that looked expensive. Boris had been a fancy lawyer before New Orleans.

"It was one shot in the chest. Some kid fucked up a robbery."

"No arrest?"

"Not yet."

Ben tucked two disposable pens in an inside pocket, one for himself and the other in case a client needed to sign something. He chewed his pens and didn't want to give a client something he'd drooled all over. Or put something in his mouth that a client had held. He said:

"This one's yours."

"I covered for you last week, my dude."

"I was in trial. Which I lost. Pity me."

"I bought you a drink."

So there was Ben when the arrest was announced later that day— *7th Ward Arrest in Scott Killing*—and the van pulled up outside the jail's sally port. The thick-bodied deputies in the special transport unit moved the kid slow and the reporters crowded around. The public wanted to know. In January of 2008, the city was in one of those periods of painful sensitivity to its endemic violence, like waking with a start at midnight suddenly alert to the sounds in the darkness. It was worse though than just a regular murder. The dead woman was a daughter of the city's Creole royalty. She'd been walking home from her restaurant, one of the first new places to open after the storm. The Hot Potato went out of its way to hire people who were down on their luck: Just back to town, from the storm or from prison.

Ben stopped short when the scrum broke and he saw who the kid was. He had his job to do, though. He swam through the reporters and talked directly into the kid's ear.

"I'm coming to see you. Don't talk to anyone until I get there."

The gate rolled open and the deputies and reporters paused for more shouts and camera snaps. The TV people smelled like talcum powder.

"Can you hear me?"

His head hanging down. Ben, his lips inches from the boy's ear: "Robert, it's Ben Alder. Robert. Remember me?"

Robert looked up. Ben had once gone into a jail cell and found a ten-year-old in handcuffs. The boy cried until Ben brought him coloring books. That's how it was.

"Where's Mr. Boris?"

"I'm your lawyer."

Imagine a kid, on public display for his evil, looking more dejected just because he found out you're his lawyer. Ben said:

"At least for right now."

Quiet and dry:

"Okay."

"Listen. You can't use the phone. It's all recorded."

"Okay."

"Not to your mom, not to anyone, until I see you."

"Okay."

"Say it back to me. Are you going to talk on the phone?"

A headshake you could barely see:

"No."

"Are you going to talk to anyone about your arrest?"

"No."

"What are you going to do if someone asks?"

"I could tell them I don't know what happened."

"That's talking."

"Okay."

"*I want my lawyer.* Nothing else. That's all you can say."

Robert had given what the papers called a confession and Ben called a statement. Anyhow he'd told the police, on tape, that he killed Lillie Scott. Murder was life in prison, and life meant life. A kid with wide, dark eyes. They pulled Robert away and took him in

through the gate with his head down again and walked him across
the driveway to a loading dock, the sheriff's front door. There they
stood for ten minutes, a deputy on each of Robert's elbows, Robert
with his head below his shoulders, waiting for someone to open up.
Like everything else at the jail, it was built for scale and efficiency but
operated by whim and chance.

After the reporters had cleared, Ben sat down on some steps and
called Boris.

"Did you get him out?"

"He's on his way to Disney World."

"Then this one doesn't count. You get the next one too."

"It's Robert Johnson."

"My Robert Johnson?"

"Ours."

The sheriff had a special juvenile tier. That's where they kept Robert,
in double-bunked cells where the boys went naked from the waist
up so nobody could pull their shirts over their heads and blind them
in a fight. It was just a few minutes' walk from the public defender's
office, past the police headquarters and a couple blocks of flooded-out
jail buildings and empty lots. The faded teal and beige of the sheriff's
insignia stenciled on warehouse walls; weeds climbing chain-link
fences; broken streets verging into fields of uneven green, a layer of
sediment over everything. Pocked by pools of standing rainwater and
banked by unkempt tumbles of razor wire. Over against the highway:
Rusted school buses and new dump trucks parked on a vast, cracked
concrete slab where something incalculably heavy and indescribably
awful had been lifted or scoured away.

3

Investigation

At the beginning Ben had almost nothing from the police, just the same two pieces of paper they gave him for every arrest. On top was the *face sheet*, with a blurred little mug shot and some demographic and charge information. Behind the face sheet was the *gist*, because it gave just the gist of what happened, according to the detective who made the arrest. A paragraph written in long-hand and signed to attest to its truth, such as it was. *On January 12, 2008, Lillie Scott, B/F, age 36, found on Kerlerec Street with a single gunshot wound to the chest. DOA. On January 14, the undersigned received information that led to the development of a suspect, Robert Johnson, B/M, age 16. Robert Johnson was questioned and, upon being advised of his rights, gave a recorded confession.* Ben needed to run all the rest down himself. It could be months before the police told him anything more about the case, and even then they couldn't be relied on to tell the truth or turn over all the evidence. Because they were harried and didn't have time, or arrogant and thought it was all wrapped up, or corrupt and deliberately hiding things, or just bad at their jobs.

He went to see Robert that same night after the perp walk. Robert was handsome: Tall and square-shouldered and square-jawed. He had hair on his upper lip; a pencil mustache, not like the ratty scruff of other kids. A thin scar on his forehead, across his right temple. They sat down across from each other in the juvenile unit, plexiglass between them. Robert still mostly looking down.

"It looks like we're going to have to fight, Robert."

Robert leaned back just a little bit.

"Not against each other. On the same team. We're going to have to fight hard to try and beat these charges."

Robert nodded and didn't say anything. You could have mistaken him for slow, but he wasn't. This was just the way some kids got. It was just shock.

There was no reason to ask if he'd killed Lillie Scott. The police thought he had. Ben only asked about the things he needed to know, and innocence wasn't one of them. How did Robert get picked up? They came to his school and talked to him and then arrested him. Where had he been the night of the shooting? Down Bourbon, into the Seventh Ward—the Marigny? *Yeah, the Seventh Ward, you know?*— then back home. Ben didn't ask why Robert had been out there. Kids always heard *why* as an accusation. What other people did Robert see that night? Nobody. He'd been alone all night. That didn't sound right—what kind of a kid goes out alone to the French Quarter on a Saturday night?—but it wasn't time to push him. Did Robert have anything else he needed to ask, or say? *I need to talk to my dad.* Your stepdad? *My real dad.* Where can I find him? *He's not always in the same place.* What are his places? *He has a lot of places.* What's his name? *I have his name.* Robert Johnson? *Johnson's my mom. McTell is my dad.* McTell? That's your dad? Robert McTell? *You know him?* No, no. The name sounded familiar, that's all.

Of course it didn't really go like that. But everything is entered into evidence through a witness, and every witness has his biases. A witness doesn't see or hear or say things exactly as they are but instead as he is. That's a truism. Robert Johnson wasn't the witness. That was Ben Alder, a Jewish guy from a college town in Massachusetts, former seminarian, child to a linguist since passed on and an employment lawyer who was proud of the work that Ben did for *those unfortunate people* in New Orleans. Robert was one of the unfortunates. He didn't talk like Ben. But some things you can't really even bear witness to, because they're not yours to see, and some words you can't say because they're not yours to speak. It's just what's possible and what isn't.

Ben didn't try to talk to the boy's dad, at least not just then. Instead, the next night he and Boris went to Bourbon Street at the same time Robert Johnson himself had walked down the street before the shooting. They could talk to the bouncers, the dealers, the beggars, whoever might have been out there and seen something. The street was neon and shadow, the air orange and lime green, the revelers like actors on a stage walking through pools of light and darkness. Three kids, fifteen or sixteen, tap-danced outside a restaurant. It was after curfew, around 10:30 p.m. One of the kids did a row of backflips on the cobblestones. A small, tipsy crowd applauded and threw money in the kids' top hats. Ben waited until they stopped for a minute and went to lean against the wall, mopping their foreheads.

"I'm with the public defender's office."

Blank looks. But Ben wanted to build sympathy:

"I work for a young man about your age who got arrested. I'm his lawyer."

The kids looked at each other. One said:

"We don't know anything about that."

"I'm trying to help him. He was arrested Saturday night. Were you out here then?"

"The police already asked us."

"I'd like you to tell me about that."

The kids looked at each other. They seemed to shrug without using their shoulders.

"I told them the same thing I'm telling you," said one of the kids. He put down his water bottle. "I don't do that."

"I'm not asking you to snitch—"

"I mean, sir," said the kid, talking louder, "that I don't perform sexual favors in exchange for monetary remuneration."

"He's just a child," said another of the kids. "Don't proposition him, sir!"

Very loudly. A couple of people walking by looked in their direction. Ben took a step away.

"I get it," he said.

"No," shouted the first one, drawing back in horror. "I'm not going to suck your dick in an alleyway for five dollars! Sir!"

Ben walked quickly away. Boris stayed a second to laugh with the kids and slap a couple of hands.

Ben showed Robert's picture to some of the bouncers. The ones who knew what a public defender is just moved him out of the way so they could check IDs and usher customers in. Others got confused between public defenders and prosecutors, and treated him like law enforcement. Made a big show of being strict on IDs as long as he was around. But they hadn't seen Robert Johnson on Saturday, and wondered what he's accused of, anyhow.

It was almost one in the morning when Ben and Boris got downriver to the place Lillie Scott was shot and died. You want to go to the scene at the same time it happened, to see foot traffic and lighting. Nobody was around. Boris took pictures. With a measuring wheel he counted off forty-six feet from the corner. They went up to the St. Roch neighborhood and walked from the restaurant Lillie Scott had owned to where she was killed. It took fifteen minutes, going slow. The ground was littered with cans and fans, wet paper, left over from earlier that day when Lillie's friends had mourned her with a second-line parade. Like in the French Quarter, Ben and Boris made a list of all the security cameras along the way. Ben would come back in daylight and try to collect footage.

These kids were their shared project, Boris and Ben. Kids sixteen years old and younger started out in juvenile court, but some were sent to be prosecuted as adults. They'd face adult punishments, too—twenty or forty or ninety-nine years, or life for a murder. The prosecutor chose which ones graduated to adult court. Mostly fifteen or sixteen years old, mostly accused of murder or rape or armed robbery. Ben and Boris had asked to represent all of them. They were both still pretty new to the job—they were post-storm arrivals who thought they could do better, new organs transplanted into the sick body with no mind paid to the toxicity and the rejection—and these were heavy cases. But the public defender's office was hard up. Since Ben and Boris were looking for more work, they got what they wanted, all the kids.

Boris sat on some steps and looked through Ben's interview notes. He was sulking.

"It's on me, huh?"

"Don't give yourself too much credit."

"Okay. It's on us."

"Who do you think we are?"

"He wants to talk to his dad?"

"The real dad. Not the stepdad."

"That's better."

"We don't know that."

"Who's the real dad?"

"A homeless guy."

"What does he want with him?"

"Boys and dads, Dudophilus. Who knows?"

"There's a lot of things a kid in trouble might want to say to his father."

"We're sort of the last guys who'd know about that."

Boris had a pelt of almost-black hair encroaching onto his forehead. He liked to puff upward and blow a hank of it in the air when he was thinking. Ben didn't have as much hair anymore and it made him jealous. Boris blew on his forelock. He said:

"Or the first. You don't have a whole list of things to say to yours?"

"I've never been in trouble."

Boris looked down the street and thought for a while. Ben leaned against a house and wished he had a beer. Boris said:

"This could be a winner."

"It's not."

"It would be if he hadn't talked. He told them everything?"

"I don't have the statement yet. But I don't think so. I don't think they have the gun."

"False confession?"

"They didn't beat it out of him."

"We need to start a PR campaign. *Stop snitching on yourself.*"

"We can make T-shirts with stop signs. We can sell them to fund Robert's defense."

"We can buy him some real lawyers."

They didn't find anything on their investigation, of course. Ben hadn't expected they would. It was just a ritual of precaution. Ben liked investigating. He liked that it was systematic, methodical, slow going. He liked that it was secrets, too.

Ben had been in high school when his father didn't come back one night. Ben and his mother drove out and there was his father's car, parked where it always was when he went fishing. In the failing light it took a while to find the boat on the empty lake, drifted into the thin, spoked branches of a fallen pine. The police came out, and early the next morning as soon as light hit they found his father without even dragging. The lake shallow and clear, the body covered in water not ten feet deep. In keeping with the tradition there was no autopsy. Maybe his father had counted on that. They had him in the ground the next day.

That was Ben's first investigation. Then, too, it was a calming ritual for him, like going into every bar or talking to every bouncer, a way of giving order to the things you don't know and can't understand. So while his aunts and his grandparents made phone calls and covered the mirrors, and while his mother sat on their big couch pressed up against the armrest, one arm wrapped around and holding on tight as though wrestling it into submission, Ben went through his father's study. Modern German and ancient Greek texts; a Ben Shahn print, brush and ink, a translucent gray dove with wings curled like beckoning fingers;

an etching of the Kabbalistic tree of life, sephirot and seraphim; a big, heavy-breathing old computer, left in standby but with nothing open on the screen. Dim brown light from old lampshades, reflected dully on greening copper from some Bedouin market in the deserts outside Be'er Sheva. The smell of pipe smoke and surrender. He found the bottle of sedatives in the velvet bag where his father kept his phylacteries, the leather straps and boxes that the devout wear in prayer. He poured the pills out on his father's desk and counted, using a letter opener to move them like he'd seen pharmacists do. Thirty out of sixty missing.

His mother never talked about it, but he guessed she assumed it was a suicide. An otherwise healthy man might fall off a fishing boat on a flat and placid lake but doesn't usually die unless that's what he wants. His mother was at loose ends for a while, so thin you could see through her, but after the first couple of years she coalesced into a person again and she did seem a little bit lightened. His father had always been leaving. He retired at barely fifty from his work and dreamed always of moving from their college town. It was something in him, an otherwise strong and competent man, so afraid of abandonment that he'd rather just go. Ben threw the drugs in that same lake. He never told his mother. There was no reason to. And from that place of secrecy and silence, a defense case, everything else came.

When they were done, Boris went home to type a memo and then drink five beers on his balcony and fall asleep in a vinyl lawn chair with a ratty blanket pulled over him. Ben walked back across St. Claude and into the St. Roch. He sat at the bar at the Hot Potato. A Polaroid of the late Lillie Scott smiling was taped to the mirror above the bar. It already looked faded and old. The other three people in the room were the bartender and a couple who sat on their stools like regulars. All were drinking, and none seemed like they'd just started. The bartender gave Ben a beer in a cold bottle and told him he looked like he had himself a serious pair of glasses. This he acknowledged, and he sat for a little while. Perhaps he meant to pay respects. Anyhow he wasn't ready for bed. After a while, the bartender's friends left.

She yawned:

"You want another?"

He was only halfway through his beer.

"I'll have what you were having."

An abomination of rum and Pepsi. Ben waved at the photograph:

"I read about the owner. Miss Scott."

"I didn't know her that well."

"Were you working that night?"

"The early shift. I wasn't here."

"I'm sorry."

"They caught the guy who did it. You saw that?"

"They arrested a kid, yeah."

"When does a kid become a guy?"

"Sometime after he turns thirty-one, I think."

He took the rum with him in a plastic cup back to his place in the Bywater, right up against the Mississippi. He stayed alone in one half of a single-story cottage with almost no furniture. Each room had its own gas heater, lit with a match. That January, in his bedroom at the back of the empty house, the heater would burn all night with a blue flame, the bare wood floor cold over the open crawl space. In the night, trains moved up from the river along the Public Belt Railroad. Early mornings he would wake and lie completely motionless under his blanket, in the cool flame before the sun. He would wait for his alarm, sometimes for an hour, with slowed breath and open eyes in the loud dark.

4

Confidences

The things to do right away: See the scene close to the time of the shooting. Done. Look for witnesses. So far unsuccessful. Collect security video. In some places the cameras record on a loop every twenty-four or forty-eight or seventy-two hours, so you need to get it quickly or you'll never get it at all. Next: Hire an expert, an adolescent psychologist or a neuropsychologist who works with kids. She would interview Robert and give him a battery of tests. Did he understand his rights when he confessed? Did he know he could have asked for a lawyer, or refused to talk? Did he have the capacity to know? If not, his statement couldn't be used at trial. Here speed was important, because the question was what Robert understood when he gave up his rights and made a statement, not what he might understand after months of thinking about his court case and talking to his lawyer and the guys around the jail. You want to capture that stupid inexperience.

So after court Ben got his usual expert lined up to see Robert. Then he went over to the jail. Robert had been one night at the juvenile detention center before his transfer and now two nights at the Orleans Parish Prison. Not long enough to get wise. He rested his chin in his hands and looked at Ben. Ben thought of a little boy sitting at a dining room table, waiting on a surprise that he feared but didn't know would hurt him and how and for how long, like a family meeting to announce a divorce.

"Where's Mr. Boris?"

"He's working with me, but I'm the main guy on this one."

"Why?"

"It's the way we do our job."

"Like you take turns."

"Not exactly that."

"Is he going to come see me?"

"He'll come with me sometimes."

"Did you find my dad?"

"I'm sorry."

"I've got to see him."

"I know you want to see him."

"You'll find him soon?"

"I'm working hard on your case, Robert. I need you to help me."

Robert pushed up out of his slump and raised his finger with a little wave and a tilt of his head like he was going to make a nuanced but important distinction in some ongoing argument. Ben saw that he liked to keep one hand on his face, on his cheek and mouth, like he was pressing down on a rotted tooth.

"You checked all the places where he stays, though?"

"It's going to take some time."

"My mom might know."

"You think?"

"Maybe not. They're not so good together."

"Did you talk to her?"

"You told me not to."

"But did you?"

"No."

"Thank you for paying attention, Robert. We're going to have to be a team. I know it's hard."

Robert didn't roll his eyes, exactly. Just a flitter of his eyelids. What you don't ever do is pretend you understand. Ben corrected himself:

"I can't even imagine how hard it is. She can come see you, though."

"Can she bring my sister and my baby brother?"

"I'll talk to her about that. I'm looking forward to meeting them."

"They're funny."

"Do you want to tell me about them?"

"I help with them, when I'm at home."

"That's good."

"I did."

Robert seemed to be right on the edge of something he didn't want to think about. So instead, he said:

"Do you have kids, Mr. Ben?"

Even if he'd had his life together, maybe especially then, Ben wouldn't have talked much about it. Most of the public defenders didn't. They worried the contrast would seem unkind or presumptuous. They didn't talk about the future, either. What for? So most of the time, no matter how long Ben knew his clients, they were nothing but a foreshortened past—the single moment they did a terrible or a stupid thing—while Ben himself had no past at all. His clients usually seemed fine not knowing about him. Your lawyer sees a tiny but very deep cross section of your life. A core sample. Ben assumed his clients mostly preferred not to know anything about him, because then it's a real person watching you.

But sometimes the kids, especially, wanted more. They'd ask whether he had children, or was married, or something else about his life and his past. *Where were you for the storm?* There was no point in sharing the literal truth, which was so foreign that it sounded like a lie: *In a vacation house on Cape Cod, with a woman.* So he usually just deflected: *I wasn't living in New Orleans yet.* They already knew he wasn't from there, of course. Some kids weren't satisfied, though. They were used to social workers and probation officers and everyone else getting in their business. *Tell me about your mom, your school, your doctors, your girlfriend. Your boyfriend. Sorry. I shouldn't have assumed.* Why should that only go one way?

"I need to visit with you about a few things. There's a doctor who's going to come see you."

Robert sat back. This wasn't the tough guy pose. It was just teen-agers. Ben thought it might have been almost the same at a school or a camp or wherever kids hang out that isn't jail. Robert muttered:

"You're supposed to work for me."

"I do."

Robert bored in a little:

"You try to help with my case and you tell me things. That's what you said."

"That's right."

"You didn't find my dad and you didn't bring Mr. Boris and you didn't tell me anything."

"I'm trying to help you get ready for something important."

"I'm supposed to trust you."

"I don't expect you to—"

"But you don't trust me."

They weren't going to talk about the expert. That was okay. Ben could wait a couple days to tell the kid that he'd be tested by a neuro-psychologist in the hope that he was too young and too screwed-over by the public school system to understand his rights. Ben had given up on the dream scenario, that Robert was intellectually disabled. Or, almost as good, psychotic. But there was something else Ben needed to know right away, and Robert was the only one who could tell him. So Ben thought there could be an easy way out. What difference did it make, anyhow. Ben said:

"I have kids. Two sons. They're small. The big one's just six years old. The little one's four."

It wasn't the first time he'd told that story. He told himself the lie was solidarity. Having kids in the city gave him skin in the game, some kind of authority to interfere in a life that was beyond his ability to conceive. He thought the fiction of having a real life here made him seem a little less different. He raised his eyebrows at Robert, as though asking for understanding. Robert nodded with him.

"Do they stay with you?"

Even with kids and dads: You never said *live with*. When Ben talked with his clients, it was always *where do you stay*. Remembering that made Ben want to pour it on a little bit. Why shouldn't he suffer, too. He said:

"I don't like to talk about them. My little one is pretty sick. That's why."

Robert leaned forward. He closed his eyes a little bit and shook his head:

"I'm sorry. I'm sorry he's sick."

"The doctors think he'll be okay. I don't want to bother you with this. You have your own things to worry about."

"That's good, though. About the doctors."

"Yeah."

"Is your son in the hospital?"

"No. Not now."

"Hey, do you have pictures? Like, on your phone?"

"I don't have my phone with me now, because of the sheriff's rules. Robert, right now I need to visit with you about your case. Did the police say they found a gun anywhere?"

Robert in his turn didn't want to answer. But now maybe he felt like he owed Ben something. He muttered:

"I don't know what they say."

"Do you know if they have a gun they say was yours?"

Shrug:

"I don't know what they say."

"Do you know if they found a gun at all?"

"I don't think they found it."

"If there was a gun and I wanted to see it, where do you think it might be a good idea to look?"

Robert pursed his lips. He said:

"You're not gonna find my dad."

"Is there something you want your dad to help with? Could I help you instead?"

Robert and Ben both waited a minute. What did he know about fathers and sons. He lied to get what he wanted, just like a fucking cop:

"Robert? If one of my kids ever got into trouble, big trouble like this, I'd want him to talk to his lawyer."

Robert half-smiled:

"They're not in here, though."

"I'm not saying it's the same. But I'd want them to get help from someone on their side."

Robert wasn't dumb but he was a mark. Ben didn't know if it was his dad or not but someone had loved Robert enough that he trusted people. At least he wanted to. It's a place full of lies and concealment, but some people are just waiting to tell the truth. Robert:

"You want to know where it is?"

5

Docket Duty

Ben's mom was calling. She wanted him to come home for a weekend. Ben's sister and her husband and their son, Ben's nephew named after his father, would be there too. Ben wouldn't answer, or he'd wait until he was on his way into court and then pick up and say a few little things and get off in a hurry. Ben was afraid of visits with his mother and sister. He was quiet and maybe they assumed he was preoccupied with his work, or sad because of his work, all the dead boys, but it was only that he had nothing to say. He knew a little bit how to talk to clients and judges and jurors, how to get something out of somebody. He didn't have words for much else. When he went to his mother's house, he felt he'd become thinner and lighter, light enough to skim over the surface of things.

The public defenders had a rotation set up so every day each courtroom had an assigned lawyer. The courtroom defender didn't represent everyone on the docket. Some had hired private lawyers. Others, like the kids Ben and Boris worked for, had particular public defenders assigned to them. But some fell through the cracks. Their private lawyer stopped showing up, for instance, because he was holding out for more money. Or the public defender's office just missed them and failed to assign someone. That's where the courtroom defender came in. Someone had to grease the wheels.

There were thirteen judges in the criminal courthouse. A few were sometimes capable of empathy, even if they acted like vaudevillians: The judge who was rumored to keep a list of Jewish public defenders; the judge who sometimes held a dog in her lap in court; the judge who was said to be auditioning for a role as a TV judge. The rest of them weren't possible. The judge who screamed at a lawyer for reading the criminal law in court; the judge who, they said, took bribes from bail bondsmen; the judge who tried to stop you from appealing his rulings; the judge who remanded a public defender into custody for asking the wrong kinds of questions; the judge who pointed to a public defender, in open court, as an example of female beauty; the judge who yelled at you for talking with your hands.

That Friday Ben was the courtroom defender in front of a judge who on Fridays at exactly 7:45 in the morning sat in chambers and replaced the shoelaces on his dress shoes. He had 26 pairs of dress shoes, he explained, and each one got a new pair of laces twice a year. The public defenders and prosecutors would attend this ceremony like they were waiting on some augury, to see what the day would bring. He put the laces into a wooden box that sat on his desk. When it was full, he explained, he would bring the laces home. Unclear what would happen then. The judge was trying to set a record for the most trials held during his time on the bench. He wasn't going to, because he was approaching his mandatory retirement and because of another judge, who goosed his own numbers by paying a public defender extra money for his diligence in always declaring ready for trial and sometimes conducting two trials simultaneously, with the juries rotating out every couple of hours.

To Ben it sometimes seemed like there was nothing much beyond what he saw in New Orleans. Everything was what it appeared to be. A line of men in chains is just that. The secret was that everyone knew. The front benches full of prisoners. The tension between impatience and dread, dropping them slack and stretching them tight at the same time, like clothes on a wire hanger.

An old woman in a wheelchair was waiting at the back of the courtroom when the judge hit the bench at exactly 8 a.m. A grandmother? No, a defendant. Both, probably. Arraignments—the new cases—came first on the docket. When the old woman's case was called, a young man pushed her chair through the swinging brass doors of the court's bar. He stood at the podium, the woman sitting beside him. A pair of oxygen canisters were slung on the back of her wheelchair. A plastic mask covered most of her face. Like an astronaut coming into the poisonous alien air of the courthouse.

"Good morning, ma'am. Please take the microphone, ma'am."

The guy at the podium wore jeans, boots, and a road crewman's reflective jacket. He looked like he'd been working all night. He said:

"She can't really talk. She can't catch her breath."

"And you are, sir?"

"Her nephew. I drove her. We don't know what this is about."

The prosecutor was at his table, flipping through folders. He had thick, swept-forward hair, the satisfied jowls of a country sheriff. He sounded bored:

"It's a 14:71, judge."

The judge:

"A 14:71, if you please, sir."

"I don't know what's fourteen seventy-one."

"Where is the lady's lawyer?"

"We just got a letter."

"The lady must have a lawyer."

"The letter told us to be here, that's all."

"Unless she wishes to exercise her right to represent herself. That is her right, of course. Will she exercise it?"

"She can't."

"Is she then indigent? What is her income, sir?"

"She can't exercise anything. She's got emphysema. She's dying."

The judge read out the charges. She was accused of bouncing a $628 check two years earlier. Ben wasn't allowed to talk yet. The public defender hadn't been appointed. The judge had a protocol that he mislabeled *courtesy* or *decorum*. This courtesy, though, was just the rehearsal of manners stripped of kindness, a mechanical display without human emotion besides, perhaps, contempt.

Now the judge needed a plea. But the man said:

"She didn't do anything like that."

"The court would request the courtesy of hearing from the lady herself."

The judge was getting agitated. He began to quiver and stammer. This was a departure from protocol.

"Mr. Judge—"

"Please, sir. Sir, I beg of you. The lady herself. I must hear the lady's plea."

The nephew picked up the gooseneck microphone on the podium and held it down to her. He removed her mask. She gasped *not guilty* like her last words. The judge was satisfied by this incantation. You could see his whole body exhale.

"What would be a hearing date for the lady?"

"She has about two weeks."

"Two weeks will be acceptable to the court."

"To live. That's what the doctors say."

"You understand the bind that you're putting the court in. We do wish to accommodate the lady. But we must ensure that justice is done, in fairness to the court and to the State."

They set a hearing date for next Tuesday. The judge decided she couldn't afford a lawyer, so Ben was appointed to represent her. The nephew wheeled her out and Ben followed to get her address and number, but that was just habit. She wouldn't live to be convicted. So the case would end with Ben's client still not guilty. An easy win for Ben and for justice.

6

Physical Evidence

Boris's father helped design the Soviet navy. He defected in 1977, secreted across borders by the CIA before most Jews could get out. They sent him to the ironworks in Bath to lend his know-how to the construction of American warships. There, Yevgeny Pasternak met Boris's mother, Marie, a billing clerk whose first language in the parish schools of backcountry Maine was French. Pasternak knew French too, along with Russian and German and four other languages. He left when Boris was six months old, escaping again: Deeper into the country, looking for someplace warm. Never heard from since.

Boris's Catholic mother did her best to raise their son in the tradition of his father's people—as a disaffected Jew, a permanent refugee, a pragmatic skeptic. To her, religion was always and only ritual and misery. So during the High Holidays every fall, she drove him into Portland to stand by himself in a corner of the men's section at Maine's only Orthodox synagogue, where without intending to or even knowing it, he learned his father's robust contempt for the guttural observances of his faith. Boris didn't have Ben's Judaism of country clubs and orthodontists nor of prophets and windswept hillsides. He didn't join Ben's vain and romantic longing for an inheritance of justice. His own inheritance had better prepared him to be a public defender. He wouldn't believe what he was told, or countenance what couldn't be tolerated, or stay where he was sent or even where he was wanted.

Just then he wasn't wanted: Leaning back against a pillar in the courthouse hall, squinting at a bald, white detective, half incredulous and half disgusted like the guy wasn't wearing pants. The detective was one of the full crazy ones, and he was sneering back at Boris. A little while later it came out that this detective had a thing where he'd text a prostitute he was sleeping with whenever the police were going to do a drug raid in the neighborhood. The courthouse's upper floor was high, bright, marbled, hot. Grand like an old-fashioned train station, and likewise filled with people waiting to be taken somewhere, but without a ticket or a schedule.

Ben stepped in Boris's line of sight. Boris sighed. Ben reached into his jacket and pantomimed offering him a flask. Boris pantomimed injecting heroin, tying off with his necktie wrapped around his bicep. Ben said:

"Stop provoking them. It's like tapping on the glass at the aquarium. It messes with their circadian rhythms."

"You're coming out tonight?"

"It's Friday."

"That's the idea, Duderonomy."

"I'm going to *shul*."

"Pray for me to get lucky."

Boris: Still built like a college shooting guard, about six foot three with square shoulders and long muscles. Big, rough features layered on top of each other like they were laid in brick. Eyes pale gray. A schoolgirl's dream of a sensitive, working man. He didn't much rely on luck.

"I'll pray for you."

Used to be, every Friday night and Saturday morning, Ben would walk with his father to synagogue. A dim yellow room, too low for its length. He'd hated the utilitarian prayer of Orthodox Jews. There was no romance in it, two or three hours to speed-mumble through a couple hundred pages of blessings and medieval acrostic poems, afterward herring and Danish in the windowless, linoleumed basement.

Now most Friday nights he went to a spare and dusty old synagogue left behind in a neighborhood where Jews used to live in the 1950s, at the edge of the Garden District. When they fled, they sold most of the old synagogues to churches. This one lingered on but only barely, with a handful of old men, university professors, Israeli emigrants, and Hasidic emissaries chanting in the liturgy of the Jews of the Spanish diaspora who first settled in the city two hundred years earlier. It wasn't that he was comfortable there on the wooden benches, under the lines of bare light bulbs. The hush and repetition of prayer were conducive to a blank mind.

Ben didn't go to synagogue that Friday, though. When court was over, he went back to the office and picked up the messenger bag that he and Boris took on investigations, with tools and gloves and a camera. He changed out of his suit. There was already a pretty good chance a white guy would be mistaken for a cop, even though Ben's glasses and build didn't really fit the bill. He'd lost his last fistfight, in the second grade. Since then he'd grown a little, but still didn't look like he'd do better in a rematch.

Angeline Johnson stayed in the St. Roch, not too far from Lillie Scott's place. Robert probably passed the restaurant a couple of times a day, on his way to and from school, but never would have gone in to eat. Angeline was a little elf of a woman—tiny, skinny, with Robert's huge eyes. She stood in her own doorway like she was the one visiting, like she didn't know if she'd stay or not.

"I'm Ben Alder. We met before—"

"I remember you."

"I'm here to visit with you about Robert."

"You can come in."

She sat on the couch in the front room. Shotgun single, one room wide, bare floorboards and a couch, nothing on the walls. She was holding the baby, about eighteen months old now. He didn't look like Robert.

"Your baby got big."

"He's my fat baby."

"Is his father around? Robert's stepdad?"

"No."

"I wonder—"

"He got arrested a few months back."

"I can't say I'm sorry to hear it."

She shrugged. She didn't look any kind of way about it. Instead, she said:

"I hope Robert's doing alright."

"He knows you care about him."

She told him the police had been there a few days ago and left without taking anything. How did she know? Well, she said, aren't they supposed to give you some paper when they do? That's what they'd done when they went to her sister's house. No receipt, nothing taken. Ben asked to look around. She showed him Robert's little room, almost bare except for a bed, an old military-style trunk, and a pile of clothes on the floor. There was a photograph taped to the wall by the bed—Robert, smiling. Ben took pictures to look at later.

"The police made that mess and I haven't had a chance to clean it up."

"What about the back? Do you have a yard?"

Through the kitchen there were rotted wooden steps down into a little yard thick with ragweed, saltbush, bull thistle, mare's tail. The tall weeds grew over and around the trash dropped by waves of tenants and non-tenants. Boards, a stove, an old picture tube TV.

"They came back here?"

"With a machine."

"A metal detector?"

"I guess."

"I need to measure some things."

"Go on."

Ben went to a knee and played with the little two-button computer on his measuring wheel. She sat and watched him through half-closed lids. The kid started to squirm and then fell asleep against her chest. Eventually, after Ben looked up at her four or five times and she looked down at him, too, she asked:

"Is something wrong, Mr. Ben?"

"Sorry this is taking so long."

She said flatly:

"That night after Robert came home, he came back here. It was late and I was trying to sleep but he kept making noise. He was banging around for a while."

Ben kept looking down at his toy:

"And what happened?"

"Nothing. He went to sleep."

"If you want—"

"I'll take the baby inside," she said. "No, we'll go for a walk."

Alone, Ben put aside the measuring wheel and pushed through the weeds to where the TV was sunk into the green thicket. He put on a pair of purple nitrile gloves from the bag. He got down on his knees and the weeds screened him off from the neighboring yards. Ten screws held the TV shut. Eight came out easy enough; the other two were badly stripped. He bore down and took his time, and eventually coaxed them out so that he could grab the head with a pair of needle-nosed pliers. Sweat from his forehead dripped onto his glasses and smeared.

Inside the box was a little revolver, three-inch stainless-steel barrel and black grip. He picked it up with a pencil through the trigger guard like he'd seen a cop do on a show, put it in a brown paper bag and wrote the time and date on the outside with a marker. He put the TV back together, driving the stripped screws as best he could. When he got inside the house he stopped, took the gun out of the bag, without a pencil this time, and opened the cylinder. He'd gone online earlier to watch a video showing how to do it. He counted with his finger four live rounds, one spent casing.

There's a way to do this. You can bring the gun back to your office and put it in the bottom of your locked desk drawer, or in an evidence safe if you have one. The next day you can bring it to a fingerprinting expert and ask him to try to lift prints. If he can't find any, you have him sign a statement saying so. Then you go hire your own lawyer, someone outside the public defender's office, whom you trust. You give him the gun. Before the end of the day, he drops it off with the chief of investigations for the DA's office. *Got a gun here*, he says. *You might want it. Everything else is confidential.* How'd you get it? *Including that.* They'll run the ballistics and probably figure out it's consistent with the gun that killed Lillie Scott, but that's as far as it will go. No concealing or tampering with evidence. No connection with Robert Johnson or Ben himself. Everything has to go right, though. And the police still have the gun. And Robert Johnson is no closer to anything like freedom.

7

Failure to Appear

Robert told Ben he'd not just hidden the gun in the backyard but found it there, too. Maybe. Maybe a big cousin or someone had hidden it and bragged about it to Robert or just confided in him. But Ben knew Robert could find a gun if he wanted one. He knew it because of how they'd met the first time—six months earlier, in a room without electricity in an abandoned hotel in a part of the city that was about to be torn down.

One night back then, Ben got back from court and found Boris writing a memorandum of law and researching dinner options. When Boris ran out of ideas for either law or food, he stopped and picked up a fork with a cylindrical handle that sat on his desk. It telescoped out to about three feet. He'd collapse and extend it a few times to get his creative juices flowing. It was a camping fork they'd found lying on the floor during an investigation at one of the third-tier strip clubs, off Bourbon Street. Boris had accused the manager of entertaining Boy Scouts. He'd explained that the fork was evidence and he needed to have it. He used it to control his fidgets and to eat food off Ben's desk.

Ben had been visiting clients at the jail, and he started putting together files. That's step three: First Appearance; interview; organization. Each client's little clutch of papers, along with Ben's interview notes ripped out of a notepad, went into a legal-sized folder. Ben wrote the case number and client name on the cover. On the inside front cover of every folder, he stapled a checklist with all the usual steps to take. Then he printed up his standard set of filings and his investigation request. He had 136 open cases. The trick was systems. He'd touch each case as infrequently as possible. When he touched it, he'd do everything he could right then and calendar every due date. Then he'd put the file away and try not to think about it, or the person behind it, until one of the dates came up. Ben hole-punched and dog-eared and alphabetized. This was the best part of the job since anyone could do it and there were no tears or arguments but he still got to feel good about himself.

Boris said:

"You want dinner?"

Ben had a Diet Coke and a vending machine honey bun.

"I have dinner. What are you working on?"

"A brief. Possession of a concealed weapon by a juvenile. They say they surrounded him and he took out a gun and threw it in the gutter. What about a beer?"

Boris had a little fridge. He opened one for each of them. Ben put up his feet to talk shop:

"What's your issue?"

"The cops made him throw it down. They can't just surround you and intimidate you until you throw down. You have a right to freedom of movement. Fourth Amendment, son."

"Did they put their hands on him before the throwdown?"

"No."

"Are they lying?"

"One of the cars had its camera on."

"That's a loser."

"It's all I've got for legal issues."

"Sorry."

"But I have a trial theory."

"Hot."

"You want to hear it?"

"I'm going to."

Boris took a drink. He closed his eyes until he found his center. Then he pivoted his torso toward Ben and struck and held a pose—left arm held out and crooked upward at the elbow, palm perpendicular to the ground and rotated inward, spread fingers to the ceiling—like an old-time hero. Boris, with deep sincerity:

"This is a case about responsibility."

"You know what you really understand?"

"Posturing."

"Values," Ben said. "You would have been a great conservative."

"I would have been great at all kinds of things, but instead I'm a public defender. Let me tell you about a kid who was trying to help a neighborhood heal. A young man. A kid?"

Ben finished his can of Budweiser quickly: "How old?"

"Sixteen next month."

"A child."

"A boy?"

"A child."

"A child," Boris agreed. "Robert Johnson."

"Like the musician?"

"Just a teenager, but already someone who cares. Cares about the community. His community. I'll say his community, it's less presumptuous." Boris made a note on a legal pad. Then he asked: "Wait, who's the musician?"

Ben liked to know things that Boris didn't know. "Blues. He only recorded a few songs. Nobody really knows anything about his life. He's a mystery. That's why white people love him. He's romantic and blank."

"Everyone likes my kid, too. He's a Good Samaritan and a hard luck story. An orphan. Half an orphan. Well, he doesn't know where his father is. Most of the time. His dad's homeless. Anyhow, Robert was walking along through the Seventh Ward, on his way home from Bible study."

"Son of a bitch," Ben exulted. "Really?"

Boris was pleased with himself:

"Who's to say he wasn't? It was a Wednesday night."

"That's convenient."

"Everything about this kid's life is convenient. He's a lucky duck. Anyhow, he sees a glint in the bushes, does our Samaritan."

"The present tense is good."

"My dude. You're ruining my flow."

"Not possible, Mayor Van Dude of Dudetown. Your flow is so ice cold."

"Thanks. You heard that in a rap song by one of those rap artists?"

"It was in a clip on NPR."

"He goes over and finds this gun. It's a rough neighborhood. Too many people carry guns. That's a tragedy in our city, which is trying to rebuild. Violence is our original sin."

Ben got another beer. He cracked it open and Boris opened his eyes, looked over. Ben ventured:

"Can I just offer one more thing?"

Boris got another beer, too. He had a few empties already on his desk. Boris did his best work at night. "You're not making this easy," he said.

"It's a judge trial, yeah?"

"He's fifteen, my dude of dudes."

"You're overdoing it with original sin."

"Noted. Now you will be silent. He picks it up, this instrument of evil, because there's little kids in the neighborhood. Babies. There's a day care just a few houses away. That's true, by the way. I have pictures. And our Robert doesn't want a child getting hurt. He loves kids. He has a little sister and a baby brother. An infant."

Ben couldn't help himself and Boris didn't really want him to. He wanted Ben to be impressed. Ben asked:

"How will that come in?"

Boris, grinning:

"I'm gonna put the mom on."

"To say he has a little sister and a baby brother?"

"To say he's really protective and responsible. He acted in conformity with his character. What's that? Rule 4-0-what?"

"404(a)(1)."

"That's why I love you, Benjamin Dudinsky Alder."

"She should hold the baby on her lap."

Boris was building up to it. He was going to make Ben jealous. "I got something better."

"Tell me she's going to nurse."

"Even better."

"I got nothing." Boris grinned and puffed at his hair helmet:

"She's gotta walk by Robert to take the stand. She's gonna hand him the baby."

"This is why I love you, Boris Yevgenyevitch."

"It'll come off great. Who would use a baby as a prop? Listen. He knows he's not supposed to be carrying a gun around."

"So he's choosing the lesser evil."

"Not the lesser evil. Then we're apologizing. It's good. He's good. Have I taught you nothing? Our kids our good kids. He's responsible. He makes hard choices. He's going to bring it right to the police to turn it in."

"And then. Bam."

"Bam," Boris agreed. "They pull up and stop him."

"Unbelievable coincidence. Bam."

"A happy coincidence, until the police did the wrong thing. Jumped to the wrong conclusion. Right when he was bringing them the gun.

"To save the children. Responsibly."

"Yup."

There were a couple of moments of quiet. Boris put a couple of exclamation points on his notepad. He felt good. He picked up his fork and briefly used it to conduct an orchestra of the damned while admiring his reflection in the window glass. Ben drank. Boris looked over, stopped conducting, and bit the inside of his cheek. He said:

"Well?"

"Good. Good. Okay."

"Just okay?"

"Well . . ."

"Well I am a narrative genius?"

"Well, why was it hidden? I mean, if he was bringing it to them? Why conceal it?"

"You can't just walk down the street carrying a gun. The police will stop you."

"That's gonna be a thing."

"They'll shoot you," Boris insisted. "A Black kid carrying a gun? You gotta conceal it. That's just reality."

"The judge doesn't know that."

"He does."

"He doesn't want to."

Boris collapsed the fork in frustration.

This was how they'd trained themselves. Their theories were stories—about innocence, or diminished culpability, or whatever the lawyer wants—to hold the evidence together. Facts only matter if the jury actually hears them. Those are the *facts in the case*. They're different from the *facts in the world*. A pack of nuns can see you do it. It's a fact in the world that they saw it. But if none of them comes to court, the story doesn't exist to the judge or jury. It's not a fact in the case. The world is bigger than the case, but it's much less important. It's not important at all. The police said Robert Johnson had a gun. Boris couldn't say they were lying, because they had video. So the theory had to be some kind of justification. The real reason Robert Johnson had the gun didn't matter. Boris almost certainly didn't know it. Why ask? What was in Robert's head wasn't a fact in the case, if he had the good sense to keep his mouth shut and not snitch on himself.

Bad defenders would get up and talk about reasonable doubt. But like everyone else, judges and jurors think in stories, and they start out suspecting the guy in the defendant's chair did it. Why else would he be there? His lawyer needs to overcome that. Otherwise, the jury goes with the prosecutor's theory. People like to have their questions answered, and the prosecutor is usually saying what jurors and judges want to believe. Trial lawyers don't change the way people think. There's no time for that, if it were even possible. Instead, the thing is to flatter them. Stand up and tell them how it actually happened, in a way they can hear. The trial theory accounts for bad facts in the case. It highlights every good fact. It panders to the jury's biases about how the world works and answers all their big questions. If they don't have their questions answered, they're going to convict the Black guy at the defense table. None of this "keep an open mind" bullshit. Nobody has an open mind. They believe things, and a good lawyer ratifies their beliefs. People need things to make sense.

Which they usually do, if making sense and being predictable are the same. So in the end, Boris pled the kid guilty in exchange for a sentence of probation. Saving the children was as good a theory as he was going to spin out, but it wouldn't work for a judge trial. Maybe he could have sold it to the right jury. But, outside of high school, kids don't get a jury of their peers.

Of course that wasn't the end, really. In juvenile court the case isn't closed and the lawyer isn't off the hook until the kid is done with probation. So one day not long after the plea, when Ben was at his desk ignoring phone calls from jail and from his mother, Boris jogged into the office in an orange swimsuit and in a hurry.

"Can you come with me?"

The public defender's office had some investigators, mostly women right out of college who dressed like unreconstructed hippies. They were good investigators because their whiteness and weirdness made them invulnerable. But there weren't enough of them, and you need a second person since you can't be a witness in your own case.

"Are you planning on wearing pants? Or at least longer shorts?"

"I ran up from the gym."

Boris went to a gym at the edge of the French Quarter where he'd hustle the city's professional class at basketball. The gym had a bar where the members would smoke after they worked out. Ben didn't exercise religiously, but he'd sometimes meet Boris there for a beer. There was a judge from Criminal Court who hung out at the bar, and they'd talk to him about cases and prosecutors and try to get information or just to make friends so they didn't get screamed at or threatened or actually cuffed and jailed, which happened to a few public defenders in his courtroom around that time.

"You're disgusting."

"I gave up my car. I can't afford the lease. I've burned through the corporate savings. Now I'm just living off my trust fund. You know how it is for the idle rich."

Boris put jeans on directly over his bathing suit. He was slick with sweat.

"Can you afford underpants?"

"We're in a rush."

Boris had gotten a call from Robert's probation officer. There was a new warrant out for him, domestic violence, but he was missing. The probation officer dangled the chance of leniency if the kid turned himself in.

Their first stop was the house where Robert stayed with his mom. She was out front smoking when Ben and Boris pulled up. Ben's car was a 1998 Chevy Cavalier, gold, with rolldown windows and a bad dent in the driver's side door that kept it from opening and that Ben never got around to fixing. Ben had to climb in and out through the passenger door, across the center console, like a child.

Ben stood back by the street. Boris tried to lean against the stairway railing so he didn't seem like he was looming over Angeline Johnson.

"We're here to visit with you about Robert."

Never *can I talk with you about Robert*. They didn't ask permission to talk to witnesses, and they didn't offer to stop. You present yourself, don't ever voluntarily leave until you're done, and wait for answers. If they say they don't want to talk, you ask why they don't want to talk. There's always another question.

She shrugged. It was exhaustion, not unconcern.

"Where is he?"

"He left last night."

"Where did he go?"

"He goes sometimes. Mostly when he gets into it with his stepfather."

She handed Boris her phone. Ben stepped forward to look. It was a picture of a boy sitting on a couch in a dark room, lit by the phone's flash, looking straight ahead. He was covered in blood, his face and his hair.

"What happened?"

"His stepfather."

"That's your—"

"My boyfriend. My little son's father."

He'd beaten Robert up again and then called the police to try to teach him some kind of lesson. He knew Robert was on probation. Robert ran out before the cops got there. The stepdad, or boyfriend, or whatever, lied about Robert starting a fight and having a knife, so they got a warrant. Angeline thought the stepdad had a friend on the force. She hadn't said anything when the police came by. She'd been afraid. She wanted to help now, though. It wasn't Robert's fault. None of the things that had happened. She smoked and talked, and no cars drove by nor people walked down the empty street.

Boris stepped away down the sidewalk. Ben thought he must have been thinking about leaving, returning the phone politely and getting on a bus and going away somewhere. Ben said:

"None of the things?"

"With Memphis and now this."

"I'd like you to tell me about that. About Memphis."

"Where we went for the storm. It doesn't matter."

Her eyes went flat. There was nothing to say about that anymore. So Ben said:

"He lives with you? Your boyfriend? Robert's stepdad?"

She gestured.

Ben:

"Down that way?"

"Right there. In that white house." A single, stucco-covered and painted bright white, half a block away. "He's probably home about now."

"Are you sure you don't want to go inside?"

She said:

"Either way."

Boris came back to stand next to Ben. He was standing up on the balls of his feet, like he was ready to jump at something. Ben said:

"Let's go back to our office. We can talk there. We'll get something to eat if you want. I'll drive."

"Robert's baby brother is inside. He's sleeping."

"It's okay. We'll bring him."

A few months after he started representing kids, Ben bought a car seat. Lots of moms needed rides and some had babies. Angeline Johnson looked up the street at the white house.

"He says, *I didn't put that child on this earth but I can take him out of it.*"

Boris said:

"Listen, we don't have to talk if you don't—"

But that was breaking the rules. Ben was a good partner. He interrupted:

"We can go now, Miss Angeline."

She got the baby and came to sit in their conference room. It was a poor attempt to give clients what they might expect from a law office: A few old chipboard-and-laminate bookcases held ancient and unread Louisiana lawbooks; a dirty water cooler, unplugged, languished in a corner. Paper clips and scraps of paper all over the table and the floor. Mismatched rolling chairs, some missing casters and scraping along on the thin gray carpeting.

Boris got hold of himself. After they learned everything they needed to learn, Boris wrote out a statement in Angeline's words, verbatim, while Ben held the kid. When Boris was done writing, he sat next to Angeline and they read it over. She signed the bottom of every page and initialed every correction. The statement said she knew she was talking to Robert Johnson's lawyers, that they'd identified themselves and explained whose side they were on, that she'd read and had an opportunity to correct the statement and it was all true. Some lawyers audio record witnesses, but then you're stuck with their words and their contradictions and hesitations and forgettings. Statements you can write the way you want. It's also nice to have a piece of paper you can make them read when you need to impeach them. While they talked they drank flat root beer that Ben poured from a two-liter bottle into disposable cups. Boris wrote that into the statement, too, because it showed they'd been sociable and friendly and didn't make her do anything she didn't want to do.

When they were finished and they had her statement, Boris sat with her for a while. He offered to call the police, or a shelter, or a domestic violence advocate. He offered to find her a civil lawyer and get a restraining order against the stepdad. No, no: She just wanted to go home. So they drove her back. Boris was quiet the whole way. When they dropped her off, though, the stepdad was outside his house, leaning against his porch. A fat guy, with fat calves under his capri pants, and a baseball cap down over his mean mug face. Boris walked Angeline inside, then came back and sat down in the passenger's seat. He took out his phone and looked at the picture of Robert. He must have had the mom text it to him. In the picture Robert's lips were pulled back and there was pink on his teeth from blood and saliva. Boris said:

"Who do you think that gun was for. That Robert was arrested with."

"At least he didn't use it."

"He should have."

Boris got out, closed the door, reached through the open rear window, and took out their investigation bag. Ben lunged across the seat and tumbled out of the car in time to grab Boris by the arm. Boris was holding a short prybar that they used in abandoned buildings sometimes. Gray steel, cut from hexagonal stock, with a forked, hooked neck.

Boris talked calmly:

"I'm going to break his jaw."

"You can't do that."

"I can," Boris explained. "I'm going to hit him right on the corner of his fat fucking face. That'll do it."

"Get in the car."

"I'm just defending myself. You think the police won't believe me?"

"We'll find Robert. We'll use the statement. We'll get him out of jail. It'll be okay."

Boris said, without apparent anger:

"Don't be a sweet naive little fuck."

"He won't be charged."

"Where's he going to go?"

"We'll do what we can do."

"Where's he going to go, though?"

"That's all we can do. That's our job."

8

Assistance of Counsel

Robert's mom said he had two places he went when he ran away. The first was Caroline's house. Caroline? She's like Robert's auntie. She lives in the Iberville.

All the defenders had clients in the Iberville. A public housing project, long, redbrick buildings, three stories, arranged in U-shapes around grassed courtyards punctured by tall posts with floodlights to hold back the terrors in the night. Second-story balconies of gunmetal gray with ironwork around, a dark mocking echo of the French Quarter a few blocks away. When Ben first started at the public defender's office, he'd proposed to their boss that they set up a substation in the Iberville. Build relationships with clients; get to be trusted; be closer to the action. An open-door policy so residents could come in to complain if they were harassed by the police or just needed to know a court date or whatever. But we're not out here trying to change the world, Ben. If you're looking for more foot traffic, you probably don't have enough to do.

When Ben and Boris walked into the courtyard where Auntie Caroline lived, unmarked white Impala cruisers were pulled across the grass. A half-dozen anticrime officers in the jumpsuits that they called battle dress uniforms had five kids up against the wall. None of the kids was Robert. It was probably nothing, just standard operating procedure. The police kept hands on the kids but watched Ben and

Boris, the two white guys, as they crossed the courtyard to ring the doorbell. Nobody answered.

"Okay, next place."

Boris shook his head:

"Let's sit a minute. I want to see what they're doing."

"They won't do anything while we're here."

"That's the point."

"We're in a rush, no?"

The next place was the Palais Royale. A concrete cube, a block long and wide, right next to the raised I-10 that cuts New Orleans in half between the river and the lake. It'd been run down even before the storm. A thousand rooms on the wrong end of Canal Street meant there were usually more rats than tourists. Now it was closed, but some people still stayed there. Driving past on the highway, you could look in through the blank windows and in the daytime see men and women leaning out and taking in the overpass breeze. At night, the wavering light of flame or the spitting light of stolen electricity.

Ben and Boris stopped at a pharmacy and bought paper towels, bandages, water, and new batteries for their flashlights. The awning of the marquee stripped down to its metal ribs. The glass on the street painted over but the front doors unlocked. The bank of elevators shut down, with cobwebs shrouding the steel doors. Someone had looted all the furniture from the lobby. The grime on the floor worn away in a scuffed track between the front doors and the fire stairs.

Behind the desk: Conley Bradley, about six foot four and 280 pounds, holding the twenty-inch Maglite that doubled as a club he'd use to beat money out of his guests. The empty building's owners paid him to keep watch, but instead he was running a $10-a-night flophouse. Ben had never been up in the building before, but Boris had. A witness in a murder trial had been living there. Bradley had helped Boris find him, in exchange for Boris agreeing not to subpoena Bradley to court to cross-examine him about how he made his living.

It looked like he wanted to spit at them.

"Barry the Jew. You brought another one with you. Your partner?"

"Sidekick." Boris didn't break stride: "I'm here to find someone."

"Feel free to use the courtesy phone."

Boris, still casual like he was settling onto a barstool with the guys: "I should report you before the meth guys blow the whole place up."

"You think the police don't know?"

The police knew. As long as the addicts and prostitutes and homeless weren't out on Canal Street, it was okay with the police.

Boris was regretful, almost wistful:

"I'm not talking about the police."

"You got some Jew hotline you're going to call?"

"Tell me really. How do you even know to hate Jews? Wasn't I the first you ever met?"

"Fucking Micah Isaacson in 1405 tore out all my drywall."

Boris leaned against the reception desk and turned to Ben:

"We could get a minyan going in here. You know something about this guy? He picked the name when he got his green card. He thought Conley Bradley was a good name for a guy from Uttar Pradesh. Don't look confused, my Semitic friend. That's in India."

Bradley hit the Maglite against his palm like he'd maybe seen a tough guy do in a movie. Boris didn't seem to notice. Ben wasn't sure what Boris was doing. Maybe Bradley was only make-believe tough, but he had plenty of the trappings of the real thing. The heavy shoulders weren't fake. Bradley said:

"What kind of a fucking Commie name is Boris?"

"You do know my name! Hey, here's a legal question for you, since you're smart. You think running an illegal flophouse is a crime of moral turpitude?"

Bradley's brow furrowed a little bit:

"Turtle what?"

"Close enough. It'll get you deported. You want to bet ICE will care, even though NOPD doesn't?"

Ben and Boris had both called immigration enforcement on prosecution witnesses. In Ben's case, the witnesses hadn't come to court in the end. Ben didn't know if ICE had picked them up or not. They weren't Ben's clients so he didn't have to worry about them. Bradley sneered:

"Fuck you."

"I'm looking for Robert Johnson."

"I don't know him."

"He's a kid. Looks a little like a young Gregory Hines. Never mind about that. Skinny, tall, and covered in blood. How many of those came in today? Like, a half-dozen at most, right?"

Bradley thought about it. He wasn't too happy that he was able to help them:

"He likes to go to the third floor. Uptown end."

"He's here now?"

"Let me check the computer to see if he used his keycard. The answer is *fuck you*."

Ben put a $20 bill on the desk to try to mend fences. Boris looked disappointed in him. Bradley tucked it away quick.

The fire stairs wound seventeen stories around a central well. A couple points of stale light coming down from where the stairway ended at the roof, otherwise too dark to see. They turned on their little flashlights. On the third floor someone had taken something sharp and gouged a long channel in the Sheetrock all the way down to the end of the hallway. It smelled like ammonia, from urine or meth Ben didn't know. The door at the end was closed. Boris knocked and called out. No answer.

Robert was curled up on the floor by the bed like a child playing hide-and-go-seek. He held a dirty cloth to his face. Boris pulled him to his feet. Robert drank some water and with a head shake refused bandages. He kept the cloth pressed against his face. None of them said a word. Boris motioned and turned and left. They waited in the hall for just a second before Robert followed.

In the car Boris said the hospital would be better, they might have a plastic surgeon who could help him avoid a scar, but Robert said no since there might be cops. While Robert was getting stitched up at urgent care, Ben called the one sympathetic juvenile judge on her cellphone and told her the whole story, about the stepfather and the mom's statement and the domestic violence warrant. She couldn't rescind the warrant, which she hadn't signed, but she called in a recognizance release so that Robert wouldn't have to spend the night in detention. Boris and Ben drove Robert to the juvenile jail. The cop there took his picture and vitals and fingerprints and booked him in and then booked him right out again thanks to the judge's release order. Ben and Boris bought him McDonald's and then got him a room at a motel out by the airport. Just for the night, though. Tomorrow he'd have to go back. There wasn't anyplace else.

9

Spoliation

Well, there's always one other place, and Robert got there eventually.
In the present day, with Robert in jail for murder and Boris
afraid to go see him because they'd not been able to fix anything at all,
Ben sat on Angeline Johnson's couch and the dark came up from the
ground all the way to the streetlights and hung there between earth
and sky. He thought if he just sat there, unmoving, maybe nobody
would come home or knock or ring. The windows on the street were
blinded with bedsheets. The revolver sat on the floor in its paper bag
like a schoolboy's sack-lunch.

She did knock, though, when she was too tired and cold to stay
on the stoop. Ben took the gun and put it away in his backpack. He
left and drove downriver to the foot of the Judge Seeber drawbridge.
Closed off. A few months earlier, a police officer had tried to drive over
the Judge Seeber and died because the bridge was up but the barriers
over the roadway hadn't gone down. There was another bridge a little
ways lakebound. Ben drove on and parked and walked onto it. This
was where just after the storm the police had murdered in cold blood
a seventeen-year-old Black boy named James Brissette. Ben hadn't
been in New Orleans yet but that, too, was part of his map of the city,
an archipelago of misery. A burglary in that graceful house with the
tall columns. A shooting under the overpass, where the kids and their
families watch the parades. Witnesses in that brick project building

who all saw the cop plant the evidence but wouldn't come to court. An efficiency apartment on the corner that he'd visited one afternoon: The kids sitting silent on the edge of the bed; the girlfriend leaning in the corner under a spider-web, the spider's body the size of a thumb; his client, tall and strong but with the bloodshot eyes of an addict, ready to sign away his life on a guilty plea. The whole scene, with the electricity shut off, gray-green in the light of an afternoon rainstorm.

Maybe it'd been different before Katrina. Maybe it had been the way that beautiful cities are, like a body: Organically grown, with hard places and soft, calluses and contours, all joined by durable and flexible fibers and covered over, contained and joined, with a skin that holds everything together and keeps the outside out. It wasn't that way anymore. The remaining houses, both the ones boarded up and the ones making a go of it with plastic big wheels in the driveway; the concrete slabs, FEMA trailers, sidewalks vanishing into the hungry chest-high grass like the land on the coast, just a few miles away, sub-sides into water. It had lost that proprioception of cities where each part knows where the others are, that sense that gives things—human and built and natural—balance and proportion.

Ben didn't really know how it used to be. He'd been once before the storm, for a law school summer. He fell in love there. One night they ran onto a lawn in the Garden District and sat together in a hammock, her head fell on his shoulder. That's the city, right; a quick touch that feels like a promise. It failed because she was inconstant and mean and he was afraid and mean. When he moved to the city after the storm, he looked at every brown-haired woman biking toward him or away and thought it would be the woman he lost. At first he felt that New Orleans was a place you could lose something and have it, too. Blessed with the privilege of nostalgia. Since he'd moved to the city, he'd come to see it differently. It was like living in a dig, but all on the surface, nowhere for anything to be buried, only the heavy green dark in layers to preserve everything. A remembered city, Jerusalem of mud and water. His hope had been to be there next to kids who didn't have anybody. He knew what that was like, didn't he? Since he came to New Orleans, though, he had nothing but a long docket full of loss. It wasn't even his loss. He was there and he saw it and mostly he did nothing to stop it.

Up on the bridge, the quick breeze against his scalp. Our kids: Their world so narrow with inexperience and fear that they can't even see the water that surrounds them always can be an escape, not just a trap. That way out, through the water, is always open. Instead, Ben reached out and dropped the bag with the gun down into the Industrial Canal and he ran from the water and to his car and back to his house. And he also hid in his dark bedroom like a stupid and scared child whose life is forfeit because of what he has done and what he has not been able to do.

10

First Appearances

Like all lawyers Ben owed his clients loyalty. There were limits, of course. He wasn't supposed to destroy evidence for them. But he was supposed to respect their *dignity* and *autonomy* by telling them everything he knew about their cases. So, for instance, he needed to tell clients about the witnesses against them, even if he was worried about the witnesses getting killed. To tell them the judge was likely to give them prison time, even if that meant they wouldn't show up for sentencing. He had to tell them those things because he wasn't in charge. You don't make decisions for your boss—especially decisions about what he should or shouldn't know.

So Ben should have said:

Oh, you're looking for your dad, Robert McTell.

Sure, I know him!

I even know where he is.

Five hundred yards away from where we're sitting right now.

In jail here, too.

I know it because I'm his lawyer too. Funny, right?

I've been his lawyer for months, even though I've never done any work on his case.

It's not been a priority.

No. You are a priority.

Look what I've done for you already. I threw out your murder weapon! You didn't even need your dad's help with that.

You're a priority because you're a kid.

Also because I feel like I'm to blame, since we didn't do anything about your stepdad beating on you.

But what were we supposed to do, really? Right?

I mean, we're just lawyers.

Even for priority cases.

Actually, your dad is kind of becoming a priority, because of you. The Public Defender's Office. Where everyone is family.

He didn't, though. He told himself it would sound like an accusation: *Your whole family is fucked up, huh?* Or a prediction. Like father, like son. Hey kid: Someday—best case scenario, if you don't go to prison for the rest of your life behind this murder—you'll also be a homeless drug user, grateful for all the city's empty houses. The city might change, and Ben himself might escape. But these boys and men would be forever here, son after father after son, in cells within hailing distance of each other. Or maybe he didn't want to break the illusion—the outright deception, in this instance—that what he knew about each client he knew because it was his job to know. That he worked on their cases and didn't intrude into their lives, that they had private lives and selves that he, just a lawyer, didn't have the right to be a part of, and that he respected the difference. Maybe he didn't want to admit in so many words that he had in his hands the lives of whole families. Or worse, their lives were not in his hands at all.

In fact, Ben had picked up the father a few months before the son was arrested. He got him in the usual way, through First Appearances. Each week he enrolled as counsel in six or eight or ten new cases. In the morning and evening of his rotation days, the sheriff's intake office gave him a stack of paper—face sheets and gists, recall—that he brought to a big room on the ground floor of the House of Detention. The room had a sloping floor like a swimming pool. There were metal folding chairs lined up in rows and a big TV screen at the deep end.

On one cinder-block wall, someone had painted a tropical mural, a green ocean with palm trees.

About fifteen minutes after the appointed time, a line of shackled men and a few women would be led into the room by a couple of deputies. Then the public defenders would call out names. They'd go through the rows of metal folding chairs to as many people as they could before the hearing started, trying to pull out a few facts to make each detained person unusual or special for the judge. *He takes care of his sick mother. He works at Denny's. He needs medicine. He also like every one of us is a child of God, who values his freedom and the presumption of innocence.* They'd find a few minutes to read the gists. Because it's not a trial and it's not about guilt or innocence, but the judge is supposed to look at the gist and decide whether it's reasonable to think that you did what the police say. If not, they can't hold you. Mostly, though, the judges skipped that step and took it on faith that the New Orleans Police Department had done the wise, considered, and honorable thing, like usual.

Nothing smelled worse than that room, but it didn't bother the judges. They'd be over in the courthouse, connected to the House of Detention by video link. The judge would ask each prisoner to stand in his turn. On the screen, a body would rise up, dressed in an orange jumpsuit. Neither could see the other's face, prisoner nor magistrate. The judge would read the charges and then pronounce the terms under which the orange-clad body would be jailed for the next two or eight or thirty-six months. If they could pay a bondsman—if they had a grandfather who owned a house that could be put up as collateral, for instance—they might get out. But mostly they couldn't pay.

Each hearing took a minute or two. If there were thirty names on the docket, a couple of gimmes would get released almost automatically. These would depend on the judge. The old judge with the snaggleteeth, for instance, didn't believe in domestic violence, so the guys who beat their wives had a good chance of doing it again that same night. On top of that, if Ben behaved himself and didn't waste time arguing for shooters and rapists, the judge would do him one or two favors and cut a few low-level offenders loose. Ben's strategy was to say nothing for the gimmes and the sure losers, and use his favors wisely.

Robert McTell had been arrested for burglary of the Israel Augustine school, right across the street from the courthouse. He'd been arrested eleven times before, and three of those had matured into felony convictions. If he was convicted on the new case, he'd do twenty to life as a fourth-time offender. This was more than enough reason for the duty judge to conclude that McTell might be a flight risk. But he was also on parole for one of those priors and the parole officer dropped a detention order on him, which meant he wouldn't be released no matter what happened at the First Appearance hearing. So Ben stayed quiet and hoarded his favors, and McTell went to jail.

Interview

Saturday afternoon was the worst time to go to the House of Detention. Families were there too, and they were crying or yelling or, worse, calm. The inmates and their visitors sat on metal stools, separated by double-thick plexiglass. They used handsets to talk. The lawyers got little rooms, also divided by plexiglass, but thinner and perforated. They could hear each other without handsets if they shouted. Ben could smell the jail on McTell through the holes in the plexiglass. He was forty-two and old, with a grizzled head and teeth coming off at tangents to his jaw.

McTell said:

"How's your day going?"

Ben used a rueful tone:

"Every day I get over to the House of Detention is a good one."

"Me too. I have a lot of good days."

"I'm here to visit with you again about your case. But first I need to learn a little bit more about you."

McTell smiled again:

"Like on a date."

"Well," Ben said.

"Come on," said McTell. "You're allowed to smile."

So Ben gave a little and said:

"Like a date, except the part about the lawyer and the handcuffs."

McTell was quick with an answer:

"You haven't been on the right kinds of dates, young man."

Ben had been to see McTell once before, a few days after his arrest. He'd given McTell his phone number, which McTell had never used, and explained about confidentiality and McTell's rights. He'd reassured McTell that he'd be back to talk about the case and help him prepare a defense. He hadn't said that it would be four months.

What Ben's clients usually wanted when he went to see them, in order of priority: To go home; for Ben to hear, and acknowledge, that they were not guilty; for Ben to hear, and acknowledge, that the police were lying; and for relief from cold or heat or hunger. The most common way for a client to introduce the main topic of conversation was: "I'm ready to go home." Then: "I don't have time for this." They mostly didn't want to hear about confidentiality and a lawyer's ethical responsibilities. And then they didn't want to talk about addresses and jobs and medical history.

But McTell didn't mind doing the other stuff first. Where were you for the storm? *Seventh Ward, then the Superdome, then Seventh Ward again.* He was homeless, usually slept in an abandoned building—*There's one I like right behind the public defender. On Banks Street.* He didn't have a job or a trade. He made money selling the copper that he stole out of abandoned buildings. He had two children. He wasn't trying to ingratiate himself. His laughter wasn't eager and searching, like the clients who tried to show Ben they were harmless. He didn't need Ben to like him, because he didn't think it would matter. If he didn't act defeated, it was because he knew there wasn't a fight going on, just a slow concession.

"Tell me about your kids."

"They stay with their mother. She and I don't get along. We're like earl and water."

"Like?"

"Earl and water. We don't mix right."

"Okay."

McTell, patiently:

"O—I—L. Earl."

"Earl!"

"Are you hearing me?"

"I am now."

"Where are you from?"

"Not here. I guess you can tell."

"New York?"

"Massachusetts."

"Boston?"

"No, in the west of the state."

"The Berkshires."

"Oh. Yeah."

"You're surprised?"

"I mean. You've been there?"

"Ten miles behind me, and ten thousand more to go."

"I don't—"

"I used to listen to your boy James Taylor. You look like you're going to fall out."

"I'm sorry."

"I like that country. Sort of rock-style-easy-style country. You?"

"I like James Taylor too."

"People have their own thing."

"I'm hearing that."

Robert McTell wasn't going to judge him, at least not too harshly, for being ignorant and white. It's just part of the human condition. Can you imagine a world without ignorant people? No, right? They're everywhere. Well, Ben Alder is one of them. Why get worked up?

Ben asked:

"Tell me a little more about your kids?"

"My little girl is Bobbie. She's eight years old. My boy is Robert. He's sixteen. Same name. They look just the same, too. Like their mother, which is a good thing."

"And where are they?"

"They stay with their mother. I thought I said that. Should I talk louder?"

"It's okay. I've got you now."

"You have your own kids?"

Ben didn't even think about it:

"Yeah, I do. Two boys. Isaiah and Nehemiah."

McTell didn't know about Robert's murder arrest. Ben couldn't figure out how to ask any more about the kid without seeming like he was blaming McTell for being an absentee dad. What had Ben been planning to do, anyhow? Tell McTell that his son had wanted to talk to him about a murder weapon, but it was now taken care of, so don't worry?

Back to business. Mostly, with kids like Robert, Ben didn't ask his client's side of the story. He was going to have to make something up, anyhow—and why have the facts in the world get in the way, or be constrained by his client's lies. But McTell seemed like he was on the ball enough to help with the storytelling, so Ben went right at it:

"I want to talk with you about what the police are saying. I'm going to read you their report. That's their story of how you were arrested. I'm not telling you I think it's true. I understand that it might not be. It's important that you know what they're saying, because that's probably what they're going to say in court. So I'll read it. And then I'm going to ask you what *really* happened when you were arrested, okay?"

It was. And, per McTell, what really happened was that he went into the school building with some tools to steal copper pipes, just like the police said. This was the global market made manifest in New Orleans street crime, since prices for copper in London and Tokyo and New York were at an all-time high and New Orleans had a lot of abandoned buildings that weren't using their pipes. So why shouldn't McTell? Ben made a show of writing. He tried to write all the way through meetings. Otherwise, his clients got nervous when

he picked up his pen. They worried what they might have said that
needed to get written down, and who might read it. For good reasons,
both general to public defenders and specific to Ben himself, they
mostly didn't trust him.

After McTell was done, Ben said:

"I need to explain something about burglary."

"You know something I don't?"

"About the law of burglary."

McTell was still skeptical, but game:

"Give it a try."

"Burglary is when you go inside a structure—that's a building, like
a school—with the intent to commit a felony or a theft. Intent means
it's something you want to do. It's like what you're planning when you
go in. If you went in, even if you weren't supposed to, but you weren't
looking to steal anything inside, it wasn't a burglary."

"Okay."

"You follow me?"

"What's that got to do with me?"

"Well, the pipes," Ben said.

McTell said:

"I need to explain something about burglary. The pipes are worth
three dollars a pound uptown, and three-fifteen on Poland Avenue.
But it's harder to get down to Poland without a truck. Try walking
all that way with a stolen shopping cart full of stolen copper. You get
arrested within a couple blocks."

Ben sat back. It was nice to have a client who'd work with him.
Even if the client, plainly and correctly, thought he was something
of an idiot. You could have a real, dishonest conversation with a man
like Robert McTell. Ben asked:

"You didn't tell that to the cops?"

"One cop. Should I have?"

"No. Of course not."

"He just told me to shut up."

"That's good advice when you're arrested. You didn't tell him why you were in there?"

"I told him the cuffs were too tight."

"You didn't cut any pipes?"

"The cop came in too quick."

"Where are the tools?"

"I don't know. I stole those, too. Easy come, easy go."

"Did the police pick them up?"

"Not the one who arrested me."

"While you were sitting in the squad car, did you see Crime Scene? The guys who do the fingerprints? Did they show up?"

"For a burglary? Of an abandoned school? How long have you been a lawyer?"

"Too long, and not long enough."

"Really."

"About two years."

"That's not long."

"Depends on where you sit."

"It's not even that long in prison."

"You have a longer-term view than most people."

McTell grinned. Maybe there was hope for Ben Alder yet:

"I have a lot of experience."

"Were you holding the tools? When you were arrested?"

"They were in my bag."

"Was the bag—"

"Closed. I hadn't even opened it yet."

"Great. Terrific. You weren't stealing anything. Now we just need a reason you were in there."

And maybe there wasn't hope, after all, for either of them. McTell plainly doubted that he, McTell, was the one who was struggling. Slowly:

"I wanted to take the pipes."

"A reason that won't send you to jail for twenty years. Was it raining?"

"It was a nice night."

"Did you ever sleep in there?"

"Not anymore. The roof's falling in."

"The prosecutor doesn't know that."

"Everyone knows that."

"Well, I mean, the prosecutor isn't homeless."

"It was on the news. Channel 5. The I-Team. They had a whole series about school buildings around town. *A Dream Deferred*, they call it. They were showing it at the drop-in center on Tulane."

They needed this guy to vet theories at the public defender's office. Ben ate his pen and thought for a minute. He brightened:

"Maybe you were running away from someone?"

McTell drew himself up to his full five foot seven inches, all 110 pounds of him, adjusted his orange collar, and smiled.

"No, indeed. I've got my dignity."

12

Forensics

A little more than a week after Robert's arrest, Ben went over to the juvenile unit with an eyepatch, a handful of pencils, and a set of blocks. The eyepatch wasn't for Robert. There was another client he needed to visit first. They were going to talk about a twenty-year plea deal. The kid had been shot in the eye and somehow survived. Six months later he was arrested for shooting another kid—not the one who shot him, or anyone connected with that earlier shooting—dead. It wasn't revenge, but it wasn't unrelated either. He had the anger in him from getting shot and didn't know what else to do with it. He always needed new eyepatches because they kept getting dirty or broken or stolen or confiscated in jail. If Ben didn't bring one, the kid would sit across from him in meetings with his open red socket.

The pencils and blocks were for Robert's testing—IQ, mental health screening, competency to give up his rights. The deputies wouldn't let the doctor bring them in, but Ben could. Ben wasn't allowed to stay, since Robert might look to Ben for cues and that would ruin the testing. But the doctor videotaped the interview so Ben could watch it later. She was good with kids, friendly without pretending to be familiar. Ben had a court order for a special setup—a room without plexiglass, where they could touch, and no shackles on Robert's wrists. When Ben left him, Robert reached out his arm and they bumped fists. Ben hadn't told Robert what he'd done with the gun. Robert just asked him if the police were going to find it, and Ben just said he didn't think they would.

That same night his expert sent over the video of the interview, and Ben and Boris watched it together. The camera caught Robert from the waist up as he sat at the table: the navy-blue pajama shirt of the juvenile offender uniform, the dirty, off-white cinder-block wall behind him.

"Who's your lawyer?"

"Mr. Ben. And Mr. Boris, I think. I don't know about Mr. Boris right now."

"What's their job?"

"He says it's to help me. Mr. Ben."

"What does that mean to you?"

"To me? I don't know."

"What is your lawyer supposed to do to help you?"

"He said he was going to try to find someone for me. And things."

"Things?"

"He has a word. He looks for things he needs in court."

"Do you remember the word?"

"I don't know."

"What else does he do?"

"He's going to go with me to court."

"What's going to happen in court?"

"He says it's still really early."

"What might happen to you in court?"

"He told me life means life."

"What does that mean to you? In your own words?"

"Life means until you die."

"What else?"

"But he said we're going to fight. Like, together."

The doctor walked Robert through some reading comprehension tests to see if he understood his rights before he confessed. "If you cannot afford an attorney, one will be appointed for you." What does that mean? *The guy in court whose job it is to put you in jail? The district attorney.* They talked for a few hours. Robert was trying hard: Leaning in toward the camera, closing his eyes in concentration. The last thing she did was a trauma screening. Fifteen yes-or-no questions that would tell her whether she needed to dig deeper into what had happened to him. If he answered right, he might even win the prize and get a PTSD diagnosis.

"Robert, a stressful event is something serious and upsetting that happens to you. A stressful event can also be something that you see, even if it doesn't happen to you. Stressful or scary events happen to lots of people. I'm going to read you a list of stressful and scary events that sometimes happen. Can you just tell me yes or no if one of these happened to you? Okay. So, the first one is a serious natural disaster like a flood, tornado, hurricane, earthquake, or fire. Did that—"

Yeah, and to everyone else he knew. She went down the list. Yes, with a little bit of a kid's play at toughness, to getting beaten up. Yes, but with shaded eyes, to seeing someone in his family beaten up. Yes to seeing someone close to him getting hurt. Yes to seeing someone die violently. And the final question:

"Anything else that was scary or stressful?"

"Well," he said, "you know."

He smiled at her. The question was almost as silly as the one about the flood. Robert brought his hands up in little half-circles, like he was taking in all the wonder that surrounded him. Watching him on camera, in two dimensions, from one fixed perspective, was somehow more honest than sitting there in the room with him, a child who was little more than a single moment. The night they'd found him bleeding in the hotel and silently brought him to be stitched up was the only history they had of him. It was physically hard for Robert to talk about anything that happened before his arrest. When he tried, he'd get choppy and stuttering like he couldn't hold more than a couple words in his head or mouth at the same time. The past, any of it, was the second point that fixes the line. Once the line exists, it stretches forward indefinitely into the future, all the years until his death.

She said:

"Or it can be something that's still going on. What's scary or stressful, Robert?"

"This is," he said.

"Being here?"

"Yeah."

"Is something happening to you here?"

"Nothing like that."

He shook his head a little bit. She made a note and moved on. She said:

"Well—"

"Because," he said, "it's right now, but also it's forever."

13

Document Review

The psychologist did her scoring and reported back that Robert was fair-to-middling smart. He's quick with numbers, slower with language, doesn't have a lot of words but could learn them if he got a chance. Fifth-grade reading level, which wasn't unusual for a kid who'd been bounced around to a lot of public schools, most of them in New Orleans. Not much of a fund of knowledge. Depressed, though that could just be the situation. People make bad decisions about their futures—like waiving their rights and confessing to shooting a local hero and symbol of the recovery—when they're depressed. Maybe he also had an anxiety disorder. Certainly trauma. She didn't think he'd understood what he was agreeing to when he waived his rights and gave his statement. She wanted to look at school records and do collateral interviews, to make sure it was all consistent. She talked to his mom, to learn about his childhood, but his mom didn't volunteer much. *I think she's limited. Like not intellectually limited. I think she's shut down. It would be nice to talk to his dad. Any chance?* No, I'm afraid not, Ben lied. He's homeless and in the wind.

So Ben and Boris went looking for evidence that Robert had existed outside the New Orleans criminal justice system. It would help the doctor and also help them build a mitigation case. Mitigation is when you're legally guilty but you deserve a break. At some point they might need to beg for mercy, to eke out a plea deal to twenty-five or thirty years, twice as long as Robert had been alive. They'd want to show that he was a hard luck story.

They knew from his mom that he grew up in the Magnolia Housing Development. That's where he got lead poisoning. When he was four, some personal injury lawyers had found him and signed him up for a lawsuit, alongside five hundred other New Orleans kids. Ben went to the city, which ran the Magnolia, for records. He first asked nicely and then rudely and then submitted a formal request, three times over. Each of the requests was lost, they said. But when he got a court order and they showed him the file on Robert Johnson's family, the only thing in it were Ben's own request letters.

Medical records: Charity Hospital, where Robert was born, had been closed since the storm. The other hospitals and their emergency rooms? *It's been a long time.* He's only sixteen. Couldn't have been that long. You don't have anything? If only Ben and Boris had brought him to the hospital the night they found him covered in blood. Or maybe used his real name at urgent care. There'd be a record of that to make people feel bad for him. They did find some nurse's notes at a hospital in Jefferson Parish, right outside of Orleans. He was admitted when he was five years old, after a teacher noticed marks on his body. Determined to be rat bites.

Child protection had been notified, though. So what of their files? *We can only confirm an investigation. We can't tell you more without a court order.* Serve the motion, wait, have a hearing, wait. Finally, with a court order in place: What can you tell me? *We conducted an investigation and closed it.* What results? *We don't have that anymore.* The water did wash things away, but that only sped up the process of erasing the city's children.

Three arrests as a juvenile. Two of them Ben and Boris knew about, of course. Possession of a concealed weapon; guilty plea, courtesy of Boris. Domestic violence battery on his stepfather. That charge was never prosecuted. There was a third case, from early in 2006. Before Ben and Boris knew him. The court computer entries show it was trespassing and criminal damage to property. Nothing more. Per the computer: The child admitted guilt at his first court appearance and was placed on probation. The public defender, the child's lawyer, had no file and no memory. What happened? The probation officer had moved to Arkansas and wouldn't answer the phone. The prosecutor didn't remember the case but was willing to share some mean-spirited wisdom: *I guess this is what happens when you let them off easy the first time.*

What about schools? Robert went to four elementary schools in New Orleans. One in Memphis, when his family left for the storm. The Memphis school sent Ben a report card that showed he'd been failing the seventh grade. The New Orleans schools: All closed, and nobody knew for sure where their records were. Maybe in the old, abandoned buildings, and probably rotted beyond recognition. Robert's high school, though, was a going concern: Fannie Lou Hamer Achievement and Excellence Mid-City Charter, a school with a name longer than its history. Ben needed to go there anyhow, since that's where Robert had been arrested.

The hallways were all hung with college pennants—Yale, Tulane, Alcorn State—and painted with lines down the middle. The kids walking in each direction made sure to stay on their side. The staff of teachers just out of Yale wore skinny pants, skinny ties. Whenever they passed each other in the hallways, the staff and the kids, they stopped to shake hands.

Just inside the doors, a metal detector and a bunch of kids talking. One of them looked over at Ben and Boris. A teenager in khaki pants, round face, a green high-school logo sweatshirt, a high fade. He walked a couple steps toward them. Boris smiled at him. Ben liked standing next to kids in court, or at least felt like he needed to. Boris actually liked kids. He asked:

"What's the point of a metal detector if there's no security?"

"It's not on," the kid said. He had an instrument case, Ben thought maybe a clarinet, and a Day-Glo yellow backpack. "They say they trust us."

"They don't trust you to walk down a hallway right."

The kid looked like that had occurred to him, too.

"That's quite a backpack," said Boris. "If a search party ever needs to find you in a snowstorm."

The kid was a little sheepish:

"My mom says it makes me easy to see when I walk home at night. After band. She's scared about cars."

"The office?"

"That way." The kid pointed. "Y'all aren't teachers though?"

Ben wanted in on the action:

"No. We're here to sell green sweatshirts. We heard there was a market."

The kid looked at him, correctly, like he wasn't that funny. Boris shrugged like Ben was a sad distraction that just had to be lived with:

"Are we supposed to shake goodbye?"

"We don't have to if you're not a teacher."

"We're going to punch it out, though?"

The kid didn't smile but he did extend his fist. The back of his hand was studded with thickened knobs of dark skin, keloid scars running up in a horseshoe under the sleeve of his sweatshirt, like bite marks.

Most of the city's kids went to charter schools, nonprofits that had taken over public education from a government that hadn't done its part. A lot of the charters were like the public defender's office, mostly staffed now with carpetbaggers from Away. Here was a chance to earn your combat stripes without ever going overseas and with most of the comforts of home. Just like the public defenders, too: Lots of people in New Orleans wanted the charter schools to fail, to prove it couldn't be done better by outsiders. Lots of others wanted them to succeed to prove that New Orleans couldn't do right by itself. Some just hated them because you hate the one you're with. Ben and Boris were mostly in the third group. Nevertheless, Ben thought the receptionist in the school's administrative office was maybe the most beautiful woman who'd ever smiled in his direction. Not right at him, though. He tried to get out in front of Boris, but that never worked.

"We have a meeting with Eric. I'm Ben Alder, from the public defender's office. This is my assistant—"

"Boris Pasternak," said Boris.

"Really?"

"I know," said Ben. "You never thought you'd meet a real public defender, right?"

Boris, to whom she was actually talking:

"My mother married a refugee. He went refugee from our family, too. She thought the name would make me an intellectual. It didn't work."

"I majored in Russian literature!"

"Because it's a glamorous job," Ben went on. "Mostly we just send press flacks and aides. So people don't get to see us in person."

"I've never actually read anything I wrote," Boris admitted. "Do you have any recommendations?"

She laughed, not at Ben's line. Ben, to whom nobody was paying attention:

"Great. You guys should fire up the old samovar and talk books together some time. Is Eric around?"

Even Boris's condescension was charming:

"How do you say grumpy in Russian?"

She laughed again and went to get the principal. Ben was a little resentful:

"That last one wasn't even funny."

"You're being a dick."

"The kid outside looked at me like he knew me."

"A self-important dick."

"We haven't represented him, right?"

"No, Doodlebug. For sure no. They don't all look the same."

"But he acted like he knew who we were. You saw he watched us go?"

"Nobody can take their eyes off you. You saw the way the secretary was sweating you?"

"Now you're being a dick. Can we talk about something important? Do you think the cardigans are ironic?"

"These people don't do irony. They've never even heard of liberal guilt."

"Surely they're Jewish, like the rest of us do-gooders?"

"That woman is Episcopalian. She has perfect teeth."

She showed off the teeth again—again at Boris, not Ben—when she brought them in to sit down with Eric Conover. Ben knew him from another case. A kid named John Hurt who'd gone there until he took a guilty plea to avoid going to jail for something he didn't do. Ben had been the lawyer standing next to him when he took the plea. Actually, Ben was the one who'd convinced him to take it.

"You guys know I used to be a lawyer? Legal aid. In Cambridge."

"I remember. You told me."

"I did special education law."

"I remember about Cambridge and about legal aid, both."

"So many families came through our office who just never had a chance. That's why I joined Teach for America. I so much appreciate what you do."

He always appreciated what you were doing. He'd gotten a lot of money from tech billionaires for conveying that sentiment very effectively. He had a good set to his jaw. People saw that he was resolved to do what had to be done, and also compassionate. Just from the set of his jaw. He could have been rich with that jaw. Instead, he was running a charter school network in New Orleans and he'd made promises about how fifteen hundred Black kids were all going to be first-generation college graduates.

"We appreciate you, too. Here's the release, signed by his mother."

"He'd only been with us since the beginning of this school year, just four months. We're all so devastated."

Ben thought he'd heard him say that before, about Ben's other client who'd gone to that school. John used to sketch animals and superheroes. He wanted to be a cartoonist. He had a little boy cousin who lived a few blocks away. One Sunday night the cousin's mom—John's aunt—took him in to the police and said John had sucked on his penis in the bath. He probably hadn't. He swore it, anyhow, and Ben believed him. Ben got a recording of the six-year-old cousin denying that anything had happened. John said he hadn't even been anywhere near the cousin's house when the bath happened. The aunt was all the way crazy. But for a fourteen-year-old in juvenile court, aggravated rape is prison—*secure custody* is the euphemism—until he turns twenty-one, no early release, and lifetime sex offender registration. So Ben told him to take a deal. It was the safe thing to do. Instead of aggravated rape of a child, he plead guilty to sexual battery. No sex offender registration and no jail time. A win.

But afterward John stopped going to school. He started hanging out with friends who actually did break the law. He was turning fifteen, so it might have happened anyway. Who can tell with teenagers. John was failing on probation. He'd stand there in court while the judge lectured him—for testing positive for marijuana, for skipping school, for not coming home to his mother—and he'd stare down at the same table where they'd sat when he pled guilty and press on it with his fingertips until the tips turned white up to the first joint. He never said a word to her but "Yes, ma'am."

He was shot almost a year after he pled guilty, riding with some friends in a stolen car. Ben came late to the funeral and sat in back so he wouldn't have to go up and see the coffin and the family. John's brother, just a year younger, sat up by their mother in a too-large black suit; probably John's. That night Ben had only the one beer and then felt sick to his stomach. When he drove back to the Bywater along the raised interstate, he reached into the back of the car and grabbed a bucket of softballs that he'd bought to hit around with Boris, and poured them out and threw up into the bucket driving at about seventy miles an hour. He went to slow down and pull off but the balls rolled around and one got between the brake pedal and the floor so he ended up driving on to the next exit before he got the ball out, and then he pulled off still holding the bucket of vomit. A hero of New Orleans. Afterward he went to the casino at the foot of Canal Street, not because he gambled but because the perpetual whirring of the machines was better than silence or talk, and there drank more on a now-cleansed stomach.

That's where Ben had first met Eric Conover. At the funeral, bequeathing his smile as a condolence. Now he bequeathed on Ben a slim folder, everything they had on Robert. Only a single sheet of paper from before this year, a photocopy of a lined notebook page. Lord knows how they got it. Teacher's notes from a meeting with Robert's mom, nine years earlier. He was failing first grade. The room was quiet for a minute while Ben looked at the folder and Conover waited for Ben to tell him something about the shooting. He was good at waiting. He'd probably been a good lawyer. The quiet made Boris snap back to attention from where he'd been shifting in his chair and looking back through the door at the Russophile assistant.

"What kind of student was he?"

"To be honest I didn't know him very well. Just to shake his hand in the hallway. We say here that learning is a lifelong experience for everyone. Even when we're just shaking hands, we learn respect and professionalism."

Boris tilted his head to the side. The smile wasn't going over well with him. He started trolling.

"My boy here is going to get Robert out of jail and back with you just in time for summer school."

"Well, that's extraordinary news! I had thought he confessed. Are you saying he didn't do it?"

"That's how he pled. I'm just asking if you want him back."

"Of course we want to talk about that."

"But what would be the end of that conversation?"

"I want you to know that we take second chances really seriously here. We take first chances really seriously here. So many of our young people don't get even that. Bringing someone into our community is a really intentional, conscious thing for us."

Conover gave him the jaw. It really was impressive. Maybe Boris was thinking about breaking it, and ruining the futures of fifteen hundred kids. Boris said:

"I think that means you want to save the world, but not this kid."

"I know how hard it is to be a lawyer for kids. Here I'm trying to send hundreds of kids to college. It's so invigorating. You should come sit in on our junior social studies seminar, about the justice system. Or wait. This could work really well. Would you like to guest lecture sometime?"

Boris smiled his own smile, villainously. It was time for Ben to intervene. He said:

"I understand that Robert was arrested here at school."

Conover gave them a little apologetic simper:

"I'm sure they wrote it all up in the police report."

"We're just trying to figure out what happened."

Conover:

"I can see how much you care about your client. I want to be sure to give you the right information. Why don't I talk to our counsel, and then get back to you?"

"It would be great to be able to get started defending Robert. I know how much you care about him, too. We'd love an overview of what happened when he was arrested."

"I'll make sure to get with our lawyer right away to work that up for you."

Boris went super sweet, too:

"Someone told me that you were a lawyer, though. Where'd you go, again? Hartford? Haverford?"

Whatever else had come before, this was the unforgivable offense. Conover stood up. Nobody extended a hand for a goodbye shake. They were done at Fannie Lou Hamer, but not yet done with school visits for the day.

14

Arrest

"**H**ow's my case looking?"

"Like it's just getting started."

"I tried to call you."

"I'm sorry. I'm not always at my desk."

"Were you with your son?"

"Sometimes, of course."

"He's not at the hospital, though?"

"I appreciate that you're asking, Robert. I need to talk about what happened at school, when they picked you up."

"I'm not trying to make you upset."

"I know you're not."

"We can talk about school if you want."

"That morning, when you were arrested."

"They just came to get me. Out of class."

"Who were they?"

"My English teacher and Mr. Eric, and the police officer. The detective."

"Eric Conover, the principal?"

"Yeah."

"And Miss Michelle?"

"Miss Michelle is my English teacher. She was."

"What did they say when they came to get you?"

"They wanted to talk to me."

"What else?"

"That's all."

"Who said that?"

"Mr. Eric."

"Where did he say that?"

"In the hallway."

"What else did they do?"

"They all shook my hand."

"Where did you go then?"

"The principal's office. Mr. Conover's office."

"Tell me about that."

"They said to talk to the police officer."

"What did each of them say to you, exactly?"

"Miss Michelle said I needed to tell the truth."

"Anything else?"

"Mr. Conover said I had to do the right thing. He smiled at me. You know? Like, with his whole face."

"Did anyone tell you why the police wanted to talk to you?"

"Because I shot Miss Scott."

"Did anyone say why they thought you shot her, though?"

"I told them I did."

"Right. Before you told them you did. How did they explain why they wanted to talk to you in the first place? Why did they think it might be you?"

"Miss Michelle said."

"What did she say?"

"When we all sat down. *He looks like the picture, right?*"

"Who did she say that to?"

"We were all there."

"Did anyone answer her?"

"The detective said I did."

"Tell me what they said about the picture."

"They didn't. They just told me to tell the truth. Mr. Conover said. I remember. He said about being a responsible member of the community."

"What about your mom?"

"I haven't talked to her. Not this week."

"I mean, what did they say about your mom? Did they talk about calling her?"

"No. Not till after."

"After?"

"After they arrested me. The detective did."

"And your mom—"

"She doesn't come here. She doesn't like it here."

"I know. Let me just ask you, though—"

"We talk on the phone now."

"That's okay."

"You changed the rule."

"I remember."

"Because she doesn't come here."

"Remember, though, you still can't talk about your case with her."

"Only with you."

"None of the other guys in jail, right?"

"Right. Just you."

"Okay."

"Okay."

"And then . . ."

"Mr. Conover shook my hand again. And then he put on the handcuffs. The detective. They said it again, thank you for being responsible. We're proud of you."

15

Entry and Inspection

Ben, weaving around potholes on a broken street, windows rolled up against the people who lived there, high on life and Diet Coke.

"How often do you lie to your clients?"

Boris, leaning all the way back in the passenger seat, holding his phone in front of his face and pecking at a clever text message to the school secretary with the smile and the samovar. Of course he'd gotten her number.

"Always. I tell every client I'm going to do my best. So, always. Who's the client on this next one?"

"A guy I picked up a few months back."

"Did they give him a name?"

"Robert."

"Another Robert?"

"A homeless guy. He went in to steal copper from Israel Augustine."

Boris pulled the seat lever and shot upright:

"Oh, that's a good one."

"It's not."

"It is. Did he run?"

"No. But they found him in the building."

"Oooh, it's a really good one. It's a winner."

"Okay. What's a non-felony reason to trespass in an abandoned school?"

Boris answered right away, and definitively:

"The bathroom, Yankee Doodle."

"They don't have bathrooms."

"Yeah, they have bathrooms."

"Not with water. It's been closed since the storm."

"He's homeless, right? It's that or behind a bush."

"That's where people keep their guns, remember?"

"Bathroom's a good theory. That's why he went in. Jurors will buy it. Everyone's got dignity." Boris got out of the little gold car and held the door open so Ben could climb out across the seats. "Everyone but you, I mean. I keep telling you, John Jacob Dudenheimer Schmidt. Values."

The school's big marquee, unchanged since the storm, still read: SCHOOL STARTS AUGUST 15, 8:00. The building was peach-colored stucco, all done up like a Spanish mission. Ben had a court order allowing entry and inspection. A facilities manager from the school district was waiting for them at the top of the high front stairs, holding personal injury waivers for each of them to sign. Then he took off the rusted padlock with bolt cutters and backed away.

McTell had attended the school where he was arrested, back when it was still called Commercial High. In the nineties it was renamed after the first Black judge in Louisiana, Israel Augustine. He'd served at Orleans Parish Criminal Court, right across Tulane Avenue from his namesake school. Everyone said he was a better guy than his peers on the bench. He'd started programs aimed at diversion and reentry. From what Ben had seen: judges, even the good ones, believed that the same people who daily break lives, and the institutions that help them do it, are the only ones who can fix things.

Just through the main doors was a big lobby with mirrored walls and high ceilings. Past it, an auditorium with hundreds of wooden seats and a stage, gold curtains still hanging over the proscenium arch. Works Progress Administration murals showed scenes of business and industry. In one, a man in a gray suit and hat entered a bank vault through a huge, circular steel door. The iron lighting rig had fallen from the ceiling over the stage. The ground was thick with crumbling plaster and splintered wood and fabric from ceiling panels. In the ruined school, sitting on the edge of the stage, Ben told Boris about his father and son duo, Robert McTell and Robert Johnson.

"Son of a bitch."

"Right," said Ben.

"How often do you lie to your co-counsel?"

"Not that often."

"Why didn't you tell me you represent Robert's dad?"

"I don't know."

"It's something dramatic. Some fucking—what would you call it?—psychodrama, right? It's about your dad? Or something from the Bible?"

"What's the difference?"

"Oh shit. It's some shit from the fucking Bible."

"It's not."

"It's not a conflict?"

"The cases have nothing to do with each other."

"I mean between us. That you lied to me."

"I didn't lie to you. I just didn't tell you."

Boris rubbed his head and got up and they went on with the investigation. What else was there to do? They found the hallway on the ground floor and the windows where McTell must have come in. There was indeed a water fountain. The wall wasn't torn open, and it didn't seem like McTell or anyone else had taken anything from the fountain. That was good for the case. Ben asked:

"You haven't been to see Robert."

"You didn't tell me about the dad because you're punishing me for not going to see Robert?"

"My point is you've got your own shtick."

"I grew up in Maine."

"There's only so many times I can say I'm sorry for that."

"I inherited two glorious traditions of swearing. Only one of them stuck around long enough to stick around. I only do the French swears. *Shtick* means penis?"

"You know what it means. Your own *psychodrama*."

"All my drama is right here on the surface. Are you going to tell Robert?"

"No."

"Are you going to tell the dad?"

"No."

"Are you going to withdraw?"

"No."

Neither of them raised their voices. They both made a show of poking around the hallway the whole time they fought, like they were going to unearth a clue that would exonerate a man they knew was guilty. Boris said:

"You're punishing him, then."

"Who?"

"The dad. For being a shitty dad and getting Robert beaten up. You should withdraw."

"And leave them with the guy who isn't visiting because he feels too bad to be a good lawyer."

"Instead, you can be a hero. You want to save two generations of Black men? That's the point here?"

"One generation of me."

"You *shtick*. You're now sure that you've told me everything about this case?"

Ben lied:

"Yes."

"Are you lying?"

"No."

Boris took pictures of everything in the hallway and in the boys' bathroom. Someone had gotten all the useful pipes and wires out of the bathroom already. Paint was peeling off the walls in yellow curls the size of dinner plates. They found a classroom where all the debris had been swept up and a bunch of blankets spread on the floor; they also found a classroom with a piece of wire rigged as a latch and the smell of shit in a corner. Another room had a big pile of Styrofoam take-out containers, and needles. On a broken chalkboard, someone had written: *Help us.*

Boris opened a big cabinet in the back of the room. Empty. He was still angry. He asked:

"Were people here during the storm?"

"I don't think so."

"It still smells like school."

"That's mold and rust."

They turned around and shuffled through the building, headed back up and out.

"It could be nice," Boris said. "It's got high ceilings. They could rehab it. The public defender's office could move in."

"Why would you want that?"

"The same reason I'm named Boris. Inherited misery is romantic."

"Conover doesn't think so. He doesn't have time for the misery. He just wants things different."

"Fuck that guy, though. What do you think they'll do with it?"

"Let it fester for a generation and then tear it down when they give up or get some more federal money."

"Why do you have to be such a pessimist?"

"That's optimism. Pessimism is the kids come back and get black lung, or whatever."

"What's wrong with you?"

"I'm a public defender. And a Jew."

"So am I."

"There you go."

"This job is starting to make me hate public defenders. And Jews."

"The only reason we do this job is that we hate public defenders. And Jews."

They stood in their dress shoes in the wreckage of the school, preserved in the amber light coming in through high, filthy windows. Boris, after a minute, punted a piece of plaster across the room. He said: "Anyhow, you're wrong. Pessimism is the kids come back and the school and everything else keeps going like it used to."

16

Suppression

Their first year, not long after they started representing kids, Boris had a client, a sly and smooth-talking boy named Jack, whom he loved. Jack's mom threw him out of the house for being gay, so Boris sold his car and paid the family of one of Jack's high school friends to take him in. One night Jack sat outside with his friend while the friend's dad tried to fix an old van on the lawn. A car made the corner, moving slow, and stopped in the street. A man got out, no hurry. He reached back inside to take his gun out of the passenger seat, turned, pointed it. Jack and his friend looked back at him and died right there together. It wasn't about the drugs, or anything else really. There'd been an argument earlier that day between the shooter's girlfriend and the friend's sister about loud music. That was all.

Ben bought a half-dozen tallboys of cheap beer then drove across the river to the place where Jack had been staying. The streets were too wide, as though they were laid out for parades or four-lane traffic, which there would never be, because there in the Cut Off all roads dead-ended at the Intracoastal Waterway. It looked like they'd scaled the streets and the yards up for big-ticket suburbia but most of the houses stayed in a poor neighborhood in New Orleans. Ben didn't want to go inside the house of mourning or lurk like a cop in the car, so he walked back and forth under the trees. It was summer and big cockroaches, two inches long, scattered in front of him. The door opened and Ben watched Boris and a woman hug in the dark doorway. Jack's dead friend's mom, probably. After she went inside Boris backed down the stairs like he was backing away from a sacred object, like it would be sacrilege to turn away.

Ben said:

"Where are we going?"

Boris got in:

"On an investigation."

"Where?"

"To MLK."

"What's the case?"

"It's for Jack."

"Then it doesn't have to happen tonight. Let's just go to a bar."

"It has to happen tonight."

"Or we can sit in my yard."

Boris shook his head and drummed his knuckles on the window. He squinted into the darkness of the Cut Off, the neighborhood still unsettled. A car in front of every fourth house, only one streetlight working on each block, piles of gray wood on the curbs. He said:

"You're driving like a man with a paper asshole."

"What does that mean?"

"Delicately. Go faster."

"I like it. Where does it come from?"

"Canucks."

"I don't even know where we're going."

"The coroner's office."

"We're not going to get in."

"We're not going to try."

They came off the expressway and turned onto Martin Luther King Jr. Boulevard near the shuttered Calliope housing projects. Everything was dark, an abandoned city whose inhabitants hadn't remembered to leave. They looped around the neutral ground and stopped across the street from the New Orleans Forensic Center, in front of a brick shotgun double with plywood over its windows and doors. This city is beautiful not because it's old and grand but because it's decaying in front of you, the incarnation of time passing.

"What are we looking for?"

"We're not. We're watching."

"For what?"

"Just keeping watch."

"Really, this is very mysterious."

"You're the last person who should need an explanation."

Ben got the beers from the wheel well behind him and handed one to Boris. They rolled their windows down and sat in the hot dark, drinking and sweating. Eventually, Ben, having figured it out, tried to sound hesitant but willing:

"You don't want me to say kaddish, do you?"

"Jesus Christ, no."

"Thank god."

Jews bury their dead within twenty-four hours. They're not supposed to leave the body alone until it's in the ground. Jack was still in the empty coroner's office. So Boris and Ben sat and watched over the building with this boy in it who was not their dead, and wondered at themselves and the kids who were in their charge and also entirely beyond them, and how far they all were from home and how alone in this city of exiles and refugees, this city of refuge. A police car on patrol slowed to investigate their white faces in a dark car at night on MLK, but then because of their faces kept going. Ben opened another beer.

"Can I say something?"

"Something Jewish."

"Yeah."

"Like a sermon."

"No. Well, yes."

"I guess I asked for it."

"Judaism is all about time. Regulating time. Because the rabbis didn't have a sacred place, they thought a lot about time. That's what they could control. Not control, but structure. They could structure it. There are all kinds of timebound rules and laws. When Shabbat starts and when you have to pray. All kinds of things. But the people watching a dead body are off the hook for every timebound commandment."

For a while Ben didn't think Boris was going to respond, but then he said:

"Like they get a continuance."

"There's no makeup date or next court date. They just don't have to do it at all, ever."

"You'd think they'd have nothing to do but pray."

"They can, but they don't have to. They're off the hook because being there for someone is hard. Even for a dead body. It's all the good deeds you need to do for the day."

Boris said:

"I wasn't planning on doing any others, except maybe if I can make a bartender happy later on." He flicked a finger against the sweating beer, knocking off a couple of drops. "Was there a class on dead people?"

"It didn't work like that. We'd read the Talmud all day. You're supposed to be just completely surrounded by it and things come up. Eventually everything comes up. It's like the way we learn things now. How to do cross-examination, or how to build a crack pipe."

Boris shook his head. "We don't know anything about this. Not the important things."

Ben had spent two years in seminary before college. He didn't want to be a rabbi and never liked studying the Talmud—a long and poorly punctuated transcript, an oral argument among counsel in the absence of a judge to impose order and make rulings. Back then Ben felt it was too literal, not enough inspiration. Later when he became a lawyer in New Orleans, he saw it differently. All the sacred texts bound in brown leatherette with gilt lettering, the pages expanding outward from the central text in whorls of burled commentaries accreting over the years, like a tree growing around and over some insult. Thousands of words to encase each fragment of the broken law. This is the fantasy of law that comforts the powerless: that it can be understood, or is even meant to be. In fact, Ben learned that the law is its own explanation and its own justification. It is a secret language that signifies power but has no other meaning.

He stayed, while he did, because he loved the miserable settlement where the yeshiva was set, parallel rows of trailers terraced down the side of a hill amid rocks and low scrub, surrounded by a barbed-wire fence. The armored bus from Jerusalem would leave him at the front gate of a settler town, a thousand homes of pale stone across the hilltops. From the bus stop he'd walk across the main road and over a dark hill to the outpost of the yeshiva. All the students had to take turns standing guard. They gave even the American students assault rifles for their tours of duty. One of Ben's study partners had been scared of a rustling amid the tamarisk and white broom and shot up a cow in the middle of the night.

Ben liked coming out of his trailer in the raw black wind blowing all night against the hill front. He liked winter. The desert seemed lonelier and distances across the hills seemed farther. He liked coming into the study hall past midnight and finding a few pairs of students waving their hands at each other across folding tables. He liked that his peers had chosen this cold, unwelcoming hillside, where all the prophecies about the promised land seemed so obviously wrong. This faith in things not just unseen but also contrary to what could be seen. He liked this community that took such comfort in being abandoned, together. He left yeshiva, then, took off his yarmulke and went to college, only when he saw that the people against whom the buses were armored also believed in hopeless things, and all his study did not give him the tools to parse the difference.

Boris sat in the car and looked across the street again, then back. He checked and rechecked. He looked like he was calculating an invasion, measuring the thickness of the walls and where they could be breached. He said:

"I bet there's more where that came from, Rabbi."

Ben thought, and drank, and thought.

"They're called *shomrim*, the people who watch the dead. They're not allowed to drink while they're in the room."

"We fucked that up."

"It's okay. We're across the street."

"Because it's not sad enough? That's why they can't drink?"

"Because it's taunting, since the dead can't drink."

Boris thought on this, too. He finished his beer:

"He was never allowed to drink, so it's okay. He didn't know what he was missing. None of our kids do."

17

Direct Examination

Looking up the avenue, back along the stretch of the parade, the air shimmered with a curtain of gold and red and blue, as the riders on the high floats threw down strings of glittering beads. A hundred horns joined together. Later, when most of the crowd was gone, a gang of Ben's clients in their jail jumpsuits would come and sweep up the beads and cups, overseen by deputies on horseback. But until then the night was sound and color; the city and its tragedies abstracted away. The band marched through the pink-and-orange darkness, torches and sodium lamps, in sharp lines among the crowds; nobody paid attention in between the floats, the onlookers refilled their beers and did silly dances, sagged inward toward the streets, and the marching band came right past, inches away, without seeming to notice. Some signal brought their instruments to their lips; then all the instruments sounded like they just rose up together out of the ground, burst free in one instant. It was joy or anger or both.

The weather got hot right after Mardi Gras. Robert was doing pushups in his cell and thickening a little bit. Ben told him to stop. If it comes to that, you need to be a child, not a man, for the jury. You need to stay fixed in time as you are in place. Every week, Ben went for another round of First Appearances and picked up another handful of clients. In the meanwhile, some small number of his cases were dismissed; a very few went to trial; and most everyone else took a plea deal. The deals were getting worse. The new district attorney, with real hair like a toupee and a scabrous soul, was flexing his muscles. Thirteen years for a veteran with a heroin addiction. Thirty months for a father of three who stole a cellphone off a table at his kid's day care, the phone worth more than his week's salary at either of his two fast-food jobs. Twelve years for a car burglary, a homeless man baited by the police with a handful of change and a bottle of whiskey, while they watched with closed-circuit cameras.

Robert looked like someone trying to remember a pleasant dream:

"Did you go to the parades this year?"

"I think I forgot to ask you some questions about your dad."

"You don't want to say."

"I just want to be sure to talk about all the important things with your case."

"Where did you watch, though?"

"Uptown. On St. Charles."

"A lot of people watch there."

"How often did you see him, growing up?"

"Sometimes."

"Tell me about that."

"I sometimes saw him. Sometimes he wasn't there. Which is your favorite parade?"

"What did you do together, when you saw him?"

"Did you bring your kids?"

"Hey, I'm happy to talk to you about them. We need to finish up with your dad."

"What are their names?"

"Robert, that time I found you at the Palais, on Canal Street. You remember that? Were you looking for your dad there? At the Palais? Did he sometimes stay there?"

"Are they named after you, your sons?"

"My sons are Isaiah and Nehemiah. Your dad?"

"They're not named after you."

"Those are very old names in my family."

"Like, your great-grandfather's name."

"Like that. In my family we don't name children after people who are still alive."

"Because why?"

"It's supposed to be bad luck. You'd see him there sometimes? At the Palais?"

"Sometimes he was there. We'd stay together. When I left my mom. If I couldn't go to Miss Caroline's. My auntie. What did they think would happen?"

"What did they think would happen?"

"If a baby got a name from someone who was alive."

"Just bad luck."

"Like they might die."

"I guess."

"The old guy or the baby?"

"I don't know. Just bad luck."

"So you don't have your father's name?"

"No."

"What's his name?"

"He's passed. He's dead."

"Did you name your son after him? Your big one?"

"When you asked me to find your dad for you—"

"If I had a son, he'd have my name."

"Robert, you're young for that."

"Some people my age have kids."

"All I'm saying is that you have time. Your dad?"

"I needed to talk to him."

"Do you still?"

"You think I have time?"

"You're young."

"But I'm in here."

"We're fighting to get you out."

"You think I have time?"

"Sure. Sure I do."

"So I'll get out?"

18

Competence

Ben's father, who knew the way out, had studied translation and multilingual puns. He wrote once about the way Jews over the generations heard themselves—their own language, not the mispronounced Hebrew they reserved for synagogue—in sacred text. For instance: On the harvest festival of Sukkot, there's a poem read in synagogue with the Hebrew refrain *kol mevasser v'omer*: "A herald's voice, crying out." But for hundreds of years, a lot of Jews spoke Yiddish, not Hebrew. When the prayers were chanted, they heard not *kol mevasser, a herald's voice*, but *kohl mit vaser*, "cabbage with water." That began the tradition of eating boiled cabbage, which is disgusting, on Sukkot.

Ben's clients also often misheard the language of the law:

"You've got to file a motion to squash."

"I did ask to quash the indictment, but—"

"How long have you been a lawyer?"

"Why do you ask?"

Or:

"When are we going for the arrangement?"

"Your arraignment will be on Tuesday. All we have to do is say—"

"How long have you been a lawyer?"

"Why do you ask?"

Or:

"We have to get an Afro-David."

"He's the only Black guy at my synagogue."

"What?"

"Never mind. I got an affidavit from the expert, but—"

"How long have you been a lawyer?"

And once:

"I think we should talk before you file things with the court."

"You've only been a lawyer for two years. I've been doing this a lot longer than that. I even did the porpoise."

"You did?"

"Yes indeed."

"Can you tell me about that?"

"So I didn't have to pay the filing fee. You didn't think I knew about that, huh?"

"I didn't."

"You sure it's all of two years you've been a lawyer, again?"

And when Ben pulled the handwritten filing from the court record, there it was, the pauper's oath, *in forma pauperis*, in big letters across the top: "*In the form of a porpoise.*"

For Ben's clients, like for the cabbage-eating Jews, it wasn't really a pun. Ben's father would have explained that a pun only works if you can hear both signifieds coming from the one signifier. You have to know both languages to intend a multilingual pun. The simple Jews, though: They knew they were praying in Hebrew, a different language from their own vernacular Yiddish, though with the same letters and sounds. They didn't really understand Hebrew. Why would they have imagined a Yiddish meaning in the Hebrew text? Why would something mean something else just because it sounded like something else?

The tradition is ready with an answer. When God spoke on Sinai, He taught everything there was to know, simulcast in seventy different languages and on four different layers of meaning: *p'shat*, the plain meaning; *d'rash*, the comparative meaning; *remez*, the allegorical; and *sod*, the esoteric. The Yiddish understanding, along with many others, is already there behind the Hebrew text. So it doesn't matter that I don't speak Hebrew. The words mean, among many other things, what I hear them to mean. And the student, the reader, the ignorant peasant at prayer: Each is entitled to speak and hear and know as much of it as they can, and whatever they hear is also the sacred word.

Ben's clients believed they were saying the right words. They didn't know their lawyers were speaking a different language. It sounded like their own. Maybe, because most of them were decent enough, like anybody, they assumed that a language whose incantations were used to lock them up should also be a language they were allowed to speak and understand. That would be the decent thing. Or that what they heard and said should mean something—should have its own dignity and significance—whatever the secret intent behind the mystic incantations. Not so. The law isn't an inheritance that you can make into what you want. It's a ransom note. It demands to be accepted on its own terms.

Here now was Robert's suppression hearing, where the court would inquire, at Ben's invitation, into exactly what Robert himself understood. So Ben began: Robert Johnson is sixteen years old and reads at a fifth-grade level. So far that's just being a poor kid in New Orleans. He lives with depression and anxiety. Ditto. He's unusually susceptible to suggestion and psychological coercion. He's eager to please adults in positions of authority. He didn't understand when he was read his rights. He didn't understand the words themselves or the ideas behind them. Even if he had understood, he couldn't use the information to make an intelligent and informed decision about the wisdom of giving away his rights. And when he didn't understand, he didn't ask. When his teacher told him to tell the detective what happened, he did. So, in lawyers' language: The waiver of his Miranda rights was not knowing, intelligent, and voluntary. His statement must be excluded. It can never be a fact in the case.

To go back just a minute to the cabbage water. There's another piece of it that could confuse you if you're someone who doesn't know what's up. Stipulate, as the lawyers say, that the Jews in their *shtetl* heard "cabbage with water" rather than "the voice of the herald." Still: Why should they also believe that their God wanted them to eat boiled cabbage, however diminished the old man in his tattered overcoat might be by millennia of exile? Why *do*, simply because you *heard*?

That one's easy, though. Their faith was always up for grabs. Their history and their lives made it impossible not to question, daily if not hourly if not all the time. So, you're told to eat boiled cabbage, or think that's what you heard anyhow—it's all mumbled through a thick beard—and you think how silly that is because either (if you have some money in your pocket) you know it's disgusting and you'd never normally eat it or (if you've got no money) you know it's disgusting but it's what you eat every day so you hardly need to be told. They doubted, or believed not at all, but their practice was inviolable. They endured through the questioning by disciplining their minds and bodies with the all-encompassing strictures of the commandments and the traditions that encircle the commandments, the commentaries on commentaries. Faith wasn't the thing; life was, and life was the infinitely refracted jots and tittles of the endless law. Ben had learned this lesson as a lawyer if not as a student in seminary. The great revelation doesn't matter. It's never going to happen and maybe never did. What matters instead is the preparation, repetition, the structure of daily practice—organizing file folders; scripting every witness examination in dozens of pages, one line per question, one subject per page; memorizing opening statements down to pauses and hesitations. Those aren't the demands of faith but its replacement.

So Ben had prepped for Robert's hearing. He had binders with questions for his witnesses, each of a thousand questions aligned in ranks; folders with exhibits, pre-marked with little blue stickers. This, as a hundred generations of his ancestors knew, is how to tamp down the terror of that moment when we come, bent and fallible, before the judge, and find that he also knows nothing of justice.

Ben questioned his expert for three hours. He was surprised that the judge listened the whole time, patiently taking notes. After Ben was done, there was cross-examination:

"He knows right from wrong, doesn't he?"

"Objection."

Judge:

"You can answer."

Expert:

"That's not what I was asked to explore. He's not psychotic. He knows fantasy from reality."

Prosecutor:

"Well, did you learn anything that made you think he knows the difference between right and wrong?"

"That's the same question with more words. It's still irrelevant. We're not arguing he was insane."

Judge:

"I'm hoping we'll get more words in the answer, too. Go ahead, doctor."

"One example would be this. Robert knew he shouldn't cheat on the test I gave him, like by malingering, and my opinion to a reasonable degree of scientific certainty is that he did not cheat."

"So he knows cheating is wrong?"

"Same objection."

"Same ruling."

Expert:

"Again: That wasn't what I was looking into, but I have no reason to think he doesn't. He cares about doing the right thing. Sometimes he cares too much. He wants adults to like him."

Prosecutor:

"Except he killed somebody."

"Objection."

Judge:

"Why don't you try rephrasing that."

Prosecutor:

"Is killing an adult consistent with wanting adults to like him?"

"Objec—"

"I'll let her answer."

The fix was in. They were just being cleverer than usual: Letting Ben have a full hearing, letting his expert testify, making sure he had nothing to complain about later. She was a good witness. She listened to the question and let Ben guide her with his objections. She was careful not to seem to be in the bag, but she was also careful not to hurt Ben's case. She was worth all the money Ben had paid her, which was all the money the public defender's office had for experts that month. All the other clients were out of luck.

"We certainly didn't discuss whether he committed any crime, and of course Robert is presumed innocent. Being accused of a crime against a particular adult whom you don't know is not inconsistent with wanting adults in positions of authority to like you."

The Assistant District Attorney smirked as though he'd won the exchange. He was a fat guy with a face that in profile had a perfect semicircular arc from broad, bald forehead around to symmetrically receding chin. His belly was also a perfect, larger, semicircle. Like a Volkswagen Beetle standing on end. Archly:

"You want us to believe he doesn't understand basic words? Would he, for instance, understand if someone said *please don't shoot me?*"

"Objection."

"What about making reasoned decisions? You're saying he can't do that?"

Ben, still standing:

"Irrelevant. Nobody's talking about decisions in general or in the present tense—"

Judge:

"Go ahead, doctor."

Expert:

"Again, that's not quite right. It would be more accurate to say that, like a lot of kids his age, he had difficulty in a particular very intense situation making reasoned decisions to resolve complex issues based on an analysis of his short- and long-term interests."

"So he doesn't understand his rights?"

"I'm just going to lodge a standing objection here—"

"Go right ahead. Doctor, you can answer."

"I only tested the Miranda rights: The right to remain silent. The right to a free attorney. The right not to talk without your attorney. He didn't properly understand those when I tested him, two weeks after he made his statement. Certainly, in my opinion, he couldn't have understood that he was giving up his right to counsel here. He didn't know what that meant."

"Mr. Alder introduced you to him, right?"

"Yes."

"And you heard Mr. Alder tell him to talk to you and answer your questions?"

"Sure, that's standard."

"So he knows he's supposed to do what his lawyer tells him?"

"Objection."

"We'll just assume you object to every question, Mr. Alder. Overruled."

"He knew, in that instance, to take his lawyer's advice. But he didn't have a lawyer when he made his statement. He had his teacher, who told him to confess."

"Now that he has one, he does what his lawyer tells him?"

"Irrelevant."

"I don't know that."

"Like, for instance, if his lawyer told him to lie about his level of reading comprehension?"

"Your honor—"

"If his lawyer told him that getting his statement suppressed was the way to win his case?"

"Mr. Alder, sit down."

"If his lawyer told him that suppression was the difference between spending the rest of his life in jail and going free? Between justice for Miss Scott, a hero of this city, and escaping all the consequences of his actions?"

The judge didn't need to be convinced. He wasn't going to throw out the best evidence against the kid who shot the Queen of St. Roch. Robert Johnson wasn't going to luck into a boondoggle just because he was fortunate enough to be a dumb kid who didn't know what a lawyer was and had never before seen nor heard nor experienced this creature called rights. The judge understood that Robert hadn't had a choice but to confess. But the judge didn't feel he had a choice, either. Robert had to lose because the consequences of his winning were intolerable.

Robert sat through the expert's testimony with his head down, like he couldn't hear. He only looked up and startled a little when Ben jumped to his feet to object. He didn't understand everything that happened in the courtroom, the foreign language that pretends to be the language of justice, but he did hear it when Ben began to sound desperate. Your lawyer tries to be bold and prophetic. The voice of a herald crying out to justice and mercy. What you hear is something watered-down and unpalatable. And he understood it when the judge, having denied the suppression motion, suggested that they pick a date for a discovery conference and then for trial.

An older lawyer, trying to sound wise, once told Ben that a case is like a train. It runs fast down a straight track toward trial, where your client is tied to the rails. Your job is to do everything you can to stop or slow or divert the train. Ben had no trial theory. His legal issue was gone. There was one other thing he could think to do, so he did it.

19

Restoration

They built the state mental hospital at Feliciana before the Civil War. It had six tall white columns in front and cleats for the patients' shackles mortared into the brick basement walls. Since then it's gone the other way around. Around the columned church of justice are low brick buildings, dun against the plastic green of crabgrass, but now they have far more elegant alternatives to padlocks and iron restraints.

The smell of bleach everywhere. The place seemed silent even when someone was screaming—as someone was somewhere when Ben and Boris arrived, a vectorless voice without place of origin or any direction into the world. Robert sat in the dayroom in a red plastic armchair bolted to the floor, watching something muted on the television. Seven or eight grown men also there in chairs, in rows, watching.

Robert saw Ben and smiled. When Boris came in, Robert got up and came over and Ben thought for a minute he might hug him but Boris extended his hand and they shook. Boris hadn't wanted to come. It had been ten days since the hearing. The cruelest thing was that Robert didn't even seem disappointed. They went outside and sat at a picnic table under a portico. There were men sitting in old lawn chairs on the nearby grass; men pacing back and forth from side to side on the little patio; or standing and holding on to the pillars and looking at the driveway as though they expected someone to drive down it.

Ben made himself smile:

"How are you doing, Robert?"

Robert nodded slow and thoughtful like Ben had said something profound:

"I'm good."

"How are they treating you?"

"They're treating me good."

"Are they—is there enough food?"

"It tastes good."

"Better than in Orleans?"

Robert's shoulders meandered up to his ears in a shrug. He yawned again, for the third time since they'd sat down. He was stuttering a little, his chin jerking up and down as though articulated separately from his jaw, like a wooden nutcracker doll. A man with bug eyes came to sit with them at the picnic table. He said nothing but smiled broadly, quickly; just as quickly the smile froze; thirty seconds later, he smiled broadly again and laughed, then got up and almost skipped away. Ben remembered a fifteen-year-old boy who'd laughed to himself the entire time Ben met with him, who wandered around a locked dayroom in a knee-length smock, touching his baby-fat cheek over and over with a twitching hand. He remembered a boy who would not stop hitting his head against the wall of his holding cell until he was restrained by a pair of guards; and then, lying on the floor under their weight while Ben stood by useless in his suit and wondering if he'd done the right thing by sounding the alarm, who emitted long braying calls that were not sobs and not laughs. He remembered a mother whose son, confined and left alone for two days in a cell on the jail's isolation tier, hanged himself from his window. A mother whose face didn't even register betrayal because she never expected good faith.

Ben and Boris always tried hard to talk, with clients and witnesses, like they weren't mad or sad or afraid. You ask a boy in a wheelchair who will never walk again what he saw when the van with the shooter came around the corner, or a fifty-year-old man where he went after he shot down a kid right there on the sidewalk. It's not your job to feel or to judge. There's a person with that word right there in their name who's going to take care of all that. Still, sometimes it sneaks in. Boris asked:

"Are you taking medicine, Robert?"

"For my nerves."

"What are they giving you?"

"To help with my bad nerves."

"How is it making you feel?"

"I feel okay. Tired."

Ben stood up. "Robert, I'm going to go talk to your social worker. Is that okay? I'll come back and talk to you afterward. Can I do that?"

"Okay."

Boris stood:

"I'll come too."

"You can hang out here," said Ben.

"I'll come," said Boris.

Robert went back to his red plastic chair to look at the silent TV. The social worker was a young man with short blond hair and a tie. He half stood, with one ass cheek on his desk, while he told the lawyers that Robert was a delight. Obliging and receptive. He participates, even eagerly. He's never any trouble. He's a great resident of Feliciana Forensic Facility.

The judge had decided that Robert knew what he was doing when he gave up his rights and confessed. But that didn't mean he was ready to go to trial. For lawyers those are separate questions. The first is whether Robert *knowingly, voluntarily, and intelligently* gave up his right to remain silent. That's measured at the time he was interrogated. But competency to proceed—whether they'll let you go to trial or not—is measured at the time of the proceedings. And the question that the law asks—the legal standard—is different. Right now, does he have a *rational and factual understanding* of the charges against him? Can he *assist his lawyer with a reasonable degree of rational under-standing*? If he can't, everything stops. No more hearings until he can.

So what if his lawyer says they can't really talk to each other—that a sixteen-year-old can't help him prepare for a murder trial? What if he says the kid can't really focus on the important things but keeps asking about parades? What if he says that the kid just isn't able to get past the magical thinking of childhood and into the weighing of plea offers? What if, to stop everything—the train toward conviction and the lawyer's own unbearable fear—the lawyer gets the kid declared incompetent? This is something a judge can give the kid, at his lawyer's request, having just taken away his only real shot at a win. The judge sends him to Feliciana for *competency restoration*, and after a few months the state doctors will attest that he's ready for trial. That way the judge can be extra sure that the conviction will stick when it's appealed.

"We're very proud of him here. We're going to do everything we can to restore him to competency."

Boris said:

"That's like restoring a tree into paper."

"We're helping him to be calm so he can focus. He goes to classes every day to learn about the justice system, so he'll understand better. He's doing great. Really trying hard."

Ben said:

"We'd love to understand better how you're helping him to be calm."

"A lot of it is the atmosphere here. It's therapeutic, of course, so it's different from the jail in Orleans."

"Therapeutic."

"Of course. Because it's a hospital."

"You're giving him medicine."

"His medical records are between him and his doctor, of course—"

"We're his lawyers."

"—But I can tell you that it's not unusual to help patients rest and focus their minds with moderate doses of medication. Remember why he came to us."

Boris wasn't looking at the social worker. He was looking at a poster that said, POSITIVE BEHAVIORAL SUPPORTS. It listed a set of expectations: Talking respectfully. Listening. Being on time. Boris said, still reading the poster like it was the Rosetta stone that would allow him to translate sane and insane:

"He came to you because my apprentice here panicked in court."

"I don't know what you mean. He came to us because he committed a murder."

Ben said:

"That's not—"

"It's only an accusation. Of course. But we need to be mindful of the possibility of behavioral disturbance, in a young man accused of a crime like that. Medication can help us to manage that possibility. Gentlemen, I think your anger is misplaced."

Ben said:

"It's right where it belongs."

But Boris stepped across the room and took Robert's file out of the social worker's hands. The social worker was surprised enough that he didn't say anything, with Boris's shoulder still in his face. Boris read it out loud. Risperdal, Seroquel: soothing names. A gentle lullaby, a comforting quilt. Ben didn't ask whether they had permission for the psychotropic medication from Robert's mother, because: Did Ben himself tell her that his strategy was treating Robert like he had a sickness, or like he was an idiot? What about his father, whom Ben also represented? Did Ben tell them the risks? Did they know their son would be here, where they drug him so he can sleep despite the great silence that spreads out and fills the space between the screams of grown men? Did they know that Ben's plan was to strip their son's life clean, to mine it for details that would prove he was not himself a person who could think and act? Did they know Ben would do everything to make Robert disappear from his own story, just so Ben could spin a theory that he himself could understand, where he could make himself understood?

Crossing the causeway back to the city, it's not far to the Gulf and the open water. Jump on the I-10, east to Read, and follow Read to its end at Almonaster. On Almonaster there are dumping yards and a cement factory and stacked shipping containers, and past them there's the Gulf Intracoastal Waterway. Go east on the waterway and get soon to the split. Dropping south is the Mississippi River–Gulf Outlet canal. In that triangle between MR-GO and the Waterway, there's no solid land. You can wend your way through patches of bright green into Lake Borgne, and from there into the Gulf. You can see the fiction of the city dissolve, its pretense of constraint by dirt and concrete. The holes open up in the solid land and the honest water comes up through the holes and slowly covers, slowly covers. It's not the chaos of land falling apart but the comforting order of water restoring its original law, flat and equal over everything.

20

Cross

McTell had a trial date. If they lost, the judge would probably give him the minimum, twenty years. Ben talked to the prosecutor about a deal, but there was nothing McTell could live with. The best offer was twelve. McTell had been on the street most of his life and he didn't think he had that much time in him. Ben's advice was to take the deal: "You'll feel differently if we lose." But McTell kept saying: "I'll roll the dice." This terrified Ben. All the more so when he learned that McTell had caught the phrase from a previous public defender who'd taken one of McTell's earlier crack cases to trial and lost. McTell was sentenced to sixty months behind that conviction.

Ben had already walked McTell through his testimony. They practiced until each of Ben's questions evoked the right answer in words that sounded natural out of McTell's mouth. Now Boris and Ben went together to see him and Boris would play the prosecutor. It was practice for McTell and it would help Ben see weaknesses in the story. Sometimes there were other reasons for a mock cross: A client who insisted on testifying but was likely to make a poor witness could be swayed by a taste of how cross-examination feels. Or a particularly harsh mock cross could help a client understand why not just testifying but also trial itself might be a bad idea.

The plan was for McTell to say everything important on direct examination. He'd come out and just tell the jury the bad stuff, like his prior convictions, so he didn't look like he had anything to hide. The lawyers called that inoculation. During the prosecutor's cross he just needed to stay out of trouble, and witnesses get into trouble when they talk too much. So Ben prepared him to be calm, measured, respectful, and as mute as possible. Answer the prosecutor's questions with one of five answers: *Yes. No. I don't know. I don't remember. I don't understand.* Never say more when you could say less. Never guess. Never explain. Never assume. Never fill in silences. Take a second to think about the questions. If I object, stop talking. Remember: After the prosecutor is done, I'll get a second round of questions. That's called re-direct. If I want to fix something, I'll bring you back there.

The prosecutors weren't very good at cross. They were mostly local law school graduates who were dumb enough not to get other jobs and mean enough to settle for putting people in jail. They were rewarded by their little cave-fish boss, with his big empty eyes and flat face, for being aggressive, not smart. Most of them crossed by repeating the witness's testimony in an incredulous, mocking baby voice. But they had a volume practice, and some had been in front of juries a lot and eventually figured out through a combination of trial and error and low cunning a few effective strategies for making uneducated, nervous, desperate people look all those things, and dishonest too.

Boris, though, was good at his job. Laypeople and bad lawyers talk about stirring up mud or poking holes in the witness's story. But that isn't it. You, the lawyer, are telling the story, whether it's direct or cross. On direct you're the playwright. But on cross you're the narrator. All the witness ever gets to do is agree or disagree. You build an irresistible momentum one fact at a time, in sharp, insistent beats. You walk them down a long hallway and close the exit doors one by one, so they have to go where you want them.

Boris hadn't really talked to Ben since they got back from the forensic hospital. Ben knew that Boris had only offered to come cross McTell so that he could meet him, and only wanted to meet him so he could treat him badly. The people Boris blamed for Robert—for the shooting and the arrest and the child drugged into submission at Feliciana—started with Boris himself. Next was Ben; then the stepdad; and then McTell.

"You're lying to this jury."

"No."

"You don't want to go to prison."

"Yes. I mean, that's true."

"You're lying so you won't go to prison."

"No. No."

"Let's talk about that."

"Okay."

Ben:

"Mr. McTell, you haven't been asked a question. Don't answer if you haven't been asked a question."

"Okay."

Boris:

"In prison, you go to sleep when they tell you."

"Yes."

"You wake up when they tell you."

"Yes."

"You shower when they tell you."

"That's right. Yes."

"You eat when they tell you."

"Yes."

"In prison, the guards control everything you do."

"Pretty much."

"Yes?"

"Yes."

"You live in a cell."

"Yes."

"A room that's six feet by eight feet."

"In some places."

Ben:

"The thing is that I'm not anxious to have the jury thinking about how many prisons you've been in."

"Okay."

"Great. So let's keep going. Just remember the rule. Only five answers."

"Okay."

"A room that's six feet by eight feet."

"I don't know."

"You don't—"

"I don't know exactly. It's small."

Boris:

"A steel bed."

"Yes."

"A steel toilet."

"Yes."

"A sink."

"Yes."

"That's all your furniture."

"Yes."

"In prison, you have almost nothing of your own."

"No."

"And you don't want that. Any of that."

"No."

"No, you don't."

"No, I don't."

"And family. Let's talk about family. That's another reason you're desperate to avoid prison."

"Yes."

Ben:

"Not desperate."

McTell:

"Okay."

Boris:

"Not desperate? You have a daughter. Bobbie."

"Yes."

"You have a son."

"Yes."

"Little Robert."

"Yes."

"In prison, your son Robert isn't there at the breakfast table."

"No."

"You don't kiss your daughter Bobbie goodnight."

"No."

"You can't see them at all most days."

"No."

"You get one visiting day a week for family."

"Yes."

"Just a couple hours each week for your family."

"Yes."

"That's assuming your family can even make it that day."

"Yes."

"Your visit is in a big room with lots of other men."

"Yes."

"And guards."

"Yes."

"You can't touch your kids."

"No."

"In prison, it's almost like you don't really have a family."

McTell stopped. He looked at Ben, who was looking down at his notes. McTell said:

"That's not right. They're always my family. Can I say that?"

Ben said:

"Just stick with *no* or *that's not right*. If I need to fix it on re-direct, I will."

"Why can't I say they're always my family?"

"Because the judge might let him impeach you. That means try to make it look like you're lying."

"I'm not."

Ben looked at Boris. They all deserved a little bit of punishment. So Ben said:

"You want to see where it goes?"

Boris didn't wait for the answer. He said:

"They're always your family?"

"Yes. That's right."

"Always?"

"Yes."

"You don't live with them."

"No."

"Most days, on the outside, you don't see them."

"No."

"No, you don't."

"No, I don't."

"Your daughter is eight."

"Yes."

"She lives with her mother."

"Yes."

"You don't pay any child support for your daughter."

"No."

"Your son is sixteen."

"Yes."

"He lives—he lives with his mother."

"Yes."

"As far as you know."

"I—I know."

"You don't pay any child support for your son?"

"No."

"No, you don't."

"No, I don't."

"You never have paid any child support for him."

"No."

"Or for your daughter."

"No."

"Your kids are in school."

"Yes. Sure."

"As far as you know."

"Yes. Why do you keep saying that?"

Ben said:

"Never mind. Boris, move on."

Boris:

"At school they have parent-teacher conferences."

"I guess so."

"You guess so."

"They do."

"But you've never been to a single one of your son's parent-teacher conferences."

"No."

"You've never been to any of your daughter's parent-teacher conferences."

"No."

"Your son. You don't know the name of his primary-care physician. His doctor."

"No."

"Or your daughter's doctor."

"No."

"Your son. He has a stepfather—"

Ben decided it was enough:

"Okay. So that's just an example of what I don't want to happen."

McTell, his head bobbing a little bit side to side, not like a boxer but like a drunk:

"It doesn't mean anything."

"I just don't want it getting messy. Let's stick to the five answers if we can. Okay?"

"It doesn't mean anything."

"Okay."

Boris:

"Can I go on?"

Ben:

"Yeah."

"Your son—"

Ben:

"You can't go on about the family. No more on the family."

Boris, without even pausing, just started boring a new hole:

"In prison you can't do what you want."

"Right."

"You can't have what you want."

"Yes."

"You can't be with the people you love."

Ben said:

"Boris—"

Boris said:

"All that's true."

"Yes."

"You really don't want to go to prison."

"No."

"No, you don't."

"I don't."

"You'd do just about anything not to go to prison."

"Not anything."

"You'd say just about anything not to go to prison."

"Yes."

"You'd tell a lie to keep from going to prison."

"Yes."

Ben:

"Mr. McTell?"

"I would."

"But if the jury hears that, they might think you *are* lying, not just that you *would* lie. So here we're going to make an exception to the rule. If you get asked that, how would you feel about saying this: *I'm telling the truth.*"

"I'm telling the truth."

"The truth will set you free."

"That's good."

"Someone famous said it."

"It's not really the truth, though."

"It's your truth, Mr. McTell."

"It's yours."

"It's ours, okay?"

Everyone wants a big gotcha moment but actually it's just the relentless water on rock drip of questions that gets you. When they were done, McTell sat quieter than usual. Ben and Boris sat quietly, too. Eventually, Boris said:

"I'm sorry, Mr. McTell."

"I'm sure I had it coming. Barry, right?"

"You can call me that."

"It's not Barry, though."

"Don't worry about it. I want you to know that I don't think those things."

"You're good at saying them."

"That's what they pay me for. If it makes you feel better, I don't get paid much."

Ben was looking away from McTell. McTell was looking at him for a while before Ben turned back to see. McTell said:

"You didn't tell me you were bringing in a hitman."

"It's getting late, Mr. McTell."

McTell looked at Ben for a long minute. Ben knew that he saw contempt in McTell's eyes, but he didn't acknowledge it. McTell said:

"You going home to see those boys of yours?"

Instead of an answer, Ben smiled.

"It's always good to see you, Mr. McTell. You did good tonight."

It was quiet and dark. A few blocks away, closer to the overpass, red and blue lights of police cars and fire engines. In the years right after the storm, the public defenders would gather by their windows on the seventh floor, look out across the flat city, and watch swamp fires far off in the distance and the meth fires much closer in the abandoned warehouses and motels between the courthouse and the raised section of the I-10. Four or five years later, the city tore down the entire neighborhood to build a new hospital complex that would draw sick people and their insurance from across the south.

Boris, while they crossed Tulane Avenue against traffic:

"He looks like him."

"They don't all look the same."

"You didn't see that?"

"No, because I'm not a racist."

"They both smile wider on the right. Like their face is a little off-center. It makes them look mischievous. You didn't see that."

"No."

In the lobby of their building was a little coffee shop called Legal Bagel, which wasn't really a pun or even a rhyme and which mostly didn't have bagels and when they did were stale. They stood in front of the elevators.

"Does he think you have children?"

"He's probably got me confused with his last lawyer. He's had a lot of them."

"If you had kids, I'm sure they'd be proud."

"Everyone's proud of me, even fictional children."

They spent a lot of their day calling people out, as directly as they dared: The police, the prosecutors, the judges. It was harder with each other. But in the elevator Boris said:

"You told him you have kids. So you can suffer alongside him."

"Yes."

"You did, though."

"Asked and answered."

The elevator opened on the seventh floor, where the lights were all off. They went together to their office and sat down and opened up their laptops. Boris got a beer and didn't offer one to Ben. Their desks were only a few feet apart, separated by a couple of low filing cabinets. They faced the same direction, out narrow windows that showed the dark drowned neighborhood and the interstate and beyond it the hotels of the Central Business District and the French Quarter with red neon signs on their roofs. Ben said:

"I didn't make you cross him like that. That wasn't just about me."

"Everything's about you."

21

Opening

This case is about dignity.

And I'm going to tell you why.

But first I want to acknowledge something:

This could be a hard conversation.

Everything that happens in this room is supposed to be serious.

And this trial is serious.

But—look—it might also be a little bit embarrassing.

People deal with embarrassing things in different ways.

Some laugh or giggle a little bit.

Some make faces, or cringe.

All that is okay, if that's how you respond.

I need you to try to stay with me, though.

Because we're about to have an important conversation.

It's the most important conversation of Robert McTell's life.

His future and his freedom depend on it.

I don't want to waste your time, so let's get this straight at the beginning.

Robert McTell was in the abandoned Augustine school building the night he was arrested.

The police will tell you he was in the school, and it's true.

I'm not going to wave my arms and accuse the police of lying and try to muddy the waters and all kinds of tricks.

I don't expect the police to come in here and lie.

They're just wrong. They made a mistake.

I'm not blaming them for it. People make mistakes. This case isn't Robert McTell against the police.

But now it's time to set that mistake right.

Because here's the most important thing for you to know about this case:

Mr. McTell went into the school. But he didn't go in there to take anything.

He didn't go in there to break any law at all.

The judge will tell you: If the prosecution can't prove he was in there to commit a felony, or to take something, then it's not a burglary and he is not guilty.

And they can't, because he didn't. That why Robert McTell is innocent.

He's innocent.

So you're wondering: Why else did he go in there?

It's natural to want to know.

And the truth is: I don't have to answer that question.

It's the prosecution's job to prove he was in there to commit a crime. It's not my job to prove he wasn't.

And they have to prove it beyond a reasonable doubt.

So if you don't know why he went in there, at the end of the day—if you don't know it beyond a reasonable doubt—I'm going to ask you for a not guilty verdict.

And I trust you enough to know that you'll follow the law and vote not guilty.

But I'm going to tell you anyhow.

Because Mr. McTell and I want this to make sense for you.

He went in there to use the bathroom.

Please bear with me.

Mr. McTell has a medical condition.

It's called Crohn's disease. It's not a rare condition—hundreds of thousands of people in the United States have it. Hundreds here in New Orleans, no doubt. Could be some people you know.

It causes him a lot of pain and a lot of embarrassment.

And I know you didn't come here to hear about a grown man's bathroom habits. God knows, Mr. McTell wishes that I didn't have to talk to you about this. It's embarrassing, right?

This isn't what I had in mind when I went to law school. But you know what? It's part of my job. Tell the truth even when it's, well, messy.

It's part of his sickness that Mr. McTell gets severe diarrhea. It's a chronic condition. He's been living with it for years.

That night, Mr. McTell was walking by the Augustine school building after a long day of work. He'd been gutting houses in Fontainebleau. He gets paid as a laborer to do that. It's hard work but it's honest work. He had some of his tools with him in a bag.

He came over the overpass on Broad Street and he walked back downriver on Broad.

And suddenly he really, really had to go.

He knew he wasn't going to make it. He's a grown man. He knows his body.

I'm going to show you pictures of that intersection at 8 p.m., what it looks like after business hours. At night there aren't any businesses with bathrooms open right there.

So Mr. McTell made an uncomfortable and embarrassing choice.

He went into the abandoned school building. He went in through an open window on the ground floor, right near the street.

I'll show you pictures of that window. You'll see that he could see it from the street, as he went walking by.

He started to look for a toilet. Not that the plumbing would still be working. But he thought it was the decent thing to do.

Then he realized, not too far into the building, that he just couldn't wait.

He stepped into the nearest classroom.

And he did defecate in that building.

Again, he's embarrassed.

You might be, too.

Robert McTell didn't feel he had a choice.

But he knows he broke the law.

He trespassed. He went into property that wasn't his.

And if he were accused of trespassing, a misdemeanor, we wouldn't be having this trial. He admits to that. He'd plead guilty to that right now. Right now.

But he's not accused of trespassing. He's accused of burglary. A felony offense here in Louisiana.

And that's unfair and wrong.

He didn't go in there to take anything.

He didn't go in there to commit any crime at all.

He went in because he wanted to preserve some shred of his dignity and his privacy.

Because everyone has dignity.

That's what this case is about.

That's why, after you've heard all the evidence, you'll find him not guilty.

Good lawyers help you understand a complicated world. It was raining when Ben left the courthouse. He was carrying his trial box, so he didn't have a hand for an umbrella, which he didn't in any event own. He was soaked by the time he reached the public defender's office. Boris was leaning back in his chair and rereading Robert Johnson's file for the eighth or fourteenth time. He looked Ben over like he was thinking of selling him.

"You ruined your tie."

"It's my pink tie, too. My sensitive guy tie."

"It makes you look like an overgrown child."

"This weather is God's justice on a world that serves egg salad to jurors at lunch."

"It's bad enough being lied to about diarrhea."

Ben said:

"They were out sixty-four minutes."

Boris wanted to sound like he didn't care:

"And?"

"And Robert McTell is not guilty."

Boris tried to keep being angry but couldn't:

"Jesus Christ."

"Yeah."

"Did you use the line? In closing?"

"Not this time."

"If he went in to shit, you must acquit."

"Not this time."

"You didn't think it was going to work, did you?"

"Not a chance."

"I told you so."

Boris stopped. Who else did you have but this other fatherless Jew, here in this strange empty city. Boris closed his file. He said:

"Do you want a beer?"

"I have another trial tomorrow."

"I shouldn't have been a dick about McTell. You're not the only one who makes things up for your clients."

"I make them up for myself. My clients are just there to hear it."

"Anyhow, I'm sorry."

"How many times a day do you think we say that?"

"Not enough."

"Me too."

Ben was once in a group of adults brought to a prison classroom with six students in it, ages fifteen and sixteen.

"This is Mr. Alder—"

"*Ben*," he interrupts, "*Ben Alder*."

"He's here to see how our school works."

One of them had been arguing with the teacher, a Croatian who was in New Orleans on a Fulbright scholarship, about whether this was an appropriate time to use the bathroom. Right away he turned from the teacher, who now was the less interesting target to troll, and began to question the little party of white explorers. Two other kids had their heads down on their desks. A fourth sat bolt upright. The fifth: *It doesn't work. Nothing works here.* The rest of the group of well-meaning visitors answered the troll's questions. Ben stood by the one who'd said that nothing works, trying to look serious but approachable.

"I'm sorry to hear that."

"You don't like to hear it?"

"I mean, I'm sorry that nothing works here."

"You just mean *you're sorry*, that's all?"

"Pretty much."

"You came up like this? Like we do?"

"I didn't."

"What are you going to do now?"

"When I leave here?"

"With everything you're seeing."

"Probably apologize again."

The kid nodded and seemed satisfied with this answer or at least resigned to it. Ben was, in that one instance, proud of himself for not pretending to be something he wasn't. It didn't happen a lot.

McTell had done a good job of selling it at trial, on two occasions making to dash from the room as though in urgent need of a toilet. He'd done well on the witness stand, too: *No, sir. No, sir.* He delivered his closing line brilliantly, even though he wasn't supposed to extemporize: *No, sir. Mr. Alder didn't tell me to make up a story. Mr. Alder told me that the truth would set me free.* But not really. This, because he was still on his parole. A not guilty verdict doesn't mean you did nothing wrong, just that the prosecutor didn't prove it. In McTell's case, the parole officer and the parole board were having none of the Crohn's disease theory. A couple of days after his verdict he had his parole revoked, and he was sent to Elayn Hunt Correctional Center in St. Gabriel, and thence to one of the Department of Corrections' facilities somewhere in the north of the state. Truth or no, he wasn't going to go free.

22

Discovery

The first time Ben and Boris went to juvenile court together, they were supposed to be picking up a kid who'd been arrested during a high school pep rally. The kid had tried to shoot in the air, but he was a fuckup of a kid and the gun went off sideways and a teacher went to the hospital with a perforated gut.

The juvenile court was on the ground floor of the civil courthouse. There was a waiting area with plastic seats and locked doors. The courtrooms were small, with peeling carpets and baseboards that didn't reach the floor. Because Ben and Boris were new to the court, the judge was intent on showing them something. While they waited for their case to be called, a child was brought in—a teenager, sixteen years old and taller than Ben himself. He wasn't charged with a crime. He was there because the prosecutor alleged that his family was *in need of services*. He wasn't going to school, and only the tender attention of the court could set him right. The judge was big and thick-wristed and sour. He looked and talked like an especially mean-spirited junior-varsity football coach.

His first words, as the kid came into the courtroom:

"Where are your pants?"

The kid didn't understand, because he was wearing pants. His name was Walter Lewis. The judge was angry because the pants were, in his opinion, not properly seated at the boy's natural waist. The judge:

"We have a rule in this courtroom. Fifteen days."

Walter sat down next to his lawyer, whom he hadn't yet met, at the defendants' table. The bailiff came up and put his hand on Walter's shoulder.

"Stand up."

He stood.

"Put your hands behind your back."

Walter's lawyer didn't say anything. She was a public defender, too, from their juvenile division. She may have been quiet because she was an idiot or because she was afraid or just surprised. Ben didn't realize until the cuffs were on that Walter had been sentenced to fifteen days in detention for contempt of court. Walter didn't realize it either. The bailiff started walking Walter back out again. He just went. Ben watched it happen, but Boris was always quick on his feet:

"Your honor, Boris Pasternak. I'd like to be heard—"

"This isn't your client?"

Boris argued while walking backward, just in front of Walter, toward the courtroom door:

"It's a public defender client. I'm a public defender."

"Who's his lawyer?"

"I just got the case."

He stood in the doorway so Walter couldn't be marched out. Everything that happens in a courtroom needs to be put in words. If it's not in the transcript, it didn't happen. Where the allegation is wearing of low pants, the defense attorney may want to make a verbal record of the location of the pants relative to the waist. In case a court of appeals needs to decide whether it's appropriate to jail a sixteen-year-old who isn't accused of a crime but who comes into a courtroom wearing allegedly low pants.

"Judge, I'm six foot three and wearing a suit. It's Zegna. I used to be a corporate lawyer. That's not really the point here, but, you know, for the record, it's a nice suit."

"Mr. Karloff—"

"Pasternak. You know what? That's fine. The point is my pants are belted at the waist. I'm standing right next to—his name is—Walter, who's about my height. He's wearing jeans, and his waistband is a couple inches lower than mine. So at most we're talking about—"

Comparative tailoring notwithstanding, the judge remanded Walter into custody. Boris stormed back to the office and filed an appeal that afternoon. That night they were drinking beer at their desks and contemplating an armed uprising when Boris got a call from the Fourth Circuit Court of Appeal letting him know that he could pick up Walter and take him home. The court hadn't ruled on the merits of the case—possibly, it was okay to jail a child for a pants-related infraction—but instead put a hold on the sentence while it waited for a written opinion from the trial judge. Walter's mother didn't have a car. It would have been three buses for her to pick him up at the detention center, and by then it might have been too late to get him released. So Boris and Ben put the gangly kid in the back seat of Ben's little car and drove him across the dark city back to his house in the Seventh Ward, where his mother was sitting on the front porch in slippers, smoking and waiting for her son. Walter and his mom stayed just up Elysian Fields from the daiquiri shop where Ben bought strawberry-peach blends on summer Saturday nights. Before he got out of the car, Walter extended his arm, crooked at the elbow, for a fist-bump. Ben got one too. Ben could see what Boris had in his head as they drove away. Not self-congratulation or self-righteousness or pity, but anger and optimism. Anger born of optimism: It could be better, so why isn't it? And things might go better from here. A child is free. This was one of the things that Ben loved in Boris. Furious and practical, always moving forward.

With Robert stupefied at Feliciana, Ben worked on his other cases. He went to First Appearances, did research, ate honey buns. He took a lot of guilty pleas. But Boris watched all the videos.

The violent crimes unit prosecutor had given Ben a police report, a VHS tape with Robert's statement, Robert's signed waiver form.

That was all. The police report was four pages long. According to the police: When the story of Lillie Scott's murder came out in the papers the next day, they got a call from a guy who was held up on the same block, just minutes before Lillie was shot. He said he'd been held up by a kid in a green sweatshirt. So they canvassed from the French Quarter on down and found video from a surveillance camera outside a convenience store: A tall kid in a green sweatshirt. The still went out on the news, and Robert's English teacher saw it: *That's our school sweatshirt, and that looks like Robert Johnson.* She called the police, he made a statement, and that was a wrap.

But Ben had a thick file full of compact discs that he'd collected walking down Bourbon Street and into the Marigny, in the few days after Robert was arrested. Security videos from bars and private homes. Boris put on headphones and watched a new one every night, after all his other shit was done. Hours and hours of low-resolution jackassery, spilled drinks, shoving matches, catcalls. There was nothing on any of them.

Except: One night Ben fell asleep on the couch where the investigators used to spill their coffee. He woke when Boris kicked him hard in the shoulder. Ben got his glasses on and saw that Boris was holding a compact disc with no label, just two scrawled words in thick Sharpie: *Thanks, Ben!* Ben remembered getting this one from a daiquiri shop at the corner of Bourbon and Conti. It had open archways onto the street, a few stools, and a wall of spinning mixers behind the bar. They served drinks in purple, green, and gold novelty containers shaped like huge King Cake babies. Ben got the disc from the day manager, even though their policy was to only give surveillance video to cops, because he'd once gotten the guy's girlfriend out of jail. She was a gutter punk who'd been picked up for trying to steal her dad's car.

The time stamp on the video was 10:41 p.m.; the time in their office, as Boris handed Ben a Diet Coke for caffeine and a beer for patience, was 12:17 a.m. The screen was crosshatched into four: Street left, pointing downtown; street right, pointing uptown; the counter at the daiquiri bar; the shop's ATM. Everyone moved in fits and starts like in a flip-book, a second or so of real time elapsing between frames. The street cameras showed the stumble and waver of foot traffic; bachelorettes in tight dresses and sashes; dads, too old for this, in untucked button-down shirts and khaki shorts. After a half hour in video time: There into the shop, in the stop-motion animation of the video, came three women in jeans and heels and tank tops, leaning on each other. Backs to the camera as they faced the bar, watching the swirling candy-colored drums of frozen drinks. Bartender in a black T-shirt gave them a wave; one held up her palm to him and he slapped it and she took a couple steps backward and bent over at the waist like she'd been punched but she was just laughing. She came up waving her credit card and it was drinks for everyone.

Then, the moment you've been waiting for: here he comes from the street, our boy. Tall, hunch-shouldered like he's trying to disappear. Plainly too young to order. Bartender, midway through his pours, gives him the palm that this time means stop. Skip a second. What does he want in there? The women may be hugging their purses closer, kinda looks that way from the video, they sort of half-turn toward him. But he's not there to stick up the bar; you can tell from his little steps into the room—the way he moves just a foot or two between the wide-spaced frames, tentative, exploring, not intruding. When the bartender puts up his hand in one frame and then in the next points out toward the street Robert does indeed stop, in the middle of the checkered black-and-white linoleum floor, the women looking over at him. He turns in the next frame, the bar camera right in his face under the fluorescent lights, and you can see a half-grin that you could mistake for either amusement or good-natured chagrin. What does he want in there? He's just amazed at being an adventurer in a place that's not for him.

He sees and then he goes. That's all. Skip a second. There he is outside the door. One of the outdoor cameras shows him turning and walking on Bourbon Street, downriver. Skip. There at the edge of the frame he stops right by another kid, shorter and broader. Also wearing a green sweatshirt. Must be from the same high school. Stupid fucking kids, just giving the game away. They turn to walk off the frame and it looks like this second kid is carrying a backpack slung by one strap over his shoulder. Bright fluorescent yellow in the shadowed nighttime street.

We know that kid.

23

Stakeout

"**W**hy are we playing cops?"

If they'd been better at it, they'd have brought cigarettes or dip. Instead, they were eating Doritos and Boris was sitting in Ben's passenger seat marking up a stack of files. Ben said:

"We secretly want to be what we hate most."

Boris shook his head:

"That's prosecutors, Dude of My Dreams. It's first prosecutors, then judges, then cops."

"It's eroticized fear."

"Okay, maybe cops before judges. Then sheriffs' deputies."

"Like cuckold porn."

"What the fuck are you talking about?"

"Don't be defensive. No one's kink-shaming."

They were waiting for the Kid with the Yellow Backpack to get out of school, the little gold Cavalier parked about half a block lakeside of the big brick building. Esplanade Avenue marks the downriver edge of the French Quarter, runs up through Bayou St. John in Mid-City, and ends at the gates of City Park. Shaded all the way up from the river, lined with tall houses with columns and balconies. Lovely. Ben represented a guy who did a shooting down at the base of it, outside a famous burger restaurant; farther lakebound, another couple of homeless guys arrested in a bait car scam—the cops left money and a laptop on the seat of an unlocked car and just waited for desperate people to walk by; a vicious aggravated battery under the I-10 overpass. It wasn't that there was nothing good. There was one spring Saturday when he woke up in Bayou St. John next to a woman with a nice laugh, another do-gooder lawyer, and as he walked home riverbound that morning on Esplanade the whole city smelled sweet. It didn't seem to balance out, though.

Boris was rereading Robert's statement to the police:

"It never made sense that he was alone."

"He said he was."

"Why?"

"Loyalty. Kids like secrets. He doesn't trust me. I don't know."

The last school bus pulled away.

"He didn't get on."

"Not with a yellow backpack. I can't see anything else from here."

"I got those half-blood eyes."

"He could have had detention."

"I don't think they do that anymore."

"Can you get out?"

Boris got out. Ben crawled across the shifter and Boris's seat and got out, too. It was close and warm with a high gray sky. Boris said:

"I feel like we should be smoking."

"A rueful smoke would be a good TV cop thing to do."

"A real cop thing to do would be to go talk to Robert and shake him until he explains why he didn't mention his little partner."

"That's a real cop thing to do because it's stupid. Even if he can get a sentence out with all the drugs. He wouldn't tell us. He'd shut down."

"You're right."

"Stupid is why cops are bad at their jobs."

"Brutality, too."

"Authoritarianism."

"Venality."

"That's a good one. Sloth."

Ben leaned against the car. Boris squinted at the school building like he could use his X-ray vision to see Yellow Backpack Kid moving around inside. He asked:

"Didn't you have a girlfriend who lived around here?"

"Not exactly. Not exactly a girlfriend. Right up the street."

"What happened?"

"She wasn't into my whole thing where I drink too much and lie a lot."

"She's not the only one."

"I know."

Boris made a move with his arm like he was skipping a stone. He said:

"I went on a date with Deborah."

"Who?"

"The Russian girl. From the school. The secretary."

"Her name is Deborah?"

"Half Jewish."

"Incredible. The other half is Episcopalian, though?"

"Of course. We had daiquiris on the levy. I think she loves me."

"She's not the only one."

"I know." Boris was done throwing imaginary stones. He straightened up: "Hear that?"

"It sounds like they're fucking a goose."

Boris starting walking fast toward the school building.

"There's a field around back."

Ben skipped behind:

"You fuck your geese where you find them."

"That's where our kid's at."

Band practice. The kids in green pants with white piping; white bibs over green jackets; epaulets and chinstrap hats. Ben and Boris stood behind a chest-high fence and watched alongside a scattering of parents and other students and neighborhood hangers-on. Yellow Backpack was getting his trumpet out of its case, which was sitting on the bleachers next to the eponymous backpack. Ben felt defensive.

"I did see that he had an instrument when we met him the first time, by the way. I just thought it was a clarinet."

"You don't know a trumpet case? You must not be from here."

"I'm from New York, didn't you know?"

"Did I tell you I played sousaphone in junior high? Yes, I was a little overweight."

The kids formed up and the drums started, then the cymbals. A couple of bandleaders, fat men in sweat suits in front of the rows of kids, waved their arms and shouted. The slim drum majors with tall hats and batons marched in place with high knees.

"Okay, so we talk to him." Boris kept time with his hands on the top rail of the fence: "What if he admits he was there?"

"Then he did it. That's the theory."

"What if he says he wasn't there?"

"He's got a good reason to lie. He killed somebody. That's the theory. This is a case about loyalty and betrayal, ladies and gentlemen."

The band wheeled around the field, turning sharp corners. They couldn't hear any single instrument, but they could see that Yellow Backpack moved precise and controlled, right on time.

"His world could end," said Boris.

"I get it. If it does, it's my fault."

"No, listen. I'm saying we talk to him like we don't want his world to end."

"We're kind but we're tough."

"We go at him like we're all he's got."

Afterward they followed him, moving and parking, waiting back. North Rocheblave to Orleans; along North Claiborne; then left on Conti past the brick walls and raised crypts of the cemetery.

"This is extra creepy," said Ben. "How would you explain this if someone calls it in?"

"There's this kid, Yellow Backpack Kid. We think he was involved in a shooting that we're investigating but we can't just ask our client since he'll panic and clam up. So we're stalking Backpack to find out where he lives. Then we're going to find a time when his mom isn't home, and we'll ambush him. With luck he'll incriminate himself and we can use that to ruin his life."

"You're a storytelling genius."

"You're telling the story. I'm just second chair. Could you say *I* instead of *we*?"

"He's going to the Iberville."

Boris:

"Not just the Iberville, Grand Old Dude of York. This is Auntie Caroline's place."

Caroline's place in the Iberville, where Robert's mom had sent them looking for him when he got beat up and ran away, the first time Ben met him.

"Motherfucker."

"It's her kid. It's Auntie Caroline's kid."

The next day Ben went to the New Orleans Housing Authority's office, yellow and green under bilious fluorescent lights. He walked out with copies of the housing contracts for all three apartments at 116 Conti. It was Unit #3: Caroline Thomas, 42; Willard Thomas, 16; Madeleine Thomas, 7. A web search told him that Caroline Thomas, assistant front desk manager, was a former employee of the month at the casino hotel downtown. Phone call at 3 p.m.: *Is Caroline Thomas there? Yes, please hold for her.* Great, so she works the afternoon shift. But how late? Ben hung up and called back a few minutes later: *Hi, I'm looking for the night shift assistant manager. Can you tell me when she comes on?* Eight p.m. *Oh, I thought that was just Tuesdays.* No, it's every day. *Thanks! I'll call back!*

24

Interrogation

It was still light that evening when they walked into the Iberville courtyard. Willard Thomas, the Yellow Backpack Kid, was sitting alone on his front steps. They didn't want him with friends; kids, especially boys, act crazy around friends. If they had their timing right, his mom's shift wouldn't end for another hour or more. Willard leaned forward, arms on his knees, and watched them come toward him. He had a look like he'd been waiting for them, like they were late for an appointment.

"I'm Ben Alder. I'm Robert Johnson's lawyer."

Willard said like he couldn't possibly deny it:

"That's my little partner."

"This is my little partner, Boris. It's good to see you again."

Willard shook their hands, like he'd learned in school. He leaned in with his head at an angle, peering through the reflections on Ben's glasses:

"I saw you on TV with Robert, when they brought him to jail."

"We know about you, too. Where's your sister?"

"She's with my grandma until my mom gets home."

"Mom works until eight tonight?"

"Yeah."

"We need to go inside to talk."

He just let them into his living room. He seemed almost relieved to see them. If he was nervous, too, maybe it was just anxiety to get it over with. The police had it wrong. Most of the time you didn't need a gun and a threat to get in the door. People were ready to talk. Dolls and books—*Who Was Homer Plessy?*—on the couch. Willard moved them aside and sat. Ben and Boris sat on either side of him. Ben put a printout from the surveillance video on the coffee table—a still of the boys outside the daiquiri shop, Robert and Willard, standing facing each other.

"You're famous. You're in pictures."

"Lots of people have yellow bags."

Ben took the picture and put it in a folder. He got out his laptop and put it on the table. He shrugged and lied:

"There's video up and down the street. We can watch it if you want."

Willard thought about that. He rubbed at the scar on the back of his hand.

"Are you going to be my lawyer too?"

"Right now I work for Robert. He's the one that got arrested."

Willard, to Boris:

"You're the muscle or something?"

"We're partners."

"I didn't know it worked that way with lawyers. Like with cops. You always roll with partners?"

Ben:

"We're not cops. We're on the good side. We'd like you to be on the good side too."

"Who's my lawyer?"

"You don't have a lawyer."

Willard wasn't dumb:

"Seems like if you were on the good side, I'd have a lawyer."

"You haven't been arrested yet."

"You can't arrest me, though?"

"It's not our job to get you into trouble. We just need to find out what happened that night."

"Robert didn't tell you?"

"We need to know what you have to say."

"Robert didn't tell you."

"Robert is looking out for you."

"That's my little partner."

"He wants to help you. You should help him, too."

Ben and Boris had practiced this. What to do if he acted like a little dick. What to do if he started running. What to do if he came out and confessed that actually it was him all along and he had hypnotized Robert into confessing. Now the thing to do was wait. The success of everything they did—the preparation, the searching, the intrusions into the lives of people who wanted to be left alone— all depended on their patience in these moments for the story to come out. Everyone in the city carried so much. They were ready to let it drop.

He started all the way back at the beginning.

We came up together, he said. We came up in the St. Bernard, next door to each other. He called my mom *auntie*. Popeye's mom wasn't like that, though. Robert's mom. We would call him Popeye. His mom's place wasn't the kind of place where you walk in and there's lemonade or cookies or something. When we were little, we'd walk around the neighborhood together. We stayed just a couple of blocks from the Youth Study Center, the kids' jail. He was always saying *I'm glad I'm not in there.*

We were together for the storm, too. Well, right after it. My mom got us out early. Me and my mom and my sister, we stayed in a hotel in Natchez then we went to Memphis to a FEMA motel. Robert's people didn't get out. They were at the Superdome. My mom called his mom, and then she called some police and some other people. Two weeks later they came on a bus and we all stayed together in the motel, me and my mom and Maddy, my sister, and Robert and his sister. All that fall. His little brother wasn't born yet. It was one of those places with outdoor hallways—what do you call those? Breezeways?—and all the people from New Orleans would be together in the evenings and put meat on the grill and listen to music. Popeye and me would climb the locked fence and swim in the hotel pool at night when everyone was asleep.

He went to the hospital. You didn't know that, huh? He went to the hospital in Memphis. I stayed with him. His mom couldn't. But I stayed with him. His dad, too. The two of us stayed with him. His dad liked the chair they had, you know the green kind, blue-green kind, that turns into a bed. He liked to sleep on that. Me, they brought me a cot and I slept on it. Big Robert brought us candy from down in the hospital gift shop. A heart filled with chocolates. He probably stole it. He would sing dumb songs in the shower. He'd take long showers because in New Orleans he didn't have a regular place with a shower. It had a seat for sick people and his dad would just sit on the seat and sing his dumb country shit in an accent—like, you know, like a white guy, no offense—and make Robert laugh even though he wasn't doing so good. When he made like a country singer, he'd curl up his lip and sing way down low. But Robert wasn't doing so good.

He was sad remembering it, but there was also something wistful. It was a time when he knew what he was to people, the real kind of homesickness. Ben said:

"You took care of each other."

"We tried. When we came back to New Orleans too."

"When things happened at his house, he'd come to you."

"Sometimes. Y'all knew about that. You didn't do too much about it either. With his stepfather."

"We're here to talk about what's happening right now. Robert's in jail. That means he needs your help."

"It's not like that. He knows that."

Willard had been there that day when Robert was taken out of the classroom. Watched his perp walk on TV. His mom wouldn't let him go visit in jail. It was like she thought the Orleans Parish Prison would make him sick or something. Like it was contagious. It wasn't fair for Robert to be in there. Sometimes things just happen.

"Tell us what happened that night."

Willard leaned his head back on the sofa and up at the ceiling like a bored kid, but he said:

"We just went out on Bourbon Street."

"What were you looking to do?"

"Just go out, like we do."

"You went down to the Marigny too. The Seventh Ward. On Kerlerec Street."

"Yeah."

"Then what?"

"I don't know."

"Where were you going?"

"Just going."

"Tell me one step at a time."

Willard put his scarred hand and his good hand over his face. Ben looked to Boris for help. Boris didn't want to make like cops and interrogate this kid. But this was what they'd agreed to. It wasn't their job to care about kids in general. What they did was try to help one kid at a time. Loyalty, like family and like violence, is just something that happens. Robert was their kid, and Willard wasn't. You get displaced over and over, by inclination and by history and by tragedy, and all that matters is *we came up together*, a coincidence that becomes a commitment. Boris sat forward.

"Your mom doesn't know about that night."

Willard turned to look at him. Boris didn't know much about dads but he knew moms. Boris said:

"You want to tell her? Or we can tell her. Ben and I can. You decide. We'll wait here, and then we'll tell her all about it when she gets home. We can show both of you the videos. We'll make popcorn."

Willard shook his head. Ben's turn:

"Maybe it wasn't your idea to do a robbery. Or the shooting."

Boris:

"You didn't want it to happen."

Ben:

"Maybe you even tried to stop it."

Willard:

"I didn't."

Boris:

"I think people would believe you did. You're a good kid. Good kids help their friends."

Ben:

"You didn't mean for Lillie Scott to get shot."

Boris:

"We can see that about you."

Ben pulled the trigger:

"But the gun was yours, right?"

Three things happened very quickly. First: Before the front door opened, just before that, Willard smiled just a little bit, recognition and relief, and he nodded.

Second: The sound of a key in the lock and the front door swinging open. Caroline Thomas, 105 pounds of corded-throat fury, came through like a bull out of a gate, home early by the grace of the night manager who gave her a little bit of extra time off in recognition of all her hard work, and holding in two hands, arms pressed out and driving right at them, a pistol that she showed every sign of knowing how to use. And for all her hard work and just because she was a human being, she deserved some common decency and courtesy and would not tolerate strange men coming into her house without asking her permission and talking to her son like he was some kind of criminal. Was it not enough that her own home had been burglarized not six months before and her other gun, her favorite gun, stolen from her while she was at work? Did she have to ask twice for them to leave? Did she have to raise her voice? Did she have to call the police? Did she have to use force to defend her children and her own life and her property and the safe and sane world she carved out for them all in the middle of that noise and evil out there? Boris and Ben stumbled backward out the door into the hallway with their palms outward and in front of their faces as though warding off blows.

Third: They were in the hall, the gun still on them, when she stopped yelling and just stared at them and Boris remembered that the rule was never leave unless you have to. Keep asking questions. Make it hard to say no. Boris dropped his hands into his reasonable-man negotiating posture, elbows at his sides and spread hands in front of him, gesturing *hey, can we talk*, and maybe without knowing it, took a step forward in that little space, a big and strong man closing some of the distance toward the woman standing on her own threshold. The bullet hit him just a couple inches above the heart.

25

Confession

It was Willard, inside the doorway with tears on his face, who called 911. She stood right there holding the gun on Ben until the ambulance arrived. Of course he wasn't a threat to her, though. He was useless, kneeling on the ground next to Boris, Boris with a pink froth in the wet breath bubbling up into his mouth.

The EMTs and the first police on the scene were so surprised at two white guys covered in blood that they were going to let Ben climb in the ambulance with Boris, but a detective showed up and wasn't having it. It didn't look good—the two of them walking into an apartment without an adult's permission and hijacking a kid. Ben sat on the front steps. The detective was a wry-faced woman, about ten years older than him, with her hair up in a sensible bun. He'd cross-examined her once and more or less accused her of destroying evidence, which she'd probably done. She leaned over the railing conversationally, like she wasn't thinking of arresting him.

"You need to sit and visit with me for a little bit," she said.

"You need—"

Fortunately she interrupted him:

"You're bleeding?"

"It's not mine."

But he felt at the back of his head and his hand came away with bright red blood.

"Oh fuck," he said, like it was another hassle in a regular day. "The second shot."

Boris leaned back right before she pulled the trigger, so the bullet went higher than she'd aimed. The second shot missed him entirely as he fell down and the gun stayed high. The ricochet off the brick of the stairwell had carved a shallow furrow along the back of Ben's head. The detective called over an EMT. Ben shook his head and gave the guy a stiff arm but when he stood up he swayed on his feet like he'd been hit by a strong wind, and he sat back down hard on the stairs. So he got to go to the hospital, too. And once he was strapped into the back of the ambulance, a long black flag unfurled through the middle of his skull. It rippled, and he fainted.

No dreams troubled Ben's oblivion. He didn't want them. That wasn't how Ben's people made sense of things, anyhow, at least not for two thousand years. Everything that means anything anymore is approached by inference and analogy, or echoed through ritual, but not seen directly. When he awoke then with thoughts of blood and smoke, lying sick to his stomach on the gurney, his mind went to law and practice, not to revelation.

At the center of the Temple of Solomon, in Jerusalem, was the Sanctuary, split into two chambers by curtains. In the outer chamber was the butler's pantry of the Temple cult: a candelabrum; a small, golden altar; a table where loaves of inside-out bread were left as an offering. But nobody entered the inner chamber all year—except once, on the Day of Atonement. Then the High Priest went alone into the Holy of Holies, carrying a pan of hot coals and a palmful of incense. Always averting his eyes from the Ark of the Covenant, he threw the incense on the coals so that the chamber filled with smoke. Only then, when he could see nothing, would he retrieve blood from the day's animal sacrifices and sprinkle it before God. He had to move quickly and act carefully in there. If he looked in the wrong place and the sight killed him, nobody could enter to retrieve his body.

That's the Talmud's version, a memory first written down about a hundred years after the Temple was destroyed. The Talmud isn't the only source, though. Ben learned another when he left seminary and went to college. The ninth chapter of the Epistle to the Hebrews talks about the Temple rites on the Day of Atonement—a prefiguration of Jesus' sacrifice, whose blood was said to work a far more effective cleansing. The Christian story, though, is only about the blood. It never mentions the smoke.

In the Talmud, what the High Priest took pains not to see was the emptiness on the *kaporet*, the *mercy seat*. The lid of the ark: A gold slab, with statues of two angels facing each other, the tips of their extended wings touching. During the Jews' courtship with God, in the desert, the divine spirit would appear between the wings of the angels and talk to Moses. Since then, nothing—a nothing that nobody could look at directly. The unseeable thing was God's silence, or absence. Only when that was covered up with smoke could the High Priest do his ritual of atonement. If he knew for certain God wasn't there, what would be the point?

Here's another difference between the frankness of the New Testament and the old tradition it replaced. The prophet Isaiah, in the sixth chapter of his book, gets his marching orders in a hallucination of the Temple: God, on a throne, his train filling the sanctuary. From the golden altar, in the outer chamber, a seraph takes a coal to purify Isaiah's unclean lips. And, just like on the Day of Atonement, the House fills with smoke. But too late: Before the smoke rises, Isaiah sins.

Even the six-winged seraphim who surround the throne are at pains to avoid that vision. Two of their wings, they always keep folded across their faces, so that they cannot see the God whose praises they sing: *Holy, holy, holy, the whole earth floods with his glory.* Isaiah needs to be purified because he's seen something forbidden even to angels. He says: *Woe am I. I am a man of unclean lips, but my eyes have seen God.* There's a terror of seeing, the vacancy that isn't and the emptiness that is. Why? Because if you see something, you have to say something.

Once you witness, you have to *bear witness*. And who can do it justice? The seraphim could broadcast God's praise so loudly—in voices that shook the Temple itself—only because they couldn't see Him. And notice, too, that even though Isaiah says he saw God on the throne, he never describes Him. He describes only the angels around Him. We never really know what he saw—or didn't. Purified by fire or not, his mouth still could not speak the words.

The psychotic witness in the New Testament's Revelation tells some of the same story, with some more visual detail: Rainbows, emeralds, ruby about the throne. About that throne, too, are angels—"living creatures"—who like Isaiah's seraphim have six wings and call out *holy, holy, holy*. But here's one important difference: Isaiah's angels covered their eyes. Each of these New Testament angels, though, was *covered with eyes all around, even under its wings.*

The Jews' God never walked among them as a man, redeeming them. He was always far away, unseen. And while the tradition has so many words, all the words, none of them is about the one thing Ben's people always wanted to know: What the mercy seat really looked like; what a just judge might be. The whole earth might reflect His glory, but you'll never see the moment of real atonement. Even the seraphim themselves don't really know what they're singing about. The kabbalists, Jewish mystics, gave these angels a bittersweet backstory. They were trapped, you see. God exists on four planes: The highest, the pure abode of the divine, was inaccessible to the seraphim. They live only on the second plane, the plane of creation, always at a distance. And they burn perpetually not from the terrible majesty of the Divine presence but in its absence. They self-immolate because they cannot be closer to God, because they can never open their eyes and sing the truth.

Ben gave up for a while. He leaned back and they processed him in and put a little bandage on his head. The triage nurse said it was the blood and fear that got to him, not the bullet.

When a doctor came and shined a flashlight at his eyes, Ben said: "It was a 9mm. Like a three-inch barrel. Maybe the Sig P290."

The doctor was an old white guy with a short beard. Probably another Jew. He stopped and looked closely at Ben.

"Why did you tell me that?"

"I've never shot a gun," said Ben. "I don't know what it means. Maybe it matters."

"How are you feeling right now?"

"You should see the other guy."

"Mr. Alder?"

"How is he? Boris? My little partner?"

The doctor weighed how much to say.

"Your friend is in surgery. The bullet broke his collarbone, and the bone punctured his lung. He bled into his chest."

"He has a hemopneumothorax. I don't really know about that either. Medical records, right? I google things."

"Do you know where you are?"

"I know some things about it. Like, protocols for sex abuse nurses. Medical records exceptions for hearsay. What's going to happen?"

"Who's the president of the United States?"

"Another lucky white dude with father issues."

"Can you tell me what day it is?"

"Fucking white privilege. Even bullets cut us a break."

They held him for observation. They gave him aspirin and kept him in a gurney in the hall next to a homeless guy who couldn't stop coughing. Right there were a set of swinging doors through which at intervals of minutes or months his clients and their families came and went. As always, he wasn't really one of them. He counted the raised bars on the doors' polished diamond plate. He counted grievances against prosecutors. After a couple hours the detective from the Iberville came in. Ben kept his head back and his eyes closed. He had his shit a little bit better together by then.

"Why were you in the Iberville?"

"To buy crack."

"That's not a helpful way to talk, counselor."

"To effect the purchase of a controlled dangerous substance, Schedule II, to wit, crack cocaine."

"You ever been shot before?"

"We don't do a lot of shooting in the Berkshires."

"I thought you were from New York."

"Now why did you think that."

"That's how you come off."

"Actually we live all over the place. New Yorkers. It's an ethos, not a geography."

"You went into a woman's apartment without her permission. I need you to tell me something that doesn't make it a crime."

"I needed to use the bathroom. Crohn's disease."

"Why were you there?"

"It's as close as I get to living the life."

"Unauthorized entry and forcible imprisonment. That's the life, isn't it?"

Ben kept checking his phone like he expected to get a text or a call from Boris. He had it on his chest. He picked it up and looked at the screen. His mother had called. He deleted her message. Through a glass partition into the public waiting room, he saw a TV reporter. She'd been at Robert's perp walk. She saw him, too, and waved and gestured. She wanted to come talk to him. He put his head back again and lolled some more. He said:

"Actually, it's *Georgia v. Randolph*."

"What is?"

"Come on. It was just decided last year. Maybe two years ago. Don't y'all do continuing education?"

"What was decided?"

"The case, Holmes."

"Excuse me?"

"I didn't mean it the racist way. I meant it with an *L*. H-O-L-M-E-S. But not Sherlock. Oliver Wendell. The case is *Georgia versus Scott Fitz Randolph.*"

"Does it say a public defender can bust into a house without an adult's permission?"

"A police officer, actually. But you know the difference between a holding and a rule?"

"What did you want from that kid?"

"I'm his lawyer. He's appealing a bad grade."

"Were you working on a case?"

"That's privileged. Well, it's confidential."

"You're not here as a lawyer."

"The one's a rule of evidence. The other's an ethical rule. Got it? We're having law fun tonight."

"What was your buddy doing when he got shot?"

"Mentoring. Like a big brother thing."

"Who was Willard Thomas to him?"

"Mentoring me, not the kid."

"You're lucky it wasn't you. You think what your friend did was smart?"

Ben was suddenly tired and angry. He said:

"You know what? How do the kids say it? Keep his name out of your mouth."

Somehow he thought it was going to hurt him to reach into his pocket, but of course there was nothing wrong there. He wished his body felt more like he'd been beaten up. It's important to keep a consonance between body and spirit. He got out his wallet.

"I'm pretty comfortable right here, or I'd ask if I'm free to go. You are, though."

"I'll stay for a while."

"Then here's something to read to pass the time."

He gave her his card, turned toward the wall, and closed his eyes. On the back it said: *I want my lawyer. I won't talk to the police. I don't agree to any searches. You can't come in my house.* The cards weren't standard issue for the public defenders. Ben and Boris had paid to print them up with their names and cell numbers on the front. They told their clients to always carry the cards and give them to the police if they got stopped. Nobody ever did, but it made Ben and Boris feel better. It was like giving a kid a condom. He might use it, right?

A nurse woke Ben up a while later, made sure he knew the date and his name and George W. Bush's name, and put him in a cab. The paper covered it the next day: *Public Defender Shot in Iberville Projects*. It said Ben and Boris had been working on Robert Johnson's case. No way Willard told them. Maybe they read Boris's notebook or something. Maybe Willard told mom and mom told them. That afternoon they took the tube out of Boris's throat and eased up on the sedatives so he woke up. When they let Ben in, he stood at the foot of the bed with his stupid arms hanging at his sides like an asshole. Boris lay with his head pitched back, looking at the ceiling. A sheet covered him to his neck. He sounded like a tin can dragged through gravel.

"How many tubes?"

"I count four. Chest, chest, arm, nose. I'm happy to say I can't see if there's a catheter."

"There is. Are we getting fired?"

"We're on vacation until they see if we broke any policies. But we can't get fired. You're a public defender hero now. They're going to do a monument. If you'd died there would have been an eternal flame. I'm so jealous I can taste it. I only got nicked."

Boris said:

"Fucking mom. We almost had it."

"Parents who give a shit are the worst."

Boris closed his eyes. He asked:

"How did you know?"

"What?"

"That it was Willard's gun."

Because why else would Robert, having owned all the responsibility for the shooting, still care whether the gun was found? If he was so eager to take the lick, why not give the police the gun? Maybe because it belonged to a kid he was trying to protect. The kid who gave it to him, right before things just happened. Ben sagged. Everything is concealment, but sometimes you're just too tired. So he told Boris, lying there in the hospital not twenty-four hours from almost-death, what he'd done with the gun and why. Boris was quiet for a long time. Ben thought he'd passed out. He stepped forward and looked at the monitor with Boris's vitals and he saw that Boris's eyes were open, looking at the square foam ceiling tiles.

"You went already?"

"Where?"

It was mean of him to make Boris say it. It took Boris a minute to gather himself.

"The mom said there was a burglary. You got the police report?"

"Yeah. First thing this morning. She reported a stolen gun. A revolver. With a stainless-steel barrel and black grip."

Boris, still flat on his back. Ben could barely hear him:

"That's the gun you threw in the river."

"The Industrial Canal."

"The mom's gun. That Willard stole."

"Yeah," said Ben. "He stole his mom's gun. She thought it was a burglary. She reported it that way."

"And."

"And maybe the gun that killed Lillie Scott had Willard's prints on it."

"You threw it in the river."

"I told you. It wasn't the river. It was the Industrial Canal."

26

In Limine

A few days later he went back and found Boris sitting up in bed and reading: *Ada, or Ardor*. Deborah the receptionist had left it for him. Some people from work had visited, too, and a few guys from a softball team that he played with on Sunday mornings. He was part of a synagogue league even though he wouldn't have been caught in the synagogue. Boris was someone who could have lived a normal life.

Boris sounded a little better, but gasped a little every few words so that his sentences came out like a flat tire turning around on an axel, lifting and falling. He said:

"What happened to them in Memphis?"

"I don't know. He never told me."

"Why was he in the hospital there?"

"I don't know. He never said anything about a hospital. Maybe it's not important to him."

"Maybe he thought it wouldn't be important to you."

"Maybe."

"Maybe if you don't tell people the truth, they don't tell you the truth."

"Maybe."

Ben moved a basket of flowers to the floor and sat down, uninvited. He said:

"I think I need to leave."

"We haven't even started fighting yet."

"We haven't?"

"I guess we have."

"I mean leave, leave."

"Back to Brookline?"

"Amherst."

"That doesn't make you more authentic."

"My dad died fishing. What's more working class than that?"

"On a pleasure craft."

"A rowboat."

"What's your plan?"

"I dunno. Find someplace I can really suffer. New Orleans is too nice. Maybe someplace smaller, where everyone will know me and hate me."

"You're doing okay with that right here. Think big."

Ben said:

"Our dads left."

"Does that make it better?"

"Easier."

If they'd been sitting in their office, Boris would have extended and contracted the camping fork and looked out the window to see if there were any new fires near the I-10. Instead, he looked at Ben. Ben liked the fork and the freeway better. Boris said:

"Easier's how you're gonna do it, then, huh?"

With that admonishment in mind, he instead drove six hours up to Memphis where he found a chain hotel near the courthouse and then a bar that felt familiarly shopworn. That night he met another public defender and brought her back to his hotel with the promise of its rooftop pool. He had no idea how; maybe there was a romance to men whose idea of small talk had been reduced to one-liners about prosecutors and self-hatred. She took off her clothes down to her black underwear. She had long legs and pale skin and short dark hair, and she slipped into the water like a needle into fabric smooth and quick and silent. He dived in and swam after her, but he was drunk and hit the bridge of his nose against the far edge of the pool. She stayed over anyhow but they didn't have sex. Instead, they curled up naked on the bed like nesting animals looking for warmth. The next morning she was hungover and put on her suit from the day before. Ben walked her over to the courthouse like a gentleman, stopping for Band-Aids to put on the bridge of his nose, which was split open and still leaking.

The usual shabby ecosystem of bail bondsmen and storefront lawyers and parking lots. This was one of those parts of the scattered city that feel like the outskirts of something, even though they're right downtown. Outskirts of a time when the city was different, maybe. Streets are too wide, gas stations, auto repair, all about getting you ready to drive away somewhere else. He walked up away from the river and the day got hotter. The grass was wet without any rain; probably they'd buried a bayou somewhere nearby. The slabs and tar and fences peeling up like chipping paint over the unprepped substrate of the ground. His shirt was damp when he got to the juvenile courthouse, with its outriders: Pairs of figures, almost always a boy and a woman, spaced out regularly for about a block down the street in each direction. Trying to figure out where to go and how to get there.

A secretary at the juvenile court ran the names for him even though she shouldn't have. Nothing for Robert Johnson or Willard Thomas. For a while he sat in the waiting area where families sit before they're called in to court. Best case scenario for them, the court won't make it worse, but most of the time it will. Ben sat and watched tired moms reel in younger siblings climbing the benches. The older kids slouched down and hid under their flat hat-brims. After a while he left, got in his car, and drove out to the motel where Robert and Willard had stayed those months in the fall of 2005. The motel didn't have any records because the money came straight from FEMA. The manager said they hadn't even kept lists of who'd stayed there. Ben didn't know what he was looking for and he didn't find it.

He had one more lead, the photo he'd seen pinned to the wall in Robert's room in New Orleans, its only decoration. It showed Robert with his legs spread wide, like he was looking for balance on unsteady ground or a ship's bow. Hands in his pockets, chin pointed high, eyes half-closed and a little smile like he just had a great meal that left him drowsy and satisfied. He was wearing a nice shirt, French blue, buttoned all the way up to the collar, tan Dickies, black work boots. His hair in little twists, some down over his forehead so he looked like an eager puppy. He was posed in front of a wall that looked pixelated—tiled with dots of unresolved color, most the same blue as Robert's shirt.

Ben knew what it meant. He'd seen lots of pictures like it before. Robert was wearing a uniform from some youth-at-risk program. He was posed in front of a wall of pictures just like his. Probably they took one of every kid when they started the program and when they left. Ben got his laptop and sat in the hotel lobby drinking a beer at 11 a.m. and searched the programs that did vocational training for high school kids in Memphis. It didn't take long to find the one with the Black kids in French blue shirts. Grille Life. An after-school program that taught kids the food business. Great food, life lessons. He headed over there and found a case manager. *Oh, Robert, of course I remember him. What a sad story. Whatever happened to him back in New Orleans?*

27

Making a Record

Ben went back to the same bar that night but Andrea the public defender wasn't there. He didn't have her number. While he sat at the bar, though, he got an email at his work address, where she'd tracked him down. *Do you need your bandages changed?*

She was from Denver via Seattle, and now here. There weren't as many carpetbaggers in Memphis because there was no acute disaster to lure them, just the usual chronic stuff. She'd come to town right after law school for a clerkship with a federal judge and stayed to work as a public defender. Probably there'd been a guy involved. She was tall, just a few inches shorter than Ben, and slender, and had dark eyes and dark-rimmed glasses. She lived in half a cottage in a hipster area in the middle of the city and kept a straight-shooter on her mantelpiece—a little glass tube, about four inches long, with a fabric rose inside. People buy them for the glass, not the flower, but you can't just advertise crack pipes.

"I don't even know how to use it," she said. "I mean, I know, but I don't know."

"You can watch a video on YouTube."

She sat down next to him on the couch with about a fist of bourbon in a glass.

"You never know anyhow."

167

Of course they didn't know what it felt like to sell drugs to addicts, or shoot somebody; to be addicted to drugs, or watch your little brother get shot; to be beaten by the police, or erased by a judge. Or ignored by a public defender. Of course not. Most of the time they didn't even know the logistics, the mechanical give-and-take.

Well, where *do* you hide your drugs?

Where *did* you get that gun?

What *is* the going rate for a blow job?

Maybe they didn't need to; maybe it was just prurient curiosity. Why do you have to know, anyhow? They weren't anthropologists. They were fabulists. They could research technical things. What are the New Orleans police protocols around using dogs in arrests? How do forensic sexual assault interviewers shape their questions to guide children into claiming they were abused? Some of that was in books or on the internet; some of it they learned from hiring their own experts; some of it was just trial and error.

For his first copper-theft case, Ben bought a few lengths of pipe and a pipe cutter and practiced to see how long it would take to cut all the pipes out from underneath a retired police officer's house. At first it was exciting to learn those things, like children uncovering secret knowledge. They saw glimpses; they learned what they needed to learn to make the worlds they created seem authentic; everything else they filled in with their own meanings. They learned it ad hoc, as it came up in cases, just enough to argue what they needed to argue. It was like looking up phrases of another language to navigate a foreign city. But the city was still foreign, and they were still tourists.

Andrea's client had been sixty years old and homeless, arrested for beating another homeless man to death outside a convenience store. They'd been sitting on the front step and drinking beer in the middle of the night, and then there was her client on the security video picking up something long and thin and chasing the decedent off the screen. The decedent was found dead, with his head broken in.

The police found a big metal baton, white and square in cross section, in the client's squat.

"The store owner did it," she said. "That was my theory." She leaned back against the arm of the couch and put her legs across Ben's lap.

"What about the video?"

"We got lucky. The time stamp on the video was wrong. It was like an hour earlier than the call came in. So here's the theory. My guy was a kind of informal enforcer for the store owner. He chased other homeless people away and kept order in exchange for free beer. That's what you saw on the video. But then my guy went back to his squat to smoke crack and the decedent got crazy and the owner got out the baseball bat he kept behind the counter."

"I'm not telling you he's an angel. But he didn't do this."

"Right. We found a witness to say the owner had a bat. Client's ex-girlfriend, actually. She's in a state women's prison now. But she says she was there that night. Just off-screen. She said she'd testify my guy was high with her."

"What about the stick?"

"No blood or hair or anything. You'd have expected that if he beat someone to death with it, right? *Physical evidence. The only kind that doesn't lie.* The owner sold these roses and the iron mesh pads and lighters together as a kit. So I went in and bought one from him. To show the jury what he was up to."

"This is a case about community."

"What do you mean?"

"Values. My officemate at home—in New Orleans—says cases have to be about values. This case is about a vampire who peddles drug paraphernalia in our community. Now he's trying to steal the rest of my client's life—what was his name?"

She took a sip:

"Jordan Houston. But he pled to eighteen years."

"I'm sorry."

"It was his choice."

"I don't mean the murder."

"Neither do I. I had an exoneree come in and talk to him. A guy who'd served twenty years for something he didn't do. I told him to say that eighteen years in prison is just a really long time and a bad deal and Jordan shouldn't take it."

"Fucking exonerees."

"Instead, he told my guy to take the plea so he'd have a light at the end of the tunnel to survive prison. Innocent people have no idea what's up."

"You know who knows, though?"

"White people, obviously. But it wasn't the exoneree's fault. Jordan didn't take the plea to have a light at the end of the tunnel. He took it because he was afraid."

Ben didn't have to ask what he was afraid of. Not the consequences of trial. He was going to do the time and die in jail anyhow. He was afraid of going to trial and having the jury sit in judgment of him. It was better not to be judged and to seize control of it himself, plead guilty, not have someone else decide it all. He asked:

"What was his real name?"

She said:

"You know who Jordan Houston is?"

"I know it isn't your client."

"Juicy J?"

"Oh yes, sure."

"You don't know him."

"Absolutely not."

"Three 6 Mafia?"

"Still no."

"See, that's why I like you. High-end poseur, none of your pop culture."

"It's not because I'm a good swimmer?"

"Well, where do you get your names?"

"I'm named after my great-grandfather. Binyomin Alterman. All they did was give the name a haircut."

"A bris, right?"

"That's good for a goy."

"Where do you get your client names, really?"

He put his hand on her side, under the waistband of her jeans, touching the bare smooth skin over her hip bone. He said:

"I do Delta blues."

"If you want music names, there's a lot from right there in New Orleans," she said.

"People think jazz," he said, "but it's also the bottom of the Delta."

"Plus, Delta blues is just about right for a white guy who thinks poor Black people are romantic."

"That's pretty mean."

"What are you calling him? The kid you're investigating?"

"It's a mitigation case," he said.

"Is he pleading guilty?"

"Mitigation for me, not him. His name is Robert Johnson."

"Really?"

"Yeah."

"Because he doesn't exist?"

"Were you this way before?"

"Why do you represent kids?"

"Low stakes."

"They seem more innocent than adults?"

"Are you kidding? Kids always did it."

"I mean at their core. Like, virtuous."

"I don't know anything about their core. Virtue or whatever doesn't have anything to do with shooting people."

"I think it's because the kids are used to being let down by grownups."

"That's just what I told you. Low stakes."

She pulled her knees up under her and kneeled next to him on the couch and kissed him for a while. She said:

"I want you to stay over, but I don't want to have sex."

"Me neither," he said. "I hate it."

She put her head against his shoulder.

"I mean, I like you, but I don't like you that much," she said.

"I'm great at sex, so if you want to keep it that way, we should definitely not have sex."

Robert had a nervous tic when he was little. Ben learned that from an aunt, one of the aunts that his forensic expert interviewed. He'd open his mouth and move his lower jaw to the left so the space between his lips made an irregular amoeba opening. They started calling him Popeye, because of how the sailor talked out of the side of his mouth so he could keep smoking his pipe. People called him Popeye for a long time, even after he stopped with the tic. He was self-conscious so he got the habit of bringing his hand up to cover his mouth and the bottom of his face.

That's the giveaway. Ben found a crime scene photo in the *Commercial Appeal*'s online archive. He couldn't tell for sure with the resolution and the light, but he thought it was Robert because of the hand on his face. It was a kid, for sure, with a white T-shirt and twists. He stood on the curb of a yellow-lit road, to the left of the frame. Crime scene tape and cops in the foreground, frame right. He had his right hand up over his chin and you could see him in profile. He wasn't looking toward the place where the shooting happened, but instead looking up the street like he expected something to come from that way, some new doom. His left hand was down at his side, resting on the shoulder of another figure. This other one was sitting down on the curb, its head down between its arms, its face concealed.

Ben couldn't go back to reinterview Willard, and he couldn't go to Robert yet and ask him to solve the puzzle. The kid would just shut him out. There was a reason Robert hadn't told him about Willard. So he spent that week driving around Memphis, putting together his theory. Each clue led to the next. He found the newspaper articles and internet videos. He borrowed Andrea's Tennessee bar card and the next day he flashed it at the county public records clerk and got police reports from the shooting. He went down into the basement of the hospital and looked at the sign-in logs that showed when Robert and Willard were there. He talked to anyone who would talk to him: A teacher, a violence interrupter, EMTs. At night he went back to Andrea's house and cooked dinner with her like regular people and kissed on the couch. At first, and at the end, you know nothing. In between you put together your theory; like a child's artwork, wrapping string between nails until it makes the outlines of a picture.

She said to him:

"So are you figuring it out? Whatever you were trying to figure out?"

"About Robert?"

"Sure."

"I have a theory."

"Tell it to me."

"I don't know."

She rolled over so she was lying perpendicular to him in the dark, her head on his chest, both looking up at the slow-spinning ceiling fan.

"Come on. Tell me a story."

28

Crime Scene Reconstruction

A kid from Memphis who went to their school, just a couple years older, had a car. He came by the motel a lot because he liked one of the New Orleans girls who was staying there, and then he got to be friends with Robert and especially Willard. He said it was his cousin's car and he took them all for a drive, but the girl wanted to go home after a while. She was worried it wasn't really the cousin's car. Willard and Robert thought it might not be either, but he was an older kid and it was Friday night. The three boys drove north up route 51 toward downtown. This city with its own pink-and-orange neon street; its own distractions of music and celebration; its own dead-end roads and railroad tracks; its own narrow curbless streets with single-story brick houses, just out of sight of that same river. How long will we stay or live here.

The older boy's name was Johnny Len Chatman. He pointed from the car:

"That's Elvis Presley's house."

"Who's that?"

"He's not. He's dead."

"What'd he do?"

"He sang mostly and played guitar. He danced too."

"What'd he do to be dead?"

"All the drugs."

"What songs?"

"All the songs. Look there."

A billboard advertised some Elvis-themed store. It showed that picture where Elvis is young and beautiful in a black shirt and suit on a red background.

"That's a white dude, though."

"I'd get a suit like that."

"Rich, huh?"

"All that money and he stayed right here next to Taco Bell?"

"He's buried here too."

"I'd get some peace if I was rich."

"Like in the country?"

"You mean where you were buried or where you'd live?"

"Like in a skyscraper. I'd get a penthouse so I could have the whole floor."

"You'd still have people around you."

"It's the people upstairs that make the noise. If I was rich like that, there'd be nobody upstairs."

Robert and Willard and Johnny parked off Beale and walked down the street and back. They saw kids dancing for money, just like at home. They saw women, college-aged, wearing T-shirts and jeans and dancing too, in the street in front of a club. The boys stopped and watched. It was someone's birthday. Willard had a dollar, and after Johnny Len pushed him he went up and pinned it on the birthday girl's shirt. She gave him a kiss on the cheek.

After a while Johnny asked someone the time and then he rushed them to the car and drove in a hurry back south. About ten blocks from their motel, he pulled into the driveway of a one-story brick house where a giant fat man sat in a lawn chair, drinking beer in bottles and smoking ribs in a drum smoker. He looked at his watch and took the keys back. This was in fact Johnny's cousin. *That's some shit*, said Willard. Robert couldn't stop laughing that it was a real cousin and not a joyride. Smoking ribs isn't so much of a thing in New Orleans, and Robert and Willard wanted to stick around. The cousin said he didn't blame them. *If I weighed what you weigh, I'd have a rack of ribs in each hand and one in each pocket at all times.* But he said he'd save them some ribs and sent them back to the motel because it was late. Johnny Len Chatman walked with them because he wanted to see if the girl was still up. It was warm in October in Memphis.

It turns out it was all a mistake. The two kids waiting outside the motel thought Johnny Len had shot at their friend, but that wasn't right. Another kid did that shooting—a kid named John, full stop. Anyhow, when Willard and Robert and Johnny Len came along the street the two kids pushed off the fence and started shooting, the white flare and hollow slap of gunshots on an empty street at night.

It wasn't the first time for Robert. Still he just flattened out on the ground like an idiot while Willard ran low and zigzag across the road. Robert knew that lying there wasn't the thing to do, but all he could think was they'd recognize their mistake, neither he nor Willard nor Johnny Len had done anything worth shooting them for, and they'd just stop. The kids stood only twenty feet away shooting one handed with the guns canted almost sideways, the barrels flying up and the kids jerking them back down after every shot. Like maniacs pointing their fingers over and over to identify some phantom evil.

The shooting stopped and the kids disappeared. Robert looked over and Johnny Len was still breathing on the ground near him, but real fast, so Robert ran toward the motel. The guy in the office had locked the door and didn't let him in. He banged on the glass: *Call the ambulance! You gotta call somebody Johnny Len got shot!* When Robert ran back out, Willard was there again. He had his shirt off and was holding it against Johnny's side in a way maybe he'd seen in a movie or something. Johnny Len Chatman was hit in the gut and the leg and the shoulder and the hand. The paramedics came fast enough. At the hospital they got the bullets out and stopped the bleeding and he was critical that night but by the next day it looked like he'd be okay.

Robert had been to funerals, of course. For instance, he'd had a friend as a child by the name of Reuel Burnside. Reuel was twelve when he climbed through a neighbor's window to steal a TV. The neighbor was waiting for him with a shotgun, point-blank. Robert hadn't ever been to the hospital to visit someone alive, though. But Willard's mom was making Willard go, so Robert and Willard went down to the Children's Hospital. The nurses were doing a procedure on Johnny when they got there, emptying his colostomy bag, so Robert and Willard sat in a small waiting area with Johnny's mother and his little sister. *Why are you here*, said the sister. *To visit your brother*, said Willard. *I have two brothers*, she said. *One who is dead, and one who's not dead yet.*

Johnny adopted them in Memphis. Robert didn't understand it at first or maybe ever. He was older than them. He wasn't slow or ugly or otherwise desperate for friends. He had a family. He was in school and would probably graduate. Why did he want to hang out with a couple of New Orleans kids who were younger than him and didn't know where to find girls or weed? Maybe he liked the idea of being someplace far from home. Maybe he liked being a tour guide. His own big brother had been shot and killed, and maybe he just wanted to be with kids who didn't know anything about that and weren't part of any clique or have any beefs with anyone. He was shortish and athletic, built like a little bullet. He wore sandals and socks with long gym shorts all the time, sat very straight up, and when he laughed swayed side to side from the waist like a rooted plant. Two days after they upgraded his condition to fair, his stomach wound got infected and Johnny Len got sepsis and died.

29

Lineup

You can't just arrest your way out of the problem, some people say. Memphis had tried that and was still trying. But just to cover their bases they were also doing a program called violence interruption. That's when, after a shooting, older men from the neighborhood, maybe they've been in prison, come over to your house to check on you and try to make sure you don't go kill the guys who tried to kill you. Sometimes they set up a kind of mediation, if you even know who you're beefing with. The guy who came to see Robert was tall and thin with a face that looked like it was shaped by being pressed into a corner for too long. He sat on the motel room's paisley couch, too close to Robert. Robert's mom was lying on one of the double beds with a towel over her eyes. She was having headaches since they'd gone to Memphis. His sister was out throwing a ball with some of the other evacuee kids on the second-floor breezeway. Every three or four throws someone would send it over the railing and then they'd fight about whose turn it was to go down and pick it up.

"How're you feeling?"

"I'm doing okay."

"I asked how you're *feeling*, son."

"Hungry," said Robert, not as some sort of metaphor but because he'd heard that these guys would take you to a restaurant and buy you dinner.

"You ever have real ribs?"

"I don't know," said Robert. "What makes it real?"

"Time," said the guy. Robert nodded like it was wise. The guy thought he'd already made inroads.

They went to a storefront place that had ribs and barbecued bologna and little smoked Cornish hens. The guy had barbecued spaghetti. Robert had one of almost everything. The guy said he knew he wasn't Robert's father, which he hadn't needed to say. It didn't matter what the guy knew. Robert knew it.

"Where's your dad?"

"At home."

"What does he say about all this?"

"This what?"

"Your friend getting shot."

"He got killed."

"What does your dad say?"

"He says we should come home."

"You talk to him?"

"He's got a phone with minutes. From FEMA. They're giving them out."

The guy seemed surprised and almost disappointed. He asked:

"What do y'all talk about?"

"Nothing. The food here in Memphis, sometimes."

"What do you think of it?"

"I could drink more of that sweet tea."

The guy said maybe Robert might want to do an after-school program where kids learned to prep and cook and serve food, at a restaurant run by a nonprofit. It was around the corner from the Civil Rights Museum and tourists who wanted to feel like they were really helping to make things better would eat there instead of at the famous ribs place across the street. He was trying to keep Robert off the corner, right? Willard's violence interrupter had put Willard in a program run by a blues music foundation. He'd go after school and learn to play an instrument. They wanted him to play the bass because he was thick like a bass player but he chose the trumpet so he could play in the marching band when they got home. Robert wasn't interested in cooking food so much as eating it, but he didn't mind the program. His mom was mostly just silent now, and it was hard to be with that kind of quiet all the time.

Three weeks later the police found a kid with a gun and matched the ballistics. They wanted Robert and Willard to make an ID. The violence interrupter picked up Robert and brought him to the police station to look at a photo lineup. The detective said:

"Do your best, son."

The interrupter put his hand on Robert's shoulder:

"Some people say you shouldn't help the police. But you know what? That's just being afraid."

Robert maybe smiled. The guy said:

"It's okay to be afraid. But we have to fight through it. That's what being a man is about."

Robert said:

"Can I see it?"

"See what?"

Robert looked like the detective was crazy:

"The gun."

There had been one kid with a silver gun and one with a black gun. Robert didn't know about faces. He'd been looking up from the ground, mostly, and the shooters had the lights from The King Motel behind them.

"He thought you were someone else," said the detective. "He wasn't looking for you or Johnny."

"He found us."

"We think he was looking for another kid that he was beefing with."

"We weren't beefing with anyone."

"We know you're not involved in that stuff. That's why we know we can count on you."

"It didn't help," said Robert.

"We'll look out for you. Maybe we can get you out of that motel. Maybe back to New Orleans."

They showed him six pictures, a photo array. Robert told them they didn't have the right guy. He did recognize one of the pictures though. He hadn't seen the faces during the shooting, but he knew this kid from school. Papa, everyone called him, because when he was little he used to wear his pants real high like an old man. So now Robert knew what he was supposed to do.

30

Violence Interruption

Robert played football at the school in Memphis. He was tall and strong and he ran well, so they made him a wide receiver. He had dreams about running down the field and the ball coming on a smooth arc down out of the sky toward him, but in the dreams he couldn't get his arms up over his shoulders in time. Like there was something heavy in the air pressing down against him. The ball just fell right in front of him, every time. Those weren't the only dreams where his brain didn't seem to be able to tell his hands what to do. He dreamed also about having to make a phone call—sometimes a 911 call in an emergency—and pressing the wrong numbers over and over. He would wake up and lie on the motel's greasy striped bedspreads, with his sister sleeping next to him. He'd flex his hands from fists into open. He'd look over to the other bed and see his mother lying there in the dark, her phone on and held above her, casting a halo on her skin. He never knew what she was looking for there in that pale light, all night long.

Robert and Willard kind of asked around at school but they didn't have any money or anything to trade. One evening they walked back over to the cousin's house, the guy who loaned Johnny the car that night. They thought maybe he could help them. Willard said: *We're just trying to figure out what to do about Johnny.* The cousin didn't understand, or acted like he didn't understand. But he sat them at his kitchen table and fed them pulled pork from a big plastic tub in the fridge and smoked sausage on white sandwich bread and pickles. Afterward he drove them back to the motel and left them each with a sandwich wrapped in foil. Willard said maybe they could get arrested and held at the juvenile detention center and ask one of the kids there. Robert said no because nobody there had any reason to trust them. Also once you're in maybe it's a long time before you get out.

Robert and Willard walking close like they were shackled together. They had part of a plan. Robert would come back to the motel and take off his French blue shirt and put on a black T-shirt. Willard, too, and put away his trumpet. They'd get the bag that they'd hide behind the vending machine on their breezeway. The machine hadn't been serviced since they moved in so they knew the bag would be safe there. It was November already so they could wear coats and hide it. Then they'd go to a club where they'd heard Papa liked to go, a place that had nights for kids under twenty-one. They'd wait under the railroad overpass down the block. They'd already scouted the whole thing out. The overpass was between the club and Papa's house. Willard would shoot for both of them. That would be all. But still they didn't know how to get a gun, and they didn't know anyone in Memphis who did.

Willard's mom was working the overnight shift. She'd get home in the early morning and bring the boys to school, to make sure they got there. Then she'd drop off their little sisters and come home to sleep. One morning she knocked hard on Robert's motel room door and nobody answered. The door was unlocked and the room was dark with the blackout shades drawn, the family still sleeping. Piles of clothes on the floor; microwave pizza boxes; a half-dozen mostly empty medicine bottles on top of the TV to hold down the fevers that kept coming back on Robert's sister. It was already late. Caroline Thomas shook Robert awake. She opened the shade and started picking up while he got dressed, and in one of the empty dresser drawers saw the pillowcase that Robert had wrapped around two chef's knives he'd stolen from Grille Life, where he went after school.

She picked them up from school that day, which she didn't usually do, and brought Willard to his music program. Then she drove to Grille Life. Robert shuffled his feet in the back seat of the car.

"You and I need to work this out," she said. "Your mother doesn't need this."

"She doesn't need much."

She looked at him in the rearview mirror:

"What is this about?"

"It's just something to have."

"Why do you want to have knives?"

He covered his mouth with his hand, like when he was a kid:

"To sell. For money. To buy a ticket for the bus," he lied. What could she say to that? She didn't even bother asking where he planned to go. There was only one place.

"We're going home as soon as we can."

"You think it'll be better then?"

Now it was her turn to tell a lie:

"I think things always look different when you're home." That didn't seem to work, so she then said: "I think things can get better, Robert. This is just the way it is now. It's only now. Do you believe me?"

He said:

"It's now but also it's forever."

She was doing her best. She didn't march him in there and make him give the knives back. She threw them in a dumpster and never told anyone about it. One week later he sat with his feet in the water of their motel swimming pool, still undrained and filled with leaves and scum, and cut his wrists as deep as he could bring himself to cut with a knife he'd been using that day to julienne carrots. Willard found him there, lying back and looking up at the purple night sky, and wrapped his arms around him and screamed and screamed, almost easily, almost eagerly, like it was already in his veins and just burst out like blood waits impatient to be released from a wound. Until the whole motel woke up and men, women, and children, the community of exiles, stood out on their breezeways and looked down at the two boys, locked together, still breathing together.

Caroline Thomas called Robert's dad. McTell in turn begged or borrowed or stole $54 to get on a Greyhound bus. He came in and sat by Robert's bed until the boy was released from the hospital. The staff wanted to put him in an institution for kids for a little while but McTell and Caroline and Robert's mother were all united against that. Instead, Caroline drove them back to New Orleans that next week, all of them in her five-seat car, the girls sitting on the boys' laps all the way down the flat green Delta. McTell in the middle seat in the back; Robert with bandaged wrists; Robert's mother Angeline sitting upright in the front with dark glasses over her eyes. Robert feeling as he came back to New Orleans the way he felt that other time in the van to the adult jail, that the future is the three feet of gravel just in front of your wheels.

You know who killed Papa in the end? The fat cousin, believe it or not. Just after the bell rang one day. The school security officers arrested him before he even pulled away. A grown man waiting for a boy in a school parking lot.

31

Reintegration

That last part Ben confirmed. He'd visited the cousin in jail where he was still waiting for trial two years later, still round like he was smoking ribs in his driveway every night, still smiling. He was sorry he did it but there wasn't another way. It was just something that had to happen.

Some well-meaning public defenders talked about street justice. Like: If kids learn there's no satisfaction in the regular justice system, they turn to street justice. This was a way to explain why kids weren't entirely to blame for killing each other. The fucked-up justice system was responsible for that, too. Ben thought the analogy mostly failed. Justice, if nothing else, implies intent, for better or worse. When people get what they deserve by accident, nonbelievers call it karma (jestingly) or fate (mystically), but not justice. But Ben didn't see intentionality in the way that boys and men killed and were killed until new generations of boys and men grew into their places. What happened when his clients and their friends were shot and shot each other was like a law of physics, action and reaction, strike and recoil, in a place where the regular laws of thermodynamics did not apply; a vacuum where the frictions of sorrow and exhaustion and loss did not slow the perpetual machine of violence once set in motion, and so the contained system never needed new fuel nor did it stop. The courts and their punishments can be cruel and unusual, a judge once wrote, just like being struck by lightning is cruel and unusual. But that's not right for the run of cases in either the courts or the streets, because lightning doesn't strike everyone. In real life what we call the justice system is more like a rainstorm. Whether you get hit by any particular raindrop is just chance, but everything gets wet in the end.

The last night, Ben and Andrea went over to Mud Island, where there was a planned development of winding roads and houses with porches and ceiling fans. A tiny perfect southern town in the middle of the river at the edge of the city. He told her about his lie, having his own children.

"You're trying to be special."

"I think I'm trying not to be."

"It's a fantasy."

"Of being a single dad?"

"Of having more to give."

She was good at finding something painful to say, something that hurt even through his shield of self-deprecation, and continuing to walk on with him arm in arm. The minute she said it, she always felt bad and squeezed him or smiled at him, not insincerely. He asked:

"If this wasn't it, do you think you could be nicer to me?"

"Like if it was a thing where we loved each other and we didn't both represent murderers and lie all the time?"

"Or even if we did both represent murderers, but we lived in the same place and loved each other and it was like other people do."

"I'm going to fight the hypothetical."

They drank too much and fell asleep on her couch, she facing away from him and he pressed against her back, his arm over her. She, at the end of the night, when neither of them was asleep:

"Do you have a girlfriend?"

"It feels late for that."

"Do you?"

"No."

"Why not?"

"I haven't met anyone who wants to treat me badly enough. What about you?"

"I don't know about enough. I could treat you badly, if you stayed."

"Do you have a boyfriend?"

She was still facing away from him, both of them sleeping in their jeans.

"Yeah," she said.

"What's he like?"

"He's been in trial this week."

"He's a public defender too."

"Yeah."

"What kind of case is it?"

"I'm sorry."

"You don't have to be. You didn't lie to me."

"You lie too."

"I know."

"So don't be mad at me."

"Why not? I'm mad at me."

He didn't know whether it was that the work attracted damaged people or that it damaged people. More likely it just gave them license to act out hurt that we all have. Or an imperative. Otherwise, you're too different from your clients. That's too awful to think—that there is this kind of suffering and desperation, and right alongside it joy or just regular sorrow and the usual kind of waking up and lying down. Better that we all be together in that desperation. What kind of a monster doesn't break? What would be wrong with you if you didn't?

But some of Ben's colleagues had wives or husbands and children and mortgages and seemed, most Saturday nights, to be asleep on the couch or else clapping along to a brass band on Frenchman Street. Either domestic bliss or just the regular kind of happy or even the regular kind of unhappy. He accused those people of being very good at compartmentalizing, which was damning because it meant they didn't feel deeply enough and so were probably selling out their clients in one way or another. In fact, some people take for granted that they will see and even experience difficulty and outright tragedy, and aim to defeat it when they can and coexist with it when they must, and either way not to act out perpetually a drama of lost naivete. By being always naive we proclaim that we are also always pure. But, like courage and constancy, purity is not intrinsically good; just as guilt and lies, too, have their uses. There's no virtue in innocence, nor is goodness any protection.

Ben and Andrea went into the bedroom and had sex for the first time. She pulled away in the middle and he sat back, but she motioned to him to go on and he did. She cried afterward and he got up to go sit on the couch. She came in and curled up next to him but not quite touching. In a little while he kissed her on the cheek like they'd see each other again and left.

32

Negotiation

en was back at his hotel with a Styrofoam clamshell of ribs on the
bed and three tallboys icing in the sink. He wiped the dry rub off
his hands onto a pillowcase and answered his phone.

"Mr. Alder?"

"This is Ben."

"Mr. Ben Alder?"

"This is Ben Alder."

"This is Imelda."

"Hi, Imelda."

"Hi, Mr. Ben Alder."

"Hi."

"Imelda McTell. Robert McTell's mother."

This was a new McTell in the world, about whom he'd never
thought to inquire. But there she was, calling from Lafayette, Louisiana.

"Well. Hi."

"How are you, Mr. Ben?"

"I'm okay. How are you, Miss Imelda?"

"My shingles are acting up, and I have to go downtown just about
every day. You know how it is downtown."

Ben didn't know downtown Lafayette, but he thought he should
apologize for it:

"I'm sorry."

"Robert wants to see you."

"Robert?"

"My son."

"Right."

"He's got some things to say for his case."

"He doesn't have a case. He was revoked—"

"He's got something new."

"He has a new case?"

"They've got him locked up on some kind of thing."

"He's in prison."

"*Special* locked up. He can't call you."

"What do you mean?"

"He said he can't call you. He said to come talk to him about Robert. The other Robert. My grandson."

The next day Ben drove down to Cottonport, Louisiana, population just around two thousand not counting the prisoners. He listed to Memphis hip-hop on the way down and had learned nothing about Juicy J by the time he pulled into downtown looking for a pre-prison beer. The whole place consigned to For Sale signs and cracked concrete slabs; Xstream Youth Ministries and Christian Club Café; as little glass as possible on the street—boards, butcher paper, metal grilles. McTell was in administrative segregation at the Raymond Laborde Correctional Center and the guards took their time bringing him out. They wouldn't unshackle him even when lawyer and client were alone together in the visiting room. He didn't bother pretending he wasn't mad.

Ben, pursed lips:

"How'd you find out?"

McTell, eyes squeezed almost shut like there was some kind of bright light in the dim room:

"I don't have much to do other than read the paper. There you were getting shot in the Iberville, just like a local boy."

The newspaper had used a picture of Ben from an earlier perp walk.

He'd been wearing his pink tie and walking with his head down next to his client on that one, a kid who in the end took a terrible deal. He'd driven, his little partner had shot out the passenger door, and another kid standing in his own doorway had ended up in a wheelchair for the rest of his life. Ben had been in the paralyzed kid's living room and listened to him tell his story. When you talk with victims you try to show compassion without admitting your client did anything wrong. *I'm so sorry. For what? For what happened to you.*

"The tie was supposed to make me look emotionally accessible. Kind."

"It made you look like a big baby."

"That's what Boris said."

"I didn't like Boris."

"I don't suppose you like me much, either."

"Shot working on Robert Johnson's case, said the paper."

"Doesn't that make you happy? I bled for him."

"I'm not happy."

"No."

"Well?"

"Well?"

"What happened?"

Ben told the truth, at first: I tried to show that he didn't give a valid waiver of his rights. That means he didn't understand what he was agreeing to. We were going to get the statement suppressed. But I lost. Then I panicked and raised competency to stand trial. I just wanted to slow things down and give us some time. I don't know for what. To think of something. For the judge to die. I don't know. The judge sent Robert to Feliciana, the state forensic hospital. They're giving him classes about the justice system. Teaching him who does what, and what's going to happen in court. So they'll be able to bring him back and try him and send him to Angola prison until he dies.

McTell wanted to know if that was all they were doing with Robert at Feliciana. Yeah. That's pretty much it. No medicine, or anything? Then Ben stopped telling the truth. No, none of that. He doesn't need medicine. And what next? Eventually the judge will run out of patience.

Ben said:

"Now tell me what happened to you."

McTell hadn't summoned Ben to Cottonport for that. He waved his hand, as much as he could with his wrists bound to his waist:

"I'm in the hole."

"Why? I mean, why are they saying they put you in the hole?"

"I don't know what they're saying."

"Can you tell me what happened before you got put in?"

McTell shrugged:

"There was a guy getting crazy, so I chastised him."

"What did you say?"

"I didn't say anything."

"Right."

"Right."

"That's why they said they were putting you in the hole? For chastising him?"

"They didn't say it. They just did it."

"Right."

"Right."

"Did he tell them you did something else?"

"I don't know what he told them."

"Okay. Look. Can you walk me through exactly what happened, because I wasn't there?"

McTell sighed, like he'd told the story a thousand times.

"We were in the TV area, just watching TV. He starts getting crazy on me, saying this and that."

"What did he say?"

"Why does it matter?"

"It matters because of what they say you did. In response."

"They're not saying anything."

"This conversation isn't getting easier."

"I'm not asking for your help."

"Not asking for my help on this."

"Right. Not on this."

"But it's a package deal. Can you tell me exactly what you said when you chastised him?"

"I didn't say anything."

"Oh."

"Exactly."

"But then how—"

This was, or should have been, obvious:

"I took some of that wire—"

"To chastise him."

"I boiled up the water."

"You—"

"And I threw it on him."

"Oh."

Triumph:

"And I chastised him."

"You did."

"I did."

"Is he okay?"

"Thriving."

"This is a little bit surprising, Mr. McTell."

"I've been angry."

"You're still angry."

"You know it."

"I understand."

"I don't guess you do."

"I understand that people do things I don't understand, and so do I. All the time."

Ben looked it up later. It was more wisdom that he didn't know about. You can make a heating element with wire and razor blades and matchsticks and thread. Then you can boil water to heat coffee, or cook noodle soup cups, or burn the skin off your cellmate's arms. This is aggravated (because of the weapon) second-degree (because of the extent of the injury) battery. But nobody in the cell was thought to be worth the trouble, so there was no prosecution. The punishment, instead, was ten days in administrative segregation. Nothing Ben could do to help, even if McTell had wanted it. McTell was wearing an off-white T-shirt that was supposed to be white and a pair of wide-legged blue jeans. He either didn't shave evenly or didn't grow his beard evenly, but his cheeks looked patchy. He smiled the off-kilter smile that Boris had noticed but Ben hadn't, the smile that looked like Robert, and he told Ben a new story.

After the storm, he said, the city was full of welcoming places. The police didn't tell him to move along anymore. The taxpayers of the city had moved along. Lakeside of the I-10 there were abandoned houses all the way to Broad. Some of the places that hadn't taken so much water were filled with Spanish workers who came first to put up plywood over doors and windows, and then to gut the houses, and then to install drywall and new roofs and new paint and make the city ready again for new white immigrants from New York and Boston. Over on Banks, by where the public defender's office is now, they were a little colony of men. Sitting on the porch of an abandoned house across the street, a little red double-shotgun with a waterline at about eight feet, McTell watched them get robbed three times. They were good targets because they carried cash and they didn't call the police.

Mornings, he walked down Tulane to the drop-in center behind St. Joseph Church for breakfast. Once a week he showered there too. The hippies had a clinic in the upper Ninth Ward where he could eat and get new clothes. He learned to tell the difference between hippies and gutter punks, though both were dirty and white and wore dreadlocks. Hippies were the ones with tall bikes, and gutter punks were the ones with unkempt dogs. The gutter punks had little encampments during the day on the neutral ground on Elysian Fields; at night, like him, they had favorite spots. Theirs were mostly in the upper Ninth Ward across St. Claude from the Bywater.

The painted symbol, an X with numbers and letters in the blank spaces, was a rune of invitation meaning the house was open to him. He slept one night in a house in Lakeview whose front had been pulled away, with a big shiny chandelier hanging from the roof of the triple-height entryway, bared to the rain and the wind. He walked down Paris Avenue the next day and stood in front of Spider's Market, just lakeside of the I-610, within a long stone's throw of the juvenile jail and across the street from the boarded-up St. Bernard Projects. That night he rested on the front porch of a little cottage surrounded by a chain-link fence and uncut grass. It used to belong to his family. He remembered his uncle and aunt sitting under a pop-up canopy drinking amaretto in the paved-over backyard, while McTell and his sisters with ribbon and yarn made a maypole out of one of the canopy's aluminum struts and circled it again and again.

The next day he walked on Dumaine toward the river. A car full of kids, a sedan with Texas plates, was parked on the downriver side of the street, pointed toward Broad. Four kids, all around eighteen, a girl and three boys. It was a hot day and their windows were down. McTell was on the other side of the street. A man got out of a Dodge Charger and walked up behind the car with the kids and shot maybe twenty times, maybe more, from a long gun. McTell stood still on the sidewalk and watched until the shooter got back in his car and drove off. The shooter never even looked at McTell. All four kids died. They never arrested the guy who did it, but McTell knew who it was, both his face and his name. Everyone in the Seventh Ward does.

Ben knew who he was, too. It didn't take even a second to remember all about him. Ben remembered it all the time. McTell said:

"You're not going to ask me if it's true?"

"You know that's not what I do."

"Just if you could tell a good story about it."

"There's more to a theory than just a story."

"If you can make it seem true."

"Values and texture. Those are the important things. Could I?"

"That's your job."

"You didn't tell me about any of this before."

"You didn't tell me, either. About Robert."

"Robert didn't have anything to do with your case."

"He has something to do with my life."

"I could have used this to help you before."

"It wasn't worth it then."

"It's not worth it now."

"What would the district attorney give me?"

"Nothing worth your life."

"What will he give Robert?"

"I don't know."

"What if it were your kid? Your kids. What are their names?"

"My kids?"

"Your kids. Who you told me about."

"Yeah. Isaiah. And Nehemiah."

"What would you do?"

"I wouldn't try to enlist someone else in my suicide mission."

"You told me I was the boss."

"Of your case. Your case is over."

"My life isn't."

"Not yet."

"Anyhow, it's my life."

"I'm not your lawyer for life."

"You're little Robert's lawyer."

"Getting his dad shot won't help him."

"I want to make a deal to help him."

"Eddie House will kill you if you snitch on him."

"That's my life, where you're not my lawyer."

"I knew a kid who Eddie House killed."

"That's got nothing to do with me. One client's got nothing to do with another, even if they're father and son, right?"

Ben had always thought it would be nice to tell a client the truth, but it didn't quite shape up that way:

"Doing this won't make up for being a terrible dad."

McTell bent his head toward his waist and rubbed his face with his shackled hands.

"I'm not a white guy who went to law school, so I have to find another way to make myself feel better."

This language, Ben understood. It was the tone, if not the exact substance, of his internal monologue. He agreed to go talk to the district attorney. He left after putting some money in McTell's commissary account. *You can buy honey buns. Or noodle soup or more razor blades or whatever.*

In Krotz Springs, on the way back to New Orleans, Ben found the bar he'd been looking for. He sat in a green-blue painted concrete room like the bottom of an empty swimming pool and drank cheap, cold beer in bottles.

The bartender:

"You're not from here?"

"You'd be surprised how often I hear that."

"I don't think so."

"I was visiting in Cottonport."

"Seeing a friend?"

"I guess."

"Lady friend?"

Ben took the path of least resistance and smiled ruefully. The bartender:

"How much longer does she have?"

"A while."

"You're waiting for her?"

"I'm waiting."

She leaned across the bar and confided:

"I got a cousin there."

"Oh yeah?"

"Three years on forgery. Can you believe it? Just a few checks."

"I'm sorry."

"They were my checks."

"Well, then, I'm really sorry."

"Nah. There wasn't much to take."

"I'm sorry for that, too."

"Y'all have kids?"

Why not? Ben nodded.

"That's hard. You mind my asking what she went in for?"

"Can I get another?"

"Sure. I hope you don't mind my asking."

"No, I understand." Ben took a drink and had himself a vision of pure comfort and suffering. He said:

"She made a bad mistake."

"She's not the first."

"She took a life."

"Oh, my Jesus!"

The bartender wanted to know more but didn't know how to ask. Ben wasn't going to let her down. He said, softly:

"It was a baby."

"Oh my god."

The bartender put another beer on the bar. Then she retreated to the far end of the room and started mopping the floor, which was already clean. The beer was all on her, don't worry about that.

33

Cooperation

There was a picture in Evidence: A man, shirtless and facing the sky, lay on a bed of gray gravel. He was enormous, four hundred pounds or more. Five black-rimmed bullet holes in his chest and torso, each surrounded by a red penumbra, neat and precise, clean lined. He had scraps of a beard on his cheeks and chin. Barely out of his teens. Zoom out just a little bit: The parking lot where he died, filled with identical dirty white trailers; a little bit farther, the gas stations and motels of Chef Menteur Highway in east New Orleans, the best place in the city to buy a Vietnamese sandwich or get arrested for prostitution.

The fat man was named Chester Burnett, and the crime scene photos of his body weren't in evidence in the legal sense of being admitted at trial. They were in a police department warehouse with a sign in front that read EVIDENCE AND PROPERTY. Ben had driven there on an August morning with the fat man's mother to sort through the single dusty box containing everything the police had collected in the case. She removed each item one at a time. Her son's brown cloth wallet. The contents of the wallet, individually vacuum-sealed: A non-driver's ID; $7; a sandwich shop punch card. She saw, too, Chester's own gun, recovered from the ground beside him. Casings from the bullets that killed him. She'd hold them up against the fluorescent light tubes like she might see a hidden sign; like she was looking for clues; like he hadn't died but just disappeared and she could pick up his trail and track him down. Even if she'd found some memento, she couldn't have taken it home with her. The investigation was still open, and always would be. Everything was suspended in yellowing plastic pending the trial of the man, forever to remain unknown, who shot and killed her son.

Chester had been in witness protection, but he wasn't hiding. He was killed in front of the trailer he shared with his mother and younger brother, in the parking lot where he'd stayed since returning from Katrina exile in Shreveport. Where else was he supposed to go? For Chester, witness protection had meant a week in a motel in Kenner, and afterward a suggestion that he stay with a relative out of town. Possibly the vicious little district attorney had at his disposal more generous protections than those he offered to Chester. But the social workers who were responsible for taking care of witnesses thought Chester was no better than the man against whom he offered testimony and on whose account he was killed. Ben thought the premise was right but the conclusion was wrong. Nobody is better but some people are ours.

It started with Chester in a cell alongside another kid who talked too much about what he'd done and why. Chester himself was looking at fifteen years minimum for armed robbery of a tourist couple in the French Quarter. He was a terrible armed robber because he was too big to run away and so had to climb laboriously into a waiting car, whose license plate the victims photographed with the cellphones that Chester had forgotten to steal. Since he had no good way to win his case, he thought he'd help himself out by cooperating. So Ben went to the First Assistant District Attorney: in shirtsleeves, a yellow tie, abundantly pleated pants, bald head the mottled pink of a mole rat.

Ben said:

"I have an offer for you."

"That's the opposite of how this works."

"My client heard the Waffle House killer confess."

"What's he accused of?"

"Murder, dude."

"Your guy."

"Armed robbery. He needs to do no more time."

"I'm not going to offer you that."

"I'm offering it to you, remember? That way, when he's cross-examined, he can say *they didn't offer me anything in exchange for my testimony*."

"You're good. You should have been a prosecutor."

"You said *good* when you meant *amoral*."

"I can't let an armed robber go without any time."

"Any more time. He's been in for fifteen months."

"We're ready to go to trial whenever. That's our motto."

"He'll be risking his life if he testifies. He can't stay in jail afterward. He can't protect himself."

"If he tells the truth, I'll look at his case after he testifies."

"Two months after he testifies. Nobody will be paying attention. That's when you'll look at his case, reduce his charge, and release him with a sentence of time served."

"That would be a very generous deal."

"He's a very sympathetic witness."

"He's an armed robber."

"That's who they put in cells with restaurant shooters."

Jailhouse snitches have plenty of motive to lie and nothing but time to scheme up a good story. Ben thought Chester was telling the truth, though. At least, telling the truth about his cellmate. He did lie, convincingly, when he told the jury on cross-examination that he hadn't cut a deal. He knew in fact that when everyone had moved on, he would plead to simple robbery and get probation. Ben had worked it out. The prosecutor didn't think it was his responsibility to correct Chester's lie. It certainly wasn't Ben's job. That was to help Chester get out of jail, like Chester wanted. Chester did get out of jail, and then he went home and got killed for snitching on the Waffle House killer.

In just such a way, Ben went to the First Assistant to work something out for McTell.

"You remember the murder back in 2005, on Dumaine Street? Four kids in a car?"

"Weren't you suspended?"

"I was still in law school."

"Just now. From your job. For your adventure in the Iberville."

"I took a road trip. It really cleared my head. I feel great now."

"How's our friend Boris?"

"Thriving."

"I heard he's out of the hospital."

"Don't worry about him. I promise he wouldn't worry about you. I have a guy who saw everything on Dumaine Street. He can give you a face and a name. The shooter's someone you'll be interested in."

"Who's your guy?"

"His name is McTell."

"Like the archer?"

"No. The archer? The blues musician."

"Right."

"You don't know who that is."

"No. What's his story?"

"He's a Good Samaritan."

The First Assistant pulled up McTell's record.

"I know this guy. They told me about this guy. This was the guy who shit in the school. The ADA is still salty. What does he want?"

"Just to talk, right now. He's in Cottonport."

"We might be able to find someone to go up there."

"He comes here. You can hold him at Templeman."

"There's only feds and kids at Templeman."

"And Mr. McTell, who will be there in protective custody, in the unit with the feds. My last guy who helped you is dead. You need to take extra care of this one."

The federal detainees were mostly immigrants, held on a contract with Immigration and Customs Enforcement while they waited to be deported. They weren't a threat to McTell because they weren't a threat to anyone.

"Is your guy crazy?"

"He's perfectly lucid about what he saw on Dumaine Street. That doesn't mean he makes good decisions."

"I don't know what's going on here, but I'm not promising you or him anything."

"He just wants to come to New Orleans and tell his story. Queen for a day."

"I'll see what I can do."

"Next week."

"I'll let you know when."

Ben got up to leave. He said:

"Next week? When you have him brought down? Make sure he's the only guy in the van."

"He'll be safe in the van."

"It's not him I'm worried about. He has really bad diarrhea."

"You're committed. I'll give you that."

"Consistency. That's how you know I'm telling the truth."

34

Redaction

Before Ben put McTell with the prosecutor, he needed to know all the details. Otherwise, McTell could get caught out lying or just mistaken and look like his testimony wasn't worth anything. So Ben went over to police headquarters to get the report from the shooting on Dumaine Street. It wasn't the full investigative file, of course. Only the initial gist, by the first detective on the scene, was public record: *911 from unidentified caller shots fired on Dumaine Street b/t Broad and North Dorgenois. First District patrol relocated to scene, Chevy Malibu, Texas plates. B/M, B/M, B/M, B/F, all DOS per EMS. Block taped, top and bottom. Crime scene OS. Multiple casings, .223 or 5.56. Detectives canvassing. Forensics, photographs, statements to follow.*

He lied and said he was on the case, so the cops at Evidence and Property let him look at the pictures and the bloody clothes. The car: Starry glass on the rear windshield punctured by ten black-hearted, white-rimmed bullet holes. Twenty-one casings on the street behind the car and on the driver's side. The kids in the car, at angles tossed forward and back and crosswise, like they were caught forever in uncontrollable paroxysms of laughter. The kids, now removed from the car, lying in the street on tarps all torn up. The police had their effects separately bagged, including a half-smoked joint. None had been carrying a weapon.

He ran Eddie House's record in the sheriff's computer. The guy had been in jail only a week before the shooting on an aggravated assault charge but bonded out. So he had opportunity: back in New Orleans, but not in jail. Ben couldn't get the forensics reports, but the internet told him what a lot of people who grew up around guns, legal and illegal, would have already known: .223 and 5.56 rounds have the same size casings. Either can be fired from an AR15 rifle. The internet also told him the weather that day: 85 degrees, sun. So, everything like McTell said. Four kids in a car smoking weed with the windows down. The killer came up behind and started circling around, shooting first through the rear windshield and then through the open driver's side windows. A Black guy doesn't just walk around New Orleans with a long gun, so he probably drove there, also like McTell said.

Ben ran the dead kids in the court computer. One had been arrested for weed, another for concealed weapons. They were young and they'd probably been away for the storm, so maybe they had arrests somewhere else. But nothing made it look like they were kids who might have run afoul of an actual gangster.

He pulled up the newspaper articles. Profiles of the kids. All New Orleans kids, but two—a boy, Booker, and the girl, Francesca—still living in Texas. That explained the plates on the car, probably a rental because nobody actually drives Chevy Malibus. The articles were the usual: Good kids, everyone liked them, always smiling. Bright futures. Pictures in the papers showed the shot-up car, the casings on the ground. The only box the reporters hadn't checked: No sobbing relatives hugging each other and sitting on the curb. Maybe that's because there were no relatives on scene. Nothing Ben had, in any of the kids' arrest records or the newspapers or any of the investigative databases, suggested any of them lived on that street.

So, if he were putting together the case against Eddie House, the most notorious villain in New Orleans, he would have wanted to know: Why were they there? How did House know how to find them? Why did he want to kill them anyway? Ben went out to the scene, on his own. He wasn't used to doing it alone. He started to call

Boris, four or five times, but Boris hadn't called him and he probably wasn't up for canvassing anyhow. If he'd asked for an investigator at the public defender's office he would have had to explain what he was doing and he didn't want to do that because it looked a lot like he was just creating extra work for himself. Who investigates a case for someone who isn't charged with a crime? He started with the house right where the car had been parked and moved first toward one end of the block then the other. Then the opposite side of the street, starting again parallel with the shooting scene and moving away. But nobody knew or wanted to know or would admit to knowing anything.

"I'm with the public defender's office. I'm here to visit with you about a shooting."

"I was out of town all last week."

"Last week?"

"A little girl got shot. You don't know about that? Who are you, now?"

"Not last week's shooting. I'm talking about a few years ago. Four kids were killed out here in a car."

"Aren't you supposed to have a badge?"

"Public defender means I'm a free lawyer. I help people who get arrested."

"Did they arrest someone?"

"I'm just trying to figure out what people saw."

"Who are you working for?"

"A kid. A boy. Young man."

"Is he the one who did it?"

"No."

"Well, Mr. Public Defender, I don't know anything about it."

Nothing on the block, but he had some follow-ups. A guy who'd lived right across the street but was now in prison. A woman at the end of the block who wasn't home when it happened but who had a friend who *knew all about it*. Another woman two doors down, same side of the street, who'd moved in right after it happened. She said the people who'd lived there before her, a girl and her mother, might know something. They'd seemed in a hurry to leave. She'd taken over their lease a week later, and they were already paid up through the end of the month and let her keep the change. Not only that: She still had a copy of the lease she took over, with the prior residents' names. She was the kind of person, she wanted Ben to know, who kept everything.

That, plus a quick check of a residential records database, sent Ben over the Crescent City Connection to visit Lizzie Douglas in her apartment on General De Gaulle on the West Bank. She opened the door for Ben like they knew each other. She was maybe twenty, wrapped in a bathrobe. In the living room were two folding chairs at a card table. But she sat on the gray carpet of the living room floor and he sat with her, like they were going to play spin the bottle. She was alone. Her mom had gone back to Houston after the shooting. She hadn't been ready to go back. Nothing really for her there. Still now she felt like an orphan, she said. She said it with a kind of resignation, the way you'd say that your husband doesn't fold laundry right. No big deal, the way life is, you're stuck with it. Wouldn't leave over *that*. Eventually:

"I was inside. They were outside in the car."

"Who were?"

"Frankie and the boys."

"Frankie is Francesca Van Buren?"

"She and I were together."

"Like—"

"Like we were in love."

"I'm sorry."

"She was visiting back from Houston. She drove with Woogie."

"Woogie?"

"His name was Booker."

"Booker White."

"You know this better than I do."

"I don't know anything. The names were in the paper."

"We all called him Woogie, 'cause when he was little he called himself Boogie. Like, Boogie Woogie."

She went into the kitchen and made coffee. She was tired because she worked nights at CVS and mornings at Rally's. The afternoon was usually when she slept. It was okay, though, she told him. It was okay to talk about it. Remember the rule: Don't ask if it's okay to go on. Just go on.

"What was happening when they were in the car?"

"Woogie and Frankie came from Houston, so the other guys came by. We went to school together. It was just like usual. I mean, like we used to do. They were in the car smoking weed because my mom didn't have that in the house. That's why I was inside, too. I don't smoke."

"And—"

"I didn't see it. I heard it."

"What did you hear?"

"Just the sound. The gunshots."

"Try and remember exactly what you heard."

"No screaming or anything if that's what you mean. Not from outside. My mom pulled me into the bathroom. She was yelling at me."

"What else?"

"Nothing else. I was lying down in the bathtub. That's where my mom put me. She threw a towel over me. I remember that. A red towel, like we were playing hide-and-seek. Then she lay down on top of me."

The dead girl went to Houston with Lizzie's family during the storm, like an in-law, though she was just eighteen at the time. They stayed in a little shack in a forever-wet neighborhood by a bayou. Like home, down to the nightly shootings. When Lizzie came back to New Orleans, though, the dead girl Frankie was going to stay and finish her last year of high school in Texas. So they visited on weekends, back and forth. Lizzie showed Ben a picture that they'd taken at a club one night, a couple of months before the shooting: Lizzie dressed up in heels and a little skirt, her hair straightened and the bangs dyed red. Frankie in a black suit, dreads, black shirt buttoned all the way to the neck. Ben once referred to the dead girl as her girlfriend, but Lizzie said: *She called me her wife. I know that sounds funny to you. But she called me that.*

Ben said:

"Did you ever hear who did it?"

"I don't know."

"Or why?"

"Something must have happened. Someone had some beef."

Ben didn't kid himself that he could tell what someone else was thinking. Police will tell you they know, from their *training and experience*, when the manager at Rally's is lying to them. They cultivate their instincts on the street until they know when something just smells wrong. Ben just assumed that police themselves were themselves usually lying. Even if they were telling the truth, it was his job to make it look like they weren't, so just skip the part where you try to figure out what's true and what's not. And civilian witnesses? It didn't matter if they were lying or not, since what's in someone's head isn't a fact in the case. But Ben didn't have a case here. He just wanted to know. Boris had said: *maybe if you don't tell people the truth, they don't tell you the truth.*

Ben said:

"I heard it was a guy named Eddie House. Did you ever hear that?"

It could be that she wanted to say yes. But she just shook her head. So Ben said:

"I'm not trying to make you a witness. I just want to know if you heard someone say that."

She got up and went to sit on one of the chairs, so he was still down on the floor, hugging his knees, and she was sitting higher than him. He thought this was okay. People feel safer when they're up high like that. He wanted her to feel safe, if that were possible. She said:

"It wasn't Eddie House."

"You know who that is?"

She nodded and asked:

"You work for him?"

"I don't."

"So why are you asking?"

"I don't think even Eddie House should get accused of something he didn't do."

"You're, like, a Good Samaritan, then?"

A joke, not an insult. Ben said:

"Not that. There's someone, a friend, who wants to tell the police it was Eddie House. I don't want to let him say it, if it wasn't."

"A friend?"

"Someone I used to work for."

She turned up her lip:

"Your friend is stupid. He's gonna get himself killed. You're out here asking questions for your stupid friend?"

"He's in a bad situation. He's trying to get out of it by telling the police it was House. I helped him get in the bad situation."

"You're trying to get yourself out of it too."

"I told you I wasn't a Good Samaritan. I think you want to tell me it was Eddie House. Why won't you?"

She said:

"That would be easier."

"For who?"

"Both of us."

"Why would that be easier for you?"

"I'm just talking."

"Did you ever hear that it *wasn't* Eddie House? Did you ever hear it was someone else?"

That stretch of De Gaulle was mostly car washes and Subways. Signs by the roadside offered to buy your house for cash. Everything was too far apart, like it was born a normal neighborhood and expanded; brown one-story brick buildings hurtling away from each other across a universe of shaggy, wet gray-green grass. Not even blown apart by something purposeful: Just the chaos of separation, the separation of chaos. What the fuck, the usual rules didn't apply to this one anyhow: Don't go without a buddy, don't volunteer information about your case, don't give people an out. Ben said:

"You don't owe me anything. I can't promise you anything if you tell me the truth. I can't even promise I'll keep it to myself. I need to ask you. You know it wasn't Eddie House, don't you?"

"Yeah."

"How do you know?"

"Because I know."

"Because you know who did do it."

She didn't seem like she was going to cry. Her voice didn't break. Instead it was smooth and quick, like she'd said the words so many times, maybe always to herself, that she'd carved out a notch or groove through something hard and old, and the words just slid out:

"He did it because of me."

35

Jail Visit

It was long after regular visiting hours. To punish him for disturbing their nighttime torpor, the deputies made him wait at every gate. They lost his driver's license and bar card for a while. Eventually they got him to a cement block visiting room; twenty minutes later, McTell was deposited too. Plastic chairs, a metal table between them, and a plexiglass picture window through which the duty deputy could have observed them had he not been playing on his phone. The iron bars on the door were all rusted like the place had been underwater since the storm and only recently drained dry. McTell was back in the Orleans orange jumpsuit.

"Why am I here?"

"I had them put you with the feds. To protect you."

"Nobody speaks English."

"That's what I mean. You can't snitch on yourself. We're going to meet with the prosecutor tomorrow. We need to get ready."

"Where's your buddy?"

Ben pretended he didn't know what McTell meant. But McTell persisted:

"You didn't bring that guy Barry, to make me look bad."

"It's not a trial tomorrow. You won't be crossed."

"What are they going to offer me?"

"Nothing yet. They'll offer you something later if they can use it."

"What if I go to the grand jury?"

"How do you even know about that?"

"I talk to people. In Cottonport."

"Talking to people in prison is how you get stabbed. Or chastised."

"I want them to give Robert a break. You tell them that tomorrow."

"He can't even get a break as long as he's incompetent."

"They can make him competent, right? If it's good for them?"

"Let me figure this out. There could be another way to win."

"I thought you were Robert's lawyer? What happened to that?"

Sometimes a lawyer isn't allowed to work for two clients at the same time. There's a problem if you represent a father who is seeking a stupid cooperation agreement to help his son, whom you also represent. As the father's lawyer, you need to tell him not to make a bad deal. But, as the son's lawyer, you might want the father to do whatever he can to help the son, even making a very bad deal that's likely to get him killed. So, as the son's lawyer, you might need to try to get the dad to make a bad decision. You have to talk that through with the son, first. Should I get your dad killed for you? The son might not want that. But you need to advise him on it. What you can't do is just keep the whole thing to yourself because—because of what? Fear? Guilt? Your fragile ego?

"Robert might prefer to have his father alive and well."

"That's my decision."

"Whether I help you or not isn't your decision."

"Did you tell Robert about me?"

"No."

"Why not?"

"I don't know. I should. I'm supposed to."

"You won't."

"Why don't you? Why don't you tell him?"

"You don't know why?"

"He's in jail. You're in jail. That's not going to change right now."

"See if you can get him ten years."

"Just wait."

"You want me to ask if it was your son, what would you do? So you can tell me about your son?"

"Mr. McTell—"

"You think you're better than me because I'm a shitty dad, and you're just a shitty liar?"

It's all true, about not understanding or even really seeing these other lives, no matter how many experts you bring in or moldy school records you collect or front doors you knock blistering paint off of. It's not just Jewish guys from Amherst and Black guys from New Orleans. It was true of Ben's own father. Ben lived with him for fifteen years and listened to his long silence, dug around in his old *tefillin* boxes and found the drugs that quieted his heart so he could let himself sink down deep without a struggle, saw his body on the lake bottom through the clean clear water lying on yellow leaves. Most people don't or can't write a note. You're left to figure out how someone can love his kid and also destroy himself. But some things you do know, even if you're a Jewish guy from Amherst. Of course Ben knew why McTell didn't just tell Robert. Of course he knew why it's easier to do than to speak, and so much easier to keep silent than to tell the truth.

Ben said:

"I shouldn't have said that about you. You're not a shitty dad. You're here."

McTell said:

"I wasn't always."

Ben said:

"And you won't be always. But still."

"Well, if we're being nice, you're actually pretty good at the lies. That's not the shitty part."

"My dad died when I was Robert's age."

McTell wasn't thinking about Ben's dad, but he wasn't cruel either:

"I'm sorry to hear that."

"He taught at a college about language. The way that words mean things."

Shaking his head:

"If he thought words have to mean anything then he wasn't a lawyer."

"He studied the Stoics. These Greek philosophers. It doesn't matter. But he got a thing from them. *If the smoke makes me cough, I can leave the house. The door is always open.* I didn't know what that meant for a long time, and then I did."

McTell smiled:

"I know it."

"What?"

McTell sang, in a rough voice:

"The door is always open and the light's on in the hall."

"I don't know that song."

"It's a country song."

"Not every white person knows every country song."

"This one is Waylon Jennings, though."

"I don't know Waylon Jennings."

McTell was, finally, shocked. So Ben just said:

"The saying means you get to choose how you go."

McTell was shaking his head:

"Waylon Jennings meant that she could always come back to him for sex, because her rich husband wasn't any good in bed."

"Are you even listening to me?"

"Ten years. That's the deal."

"You're not negotiating with me."

"Of course I am."

Even Ben was honest enough with himself to know that. A client always negotiates with his lawyer through yelling or crying or joking or indifference, before the lawyer says a word to the prosecutor. If this is manipulation, it's the normal manipulation of any relationship. People in prison just have more at stake.

Ben said:

"Can I tell you something I did this week?"

"If it ends with the words *ten years.*"

"I went to get the Dumaine Street police report, from the shooting. Because, like you said, it's my job to see if I can put together a theory that backs you up. I need to know the facts in the world so I can figure out the facts in the case."

"That could be a country song."

"I'm going to do an album. *Legal Tender.*"

"You sing?"

"No. So I asked for the report, and I did my investigation, and I learned some things about the shooting."

McTell was still pushed back in his chair. It was quiet there, late at night in the bottom of the jail. He said:

"Look at you, doing your job."

"After I did, I went back to the police station. And I asked them if they kept a log of who requested the police reports. And you know what? They do. So I asked to see the log, and that's a public record, too, so they had to show it to me."

"Your job is not that interesting."

"I run around a lot. When I looked at the log, I saw that one guy had written in from prison to ask for just that same report. But they didn't give it to him. Because a prisoner in Louisiana can't make a public records request. He's not a *person* under the public records law. They have a special definition of 'person' that doesn't include prisoners. That's revised statutes 44:31.1. Maybe you wouldn't have guessed that. But maybe you would have. So then a woman came in from the free world and asked for the same report. A woman you know, actually. Her name is Angeline Johnson."

"The same?"

"The same."

"We don't get along."

"Like earl and water. I know. But there's something you both care about. She got the report. It had some details, like the caliber of the bullets."

"I don't know anything about guns."

"There are guys at Cottonport who do, I bet. And lots of back issues of newspapers, with pictures of the crime scene and everything."

"It's a good thing about those. Not much else to read."

"The girl who was in the car. The dead girl. You know something else? I talked to her girlfriend."

She came back to New Orleans and started messing around with a boy—she knew she shouldn't have, she did love Frankie, and Frankie loved her—and he was jealous of Frankie. That was it. That was why he shot up the car and killed Frankie and three other people. Just because of that. It doesn't need to be a gangster, a professional, a madman. Even jealous kids, even kids with nothing in their heads but want and need and sorrow, can take life. Even kids who need so much more than they want, who don't even know how much they need.

McTell said:

"I hope you said how sorry you were about what Eddie House did to her. Like he did to your friend, your client, who you started telling me about. What was his name?"

"Nehemiah."

"That's a coincidence. Same name as your son."

"The coincidence never occurred to me."

"I wouldn't lie about Eddie House," said McTell. "It'd get me killed."

"You'd have to be crazy."

"I'm going to go talk to the prosecutor tomorrow. I'm going to tell him what happened, what that guy House did. Are you going to be my lawyer?"

Ben nodded. He said:

"It's your truth, huh?"

"And the truth is going to set me free."

The visit was over. McTell went and banged on the bars. Eventually a guard came and shackled his hands for transport. McTell turned back as he left the cell:

"The door's open now, Ben."

A guard walked Ben out and left him at the top of the hall, then just went away. Ben waited for forty-five minutes without seeing another person. Jail isn't usually quiet, but he only heard faint echoes of metal on metal from somewhere else in the building, no voices.

It hadn't taken very long for the surprise to give way. Within months it stopped being strange to him that the city had arrived at this place. Not so long after it started to seem inevitable. The smell of mold rising up and the lead dust falling on the children as they sleep on their mattresses on the floor; the boys lying in state or in triple-stacked tiers in the dank dark of the Orleans Parish Prison, this pig-iron manufactory of justice. He thought it would be strange if it were not this. Every city is built on something; even this shallow city has deep subbasements of cruelty and fear. It grows squarely over its foundations. For just a minute he missed the place he grew up, the hard ground and the sweet cold on his tongue. Hills and hollows; black sticks against snow; mud and green in the springtime woods.

There was nobody in the control room nearby. He didn't want to wander because he was afraid of finding a guard and being accused of wandering. After some time, though, he walked a little ways and looked through a window in a metal door. It was a room with about fifteen men in it. Some were sitting on the floor and a few were standing against the wall. There was no furniture. One was looking right back through the window and his face was eight inches from Ben's, breathing prison breath. Nobody in the room spoke, as though Ben had found a cell of monks or hermits. This was the room for sick call. They'd been there since 8 a.m. They waited in the room and were called out one at a time to meet with the nurse. It had been about two hours since they'd last seen a guard. *Should I try to call someone?*

That was as far as he could go. It wasn't very far. You don't promise people in jail anything about their physical comfort. Your inability to help them on that front is a blow to your credibility, which is already scarce. If he can't even get me a blanket, how's he going to fix the rest of my life? Just don't promise anything.

The prisoner said: *They'll be along.* Ben stepped away from the door. The prisoner went back to looking straight out the little window. Nobody else moved.

36

Colloquy

The judge who sometimes kept a dog in her lap: You'd think she was talking to you, but she'd be talking to the dog. Or you'd be at the podium, entering a guilty plea or otherwise bargaining away years of someone's life, and you'd hear the dog yipping away up there on the bench.

She'd just been elected and there were a lot of old inherited cases on her docket. It made her look bad on the tally of unresolved cases that a self-appointed good government group published twice a year. She wanted to clear away the brush, and the solution was plea day. They'd bring in all the defendants assigned to that courtroom, except the ones the media cared about. Get it all over with in a hurry. The district attorney himself would be there: A moral leper who believed he could make up for being short by taking a wide stance, wearing double-breasted suits, and eschewing both compassion and ethics. He'd offer a deal, good for one day only and at his idea of bargain-basement prices, to each of these men and women.

It went like this. He'd hold a case file in his hands as though physically weighing your life and prospects. He'd sometimes open it, sometimes not. The defense attorney would have a minute to make the case. The judge had already agreed to dole out every sentence that the district attorney approved. The DA would pretend to consider the merits and equities, and then decree a number of years and a "bill status"—an offer about how to consider a defendant's prior offenses. If a defendant pled as a "no bill," for instance, he'd get sentenced like a first-time offender no matter his record. It wasn't just the power to dictate the future; it was also the power to rewrite the past.

The DA wasn't really negotiating, just pronouncing verdicts. Still, a defender was necessary for the whole routine to go off properly. That was Ben, who was assigned to Judge Poodle's courtroom that day. The jailed men and women were brought into the room in groups of eight or ten. Ben would tell them their offers. If a guy didn't want it, the judge might yell at him to think about how he was throwing his life away; if he persisted, he'd be sent to the docks to await transport back to jail. There were more than a hundred cases on the docket.

Ben:

"You're in court today because the prosecutor has a plea offer for you."

Angry, tired man:

"I'm not looking for a deal."

"Let me tell you what they're offering."

"I'm going back to the docks."

"You should know what you're giving up."

"I don't even have time for this."

"Eight, with parole eligibility after four."

"I could do four years."

Once they agreed, they'd have to initial and sign a form showing that they knew their rights. Ben would review it with them, five minutes or less per form. Then four or five or six of them would stand before the court, with their forms all completed and submitted to the judge. She'd run through their rights, getting a yes or a grunt from each: "Do you understand that you're giving up your right to a free lawyer at trial? I need to hear from each of you. Okay." She'd accept their pleas and go on to pronounce the prosecutor-decreed sentence for each of them. Then everyone got fingerprinted, and on to the next round. Ben was the lawyer on forty-three plea forms that day, hundreds of years.

One of the plea forms belonged to Bertha Lee Pate, Boris's client, whose nose had been broken by the police officers of the Fourth District. She was charged with possession of cocaine and aggravated second-degree battery for hitting a cop with a bottle. Actually, she'd thrown a nip at him and it bounced off his shoe. Like an angry flight attendant, Boris said. The cop went out on disability.

Ben knew her because she used to come by the office. She was doing court-ordered drug testing as part of her pretrial release, but she didn't like to test because she was still using drugs. So she wouldn't show up and the judge would issue a warrant for her arrest. Boris started giving her $10 each time she came to the office with proof that she'd taken a test. She started testing almost every day.

The battery-by-nip happened at Cull's Grocery in Algiers, a favorite arrest spot. It sold beer and rolling papers. Cull's was near the police station, and officers would swing by whenever they wanted to goose their numbers. It had a big, empty parking lot and they'd come rolling in at fifty miles an hour, screech to a halt, and make like a commando unit by beating up a bunch of scabby old alcoholics. The police pushed Bertha against the front of a car and said they'd keep doing it unless she told them who sold her the cocaine. She would have told them if she'd known, but that night she was in really terrible shape so she couldn't say, and they broke her nose.

The public defenders weren't the only ones at the courthouse who knew about the police. They probably knew more, though. Clients would talk to them; they'd hear it over and over about the same cops. For Ben and some of the other public defenders, the whole thing was to keep the stories of their clients fractured and discrete. Fever visions: Instances of terrible cruelty that episodically illuminated with too much clarity the world like lightning reveals a broad and harborless sea. But between the flashes you could go back to the smaller, comforting darkness of your cabin. Boris, though, had kept a list. Names, dates, details logged into a chart on his computer: Boys who were beaten and bitten by dogs; prostitutes who were groped and raped;

each officer who lied, who broke the rules. He went around the office every afternoon and surveyed the public defenders for new offenses. He was planning his revenge. To file a lawsuit. To bring down the temple. Or maybe he just wanted to remember. When the revolution came, Boris would name names.

Ben stood at the side of the bench while Judge Poodle sorted through some confusion about the parole status of a would-be pleader. He called Boris's cell until finally Boris picked up. It had been a few weeks and Boris wasn't coming back in to the office. Ben had only seen him once, when he stopped by with some beer that Boris took without really opening the door.

"They have Bertha on the docket."

"She's not for another month."

"She was a late add-on. It's plea day."

"What the fuck is that? Never mind. I can't do it."

"She's here in court. They have a plea offer."

"I'm in St. Tammany."

"She pleads to two counts of cocaine possession. Four years of probation, and she gets released today. Why are you in St. Tammany?"

Boris sounded like he was farther away than just on the other side of the lake. He was silent for a second, and Ben thought he was completely gone. Then he said:

"Released?"

"She got picked up again. It's a new cocaine charge. That's why there's two counts. Why the shit are you in St. Tammany?"

"I didn't know that."

"The arrest was two weeks ago."

"How's Robert, since we're talking about him."

"Stuck. We aren't talking about him. We're talking about why Boris Pasternak, the Kevlar wandering Jew, is in motherfucking St. Tammany Parish."

Boris kept ignoring him:

"What are you doing?"

"I'm trying to get a deal for your client."

"To unstick him. Robert. What are you—Who's yelling at you?"

"It's Poodle. She doesn't want me on my cell in court. Four years of probation. And as part of the deal you tell me what the fuck is going on."

Boris did math in his head. He said:

"She's going to have trouble with four years on probation. How about eighteen months?"

"She's going to have trouble with eighteen months. She's addicted to crack cocaine. Anyhow, you're not negotiating with me. Can you get here? I'll have it put at the back of the docket. There's a few more hours of this."

"Hand the DA the phone. Can you hand him the phone? I'll talk to him."

"It's a good deal. Get back here."

"I don't have a car."

"At least I'm here and not, inexplicably, in that fortress of shititude across the lake."

"You're there pleading people out."

"Dude."

"You don't have standing to *dude* me. Take care of it. Bertha and Robert. Just take care of it."

Boris hung up. Ben talked to Bertha and she agreed to take the plea deal. It wasn't a hard choice. She wanted to get out. She stood next to four other inmates while the judge walked them through their colloquies.

"You're entering this plea of your own free will?"

Everyone said yes.

"Did any of you take any medication today that might affect your ability to understand and enter into this plea?"

Everyone said no. Bertha, loudest of all:

"No, ma'am. I didn't today."

The judge stopped:

"Didn't what today?"

"Take my medication, ma'am."

"Is that affecting your ability to understand what you're doing?"

"No. The medicine just helps me think straight."

They moved on with the colloquy.

"Were you offered anything in return for this plea?"

Everyone said no, until Bertha said yes.

"You were offered something?"

"They're going to let me out of jail."

"Anything other than that?"

"What else could I get?"

"You're not supposed to get anything else."

"Can I get my driver's license back? It's been suspended, for DUI."

Moving on swiftly now:

"Are you pleading guilty because you are, in fact, guilty?"

Four out of five said yes.

"Ms. Pate?"

"I don't have to tell you that. I know my rights."

After some legal education, Bertha Lee Pate's plea was accepted. Court went on until nine that night, when everyone on the docket had pled or refused an offer. The judge and her staff thanked Ben warmly for his help. He was the last lawyer in the building and the deputies locked the doors behind him. He had no files to bring back to his office; he'd kept no paper. None of them were his clients that day.

To his right was the city's downtown, guttering like a gas flame; to his left, Tulane Avenue ran lakebound past empty storefronts and motels used by heroin addicts and prostitutes. He stood there and saw the water rising up the steps of the courthouse, just as it did. He heard it spill into the cellar where they kept the trial evidence, amid plastic bags of cocaine and cash and rusted handguns. It was black and viscous like oil, and did not cleanse but poisoned. All along the avenue, the water left a line higher than his head on the empty buildings. He knew that, far from justice, the law is instead merely ritual;

ritual is neither good nor evil but can celebrate or rehearse either order or disorder. Order, too, has no moral valence but ends in either or both of oppression and equality. He knew that he was a celebrant in a religion without faith. He knew that the city might deserve what it gets for what it does on the backs of its people. He himself certainly did deserve it, whatever it would be. As he walked, he felt the shame of being light and free and also he felt the glory of it, and that too he could not bear. So instead of going home, he went up to his empty office and got a beer and Boris's extendable fork and made a plan.

37

Identification

The night Lillie Scott was killed, a man had been held up unsuccessfully on the same block. That was in the police report. The would-be holdup complainant told the police that he'd been approached by a *male* in a dark-colored sweatshirt. This was how reports were written: *Male* meant the witness couldn't give an age but could give a gender. The male had shown him a gun. When he saw the gun, he took off running. Because of the dark, the police report explained, he didn't think he could make an ID.

The defense didn't have the right to witness names. The names of the people who are going to put you in jail, or who could exonerate you, are among the things you cannot ever be told. So the prosecutor had tried to redact witness names from the police report with a black marker. But because she was lazy or careless or stupid or all three, Ben could still make out some of the letters: First name probably James. Last name, four or five letters, begins with an F-O. Ben figured they were talking about a youngish guy, since it was one in the morning and who else was out then. Maybe from New Orleans, since he was on foot off the big tourist streets. The night he got back to the office after plea day, Ben pulled a list of thirty-four eligible Jameses—Foley, Foti, Foss, and so forth—between the ages of twenty and fifty and with New Orleans addresses. He plotted them on a map and worked outward from the scene of the shooting. He tried to imitate Boris, just to keep walking forward. Get unstuck.

It took a few days to reach the seventeenth guy on the list. James Ford Jr., thirty-one, artisanal baker, who lived in half of a lovely little yellow house shaded by palm trees and looking like it ought to be on a sandy beach and not on a narrow, broken road across from a Victorian mansion in the Garden District. He wasn't there when Ben went by. His boyfriend, who was a big fan of the public defender's office and thought it was terrible how underfunded and overworked they were, told Ben he'd gone to play soccer and afterward to a neighborhood bar to drink. And yes, he said, Jim had almost been robbed a few months back.

The bar was only a couple blocks away, on a corner in the Irish Channel. Ben knew it. He went there sometimes because the owner was a New England expat, too, and the bar showed Red Sox games. Also he knew it because a couple of kids had robbed it that Christmas Eve prior, busting into the barroom in balaclavas, shouting code words to each other like commandos and fumbling their pistols. Ben and Boris were given the case, representing the kid whose prints were apparently left on the door handle, before he went and retained a private lawyer who took the first plea offer on the table. Twenty years.

The dark and cool of the barroom, coming out of the New Orleans midday sun, almost made the heat worth it. Ben stood against the bar with a beer and waited for the soccer team to come steaming in. The Sox were on TV. He could have been a normal person doing normal things, but with his phone already recording and a sheaf of statement paper in a folder and no clue about how to manage what was going to happen next. James, when he came in with a crew of slightly overweight soccer players, walked right over. Tall, a calloused handshake:

"Ben, right?"

James held up his phone and showed Ben the text from his boyfriend warning that a public defender might be waiting for him at the bar. The text described him as balding, thick-rimmed glasses, seemed anxious, probably Jewish. Tough but fair.

"You want to talk to me about the kid who held me up that night. The night that woman got killed in the Marigny."

James didn't mind talking but the condition was that they stay there in the bar. He got a beer. Ben got another.

"Did you guys win?"

"We never do."

"You're like public defenders, then. Also 'cause you drink when you lose. What brought you down to the Marigny that night?"

"We have a friend who had a kind of housewarming party. I was ready to go home, and I hadn't had much to drink, so I was walking to the car. I need to get up early most mornings. Shawn was going to stay later and take a cab. That's my boyfriend."

"Tell me about your conversation with the police."

"Conversations."

"What do you mean?"

"Once when I called them and went to see them the day after I got held up. Then about a week later they came to see me at work."

Ben got out his phone and showed a photo of Robert from the neck up. James shook his head:

"I know who that is. It's the kid they arrested, your client."

"Robert."

"Yeah. I saw his picture in the paper. But like I told the police officer, that's not the kid who held me up."

"You told the police officer—"

"He showed me a picture. When they came to see me the second time."

"Robert's picture."

"Yeah. It looked like this but he was wearing one of those prison outfits. And I told him what I just told you. Don't you get a police report or something?"

"No. I mean, yes. But that's not what the police report says. The police report says you couldn't identify anyone because you didn't see well enough."

Jim Ford, bless his heart, looked genuinely puzzled, like he'd never met a police officer:

"No, that's not right. I don't know why they would have said that.

I could have if it was him. It was right under a streetlight. Honestly, the kid just didn't seem like he knew what he was doing. That's why I ran. I figured he was probably more likely to shoot me by accident if I stood there than on purpose in the back if I ran."

"Did they show you any other pictures?"

"Just this one."

Ben had a few more pictures on his phone as filler. Kids who he pulled off the internet. He showed them to James in succession.

"No. No. Who are these kids?"

"They're just kids."

"There must have been two of them, since your client shot that woman and someone else tried to rob me. Can't your client tell you who was out there that night with him? It's not that one, either."

"It's important to know what other people saw."

"This isn't him. Does your client—what's his name? Robert?—say he wasn't there? Is that it? Didn't he confess?"

"I just need to know what you saw."

"This guy isn't him. Way off. What happens if I do recognize him? Are we going to tell the police?"

We're not. They'd just fix things by convincing Jim Ford he didn't see what he saw. Or they'd charge them both. We're looking for an alternative suspect here, not a co-defendant. We're gonna argue that the kid who held you up also shot Lillie Scott. Ben knew how it was going to go. He was terrified of it. It meant more of a fight and so more of a chance to fuck things up. He wanted to shut off the recorder, get another couple of beers, and sit and watch the Sox fade out of contention over the rest of the summer. He wanted to grow a beard and a potbelly and live in a revitalized mill town that climbs the side of a hill near a New England river and wear boots and flannel against the winter cold. The next one, photo number six, was Willard Thomas. Boris had snapped it when they were sitting on Caroline Thomas's couch and interrogating her son. The witness barely needed a moment. Yes, that's him. That's the one who held me up.

38

Appeal

He called Feliciana and told the social worker that he needed to have an important conversation with Robert. During the call he happened to mention his own son, the sick one, which evoked some kind of appropriate simulacrum of sympathy, and he parlayed that—a guy with a sick kid can't be driving up over and over, got to make this visit count—into an agreement to ease up on Robert's medicine so he'd be awake when Ben visited. Ben waited a couple of days for the drugs to clear Robert's system and then drove up through a rainstorm that made his little goldbug car sway side to side on the causeway. He tried Boris again along the way, but Boris still wasn't answering. He found Robert on the same red plastic chair, as though he hadn't moved, next to men who also hadn't moved. His head angled toward the same muted screen. They went outside to sit under the portico. The rain was still coming down hard and nobody else was out there. The vicious little drops hissed on the grass like fat in a pan.

Ben said:

"I'm here to visit with you about Willard Thomas."

Robert dropped his head like a child who's been caught stealing candy:

"That's my little partner."

"I know."

"How'd you find him?"

"I'm not smart but I sometimes get lucky."

Robert turned his head to the side and looked up, squinting:

"You talked to Willard?"

"I did."

"Did he talk to you, though?"

"Not as much."

Robert was a little bit more alert than last time but still his eyes were vague. He smiled like he was smiling at a memory of someone long dead:

"How's he doing?"

"He was with you the night that Lillie Scott was shot."

"Willard's not like that."

"I don't know what he's like. I just know he brought the gun."

"They're not going to find it?"

"No."

"You know that?"

"I know it."

Robert looked at Ben like he was proud of him. He just said:

"So."

"I also know he was the one who tried to rob that other guy. The baker. Just before Lillie Scott was killed."

Leaning back now, shaking his head.

"He's my little partner."

"I know."

"So."

"So let me tell you a story."

This is a story about a boy who was looking for a friend. No. Lead with values. *This is a story about friendship.* Better. It's about the desperate need we all have for family. For someone to hold on to. Maybe you feel that even stronger if your father isn't around.

In this story there were two boys who came up together. They did everything together: A bigger one—a kid so simple and straightforward that for a while he wasn't even competent to go to trial—and a littler quick one who was always pushing him, always pushing him. Always getting him into trouble and then running away. It even happened in Memphis, when they left for the storm. The littler one maybe did something that got them shot at, and then he just ran away. It was the bigger one who lay down on the ground while the bullets passed by overhead. It was the bigger one who couldn't handle it afterward, who almost killed himself and went into the hospital. In this story, ladies and gentlemen of the jury, it was the bigger one who was always taking the hits for his mean little friend.

They went out one Saturday night, just to look around. The bigger one, Robert, didn't want to go. He wanted to stay home and watch TV. That's the kind of kid he was. He always wanted to be home with his sister and his baby brother. But the smaller one, Willard, he kept at it: Let's go to Bourbon Street. Come on. I got something I want to show you. We'll get some money. We'll get some money to buy things. The bigger one went because they were friends and he was a loyal and loving friend. He needed and trusted his little friend, who helped him make his way in the world. He needed that help. He didn't have much. He was a kid whose stepfather used to beat him and whose mom couldn't make it work. He was just looking for a friend. Someone to be on his side. Willard pretended to be that. So the bigger one went.

Willard brought a backpack with him—a yellow backpack—you can see it on him in video stills as they walked down Bourbon, as he sent his bigger friend to scope things out, as he made his plans. In the backpack was a gun. The same gun reported stolen by Willard's mom. She honestly believed they'd been burglarized. But that's not what happened at all. Her son, who was good at seeming good, who was good at manipulating people, had stolen it. A little silver-barreled revolver with a black handle.

Robert didn't even know there was a gun. He followed his buddy down Bourbon Street and into the quieter areas of the Marigny, while the clever little one looked for an isolated victim. When the gun first came out, it was like something changed in the world: Like a scrim came up and things were clearer. Robert was terrified. But Willard was proud, boastful. He was the bigger one now.

Willard tried a baker, but the baker ran away. That's what the baker would say. That would be a fact in the case. Then that little clever would-be armed robber decided that he wasn't going to get shown up again in front of his friend. He picked another target, a woman: *Watch this*, he told his friend. And he walked up to her and before she could even open her wallet he shot her. He shot her, and then he tried to give his friend the gun. *You take it, you take it*, the gun pushed into his hands, his hands gone so cold it didn't feel like he could wrap his fingers around the grip, *your house is closer*. I don't know what to do with it. *Put it in your yard. No. Your TV. Put it in that old TV. In the back*. The woman lay down on the street so noiselessly, slow like a sheet in the breeze flutters to the ground. And when Robert wouldn't take it, Willard went and threw the gun into the industrial canal, where it would be even today if the canal were dragged.

Ben could sell it to the jury: The innocent kid, stupid, desperate, who took the fall for his quicker, meaner friend. It would ring true. People know about the torque and adhesion of loyalty and belonging: Its twisting force, its binding force. The only disinterested witness put the gun in Willard Thomas's hands, not in Robert's. Of course Robert snitched on himself. Ben could find a dozen psychologists who would say kids are especially likely to make a false confession, that someone like Robert can't weigh peer pressure and the desire for friends to like him against the immeasurable cost of all his remaining days in prison. This was it. It was a theory of innocence. It was a chance to go free.

Robert had stopped shaking his head about halfway through. He just looked at Ben like you look at any stranger.

"I told the detective I shot her. Miss Lillie. Miss Scott."

"You only said that to help your friend."

"I said it because I meant it."

Ben lied:

"They're not going to prosecute Willard. To try to put him in jail. They can't. They've already said they think it was you. He's going to be fine no matter what we say in court."

"He's not."

"You have a chance to spend the rest of your life free. With Willard. With your mother and your sister and your little brother."

"It's not what happened in Memphis, either."

"Your dad, too."

"My dad doesn't like this kind of thing."

Ben could have said: I know. But he did it when he had to, and he's doing it again to help you. Instead of saying that, though, Ben said:

"I went up to Memphis."

"We were there together."

Ben reached across and took Robert's right hand that was over his mouth, the kid didn't fight him or try to pull it away. Ben turned it over on the table so he could see the dark scar from the cut on his wrist.

"I went to Johnny Len's grave. I know about you going into the hospital. I know Willard was there with you. It's okay. I know."

Robert left his arm on the table, palm up and elbow down. He said it without resentment or anger, just a simple statement of fact:

"You don't know."

"Can I tell you what I do know? Sometimes it's harder when you're not to blame."

"I'll take my lick."

"I wasn't there that night. I can't say for sure who shot her. That means I can tell the judge and the jury how I think it happened."

"What you think doesn't change it."

"You feel bad," said Ben. "Right? For not doing more. You don't have to."

"Not doing more?"

"It's called survivor's guilt," Ben said. "Like if you make it through something and someone else doesn't. But you don't have to feel like that. You don't have to—"

Robert said:

"I didn't make it through, though."

Who knows in the end. There are lots of stories you can tell. We need the world to make sense. Sometimes it doesn't. You shouldn't wait until you're a grown man to figure that out. Maybe you're not a grown man until you figure it out.

There's another version of the story, another theory. Late at night on a silent street. The low wooden cottages on either side, cornflower and salmon and marigold, grayed out. The only colors wet green dark along the ground, purple dark above. The two boys just out, looking for anything to happen. First the boy Willard walked toward a man, coming home late from a party: "*Can I ask you something?*" Holding the gun down at his side. The man didn't see the gun at first. He said: "I'm sorry, I don't have any change." Then he saw the light move along the rising barrel and started to run, and the boy let him run. He couldn't do it. He didn't even know what *it* was that he was trying to do. He gave the gun to the other boy, his friend, who came up with him and to whom he was bound.

When the woman came along, Robert said nothing but held the gun out at arm's length like something he had just found and wanted her to examine. She stopped and cocked her head to the side, curious and friendly, like she saw a puppy hiding under a couch. *Oh, hello there.* He walked up close without saying anything and kept the gun out with a crooked wrist. She probably could have reached out and taken it. She looked at him like she didn't understand but she opened her purse. He stood there and he felt himself to be begging even though he held the gun. She had no money. It seemed to him there was nobody else in the street or the world, past and future. The gun was weightless in his hand. Nothing worth taking, but anything is worth killing for. Good kids killed and were killed, and all our kids are good kids.

Ben and Robert talked for a long time. Robert sometimes seeming to nod off, sometimes losing focus, but never wavering. It had never before occurred to Ben that Robert did have a choice to make, and knew it, and had made it. It had never occurred to him because he hadn't asked. He still didn't ask. It made no difference, he thought. What could he do but honor this choice, which he'd done everything he could to strip from the boy? You give and take and try to find some rough justice somewhere.

Ben got up to go. But then Robert said:

"Your son. Who you told me about. How is he?"

"My son. Who was sick."

"How's he doing?"

"He's doing better."

"That's good."

"He'll get home. Everything is going to be okay."

39

Conspiracy

On the way back, still north of the city, he pulled off the highway and parked outside the St. Tammany Parish Justice Center. There was a marble lobby, with wood benches polyurethaned until they looked like plastic. On a bench near the front door a woman was crying. Next to her sat Boris, in a pose that Ben knew too well: Half-turned, eyes attentive but not staring, trying to project patience and steadfast support and at the same time the message that we've got to have this conversation and get on with it. They watched people cry all the time. After some time she looked up and Boris gave her a tissue. He wasn't wearing a suit coat, his right arm still strapped to his chest.

While Ben watched from across the over-air-conditioned rotunda, a woman and her son walked up to him. The kid was twelve or thirteen. The mom stopped a few feet away, as though to reassure him that she meant no harm. He smiled extra wide to reassure her that he had no such need for reassurance.

"Are you a lawyer?"

This happens if you're a white guy wearing a suit in a courthouse, even an old shiny one that your mother bought you years before while you were home for a weekend in law school. Ben demurred:

"A public defender."

"He's got a case," she said. "We want to know if we need to talk to a lawyer."

"An arrest? That kind of a case?"

"It was at school."

It always told him a lot, the first time he talked to a kid in front of his mom or dad. How the kid looked at his parents, or didn't, before he answered; whether they even let him answer. How much the grownups trusted the kid, and how much they trusted Ben. How desperate and frightened they felt. How ready to fight for their kid or how exhausted. Ben asked the kid:

"How are you doing with it?"

The kid looked quickly over at his mom. He was afraid of seeming too okay, like his mom might think he wasn't taking it seriously enough. He also didn't want to show Ben that he was worried. He was a smart kid and gave a letter-perfect answer. Not an admission, not a declaration of unconcern:

"I'm just trying to understand all this."

"That makes both of us," said Ben.

He'd worked on his smile with kids. He didn't want to be creepy or overly familiar or condescending or try too hard to be cool, or all four at the same time, like a youth minister. He wasn't sure he'd succeeded. The kid and his mom wanted to know if they should hire a real lawyer or just take a plea with a public defender. The kid was accused of breaking into his school building.

"If you were my client, I'd tell you we need to have a long talk before you take a plea. I'd tell you not to rush into it. Taking a plea is a big decision. I'd tell you that you have your whole life to think about."

"You could help us?"

"I'm sorry."

They went off and eventually the woman talking to Boris left too. Boris sat back on the bench and Ben went over to sit with him. He waited and eventually Boris spoke:

"Did you just pick up a new client?"

"That kid's going to plead. His mom's going to make him plead. She's in a rush. He's not going to get a lawyer, or even a public defender."

"Fucking parents."

"How's yours?"

"She wants to give up. You can't fight forever."

"You can't or she can't?"

"Or you can't," said Boris, still half-smiling but not looking friendly. "Which is what I said."

"What are you doing?"

"I needed a break. I took a few domestic violence cases. Protective orders and shit. Nobody's dead yet."

"That's not what I meant. How do you even get out here?"

"The bus, sometimes. I took a taxi today. Protective orders are where the real money is. What are you doing?"

"I need a break too. Listen, I did some investigation."

Boris tried to sound uninterested:

"All by yourself."

"It wasn't the same. But I found the guy they tried to hold up first. The baker."

Boris searched the ceiling like he was bored. They were talking low and both sitting with their elbows on their knees, looking straight ahead and not at each other, the last two people in the courthouse, like the players who lost the game for the team sitting in an empty locker room after everyone else has gone home. Ben:

"It was Willard with the gun. The baker ID'd him."

Boris pulled back his lips over his teeth:

"But."

"But Robert won't let me say it in court."

"And you're going to let it sit like that."

"Yeah."

"He's sixteen years old. He doesn't get to decide to throw away his whole life."

"Maybe he can get a plea."

"To what?"

"I don't know. Fifteen years. Thirty years."

"Where will we be?"

Like Ben's father knew, and Boris's father: The door is always open, one way or another, the water or the road. He could find a million new ways to suffer in the middle of this broad country. He could go be the white guy in the corner of a Delta juke joint, hoping to understand misfortune. He could open a little law office in St. Louis and leave behind the romance but not the decay. Chicago, if he wanted to reclaim the promise of a corporate law firm job that was his birthright. Ben just said:

"Not St. Tammany, if we're lucky. We get to choose, though. I need you to do this for me."

"Which?"

"You're going to fuck around here in St. Tammany for a month or two and then you're going to go back to Tulane and Broad. You're going to stay."

"You want me to get him to flip on Willard."

"No. He made his choice. I want you to be there for him."

"What does that mean?"

"I don't know. But you do."

Ben could still hear the wet hiss of air escaping from Boris's chest; he could see his lips and his skin turning blue. He put his arm around Boris's neck, his hand on the back of his head. And Boris, for a second, leaned in to him and put his forehead against him like a child does when he's scared and needs comfort. Then Boris nodded again; yes, he would do it; and Ben left.

The interstate through east New Orleans, past the bayous that hadn't yet been filled in by a city that suddenly stopped getting bigger but never stopped pulling apart. Then up on top of the bridge again. Beneath him the sweet, welcoming, corrupt river that runs through the fraying land down to the poisoned Gulf. Beneath him the city was a thin overlay on the water and the wildness. The air tasted sour.

Eager drillers had opened something at the bottom of the ocean that they could not close, and now there was oil in the air, on the surface of the water, sinking down among the roots of the seagrass and the swamp grass. Lazy, greedy people. We betrayed everything, the water and the ground. Then the little Cavalier crested the high rise over the Industrial Canal and made ninety down into the city, for the last time.

40

Release

In January of 2006, when Ben got to town, there were houses parked across roads in the Ninth Ward; houses still on their concrete pads, but with their frames all forty-five degrees skew; long low houses, undulating like living things, crawling down off their pads as though to burrow for shelter in the huge piles of plank and drywall; houses split in half to show dioramas inside of a past age's life, like in a museum exhibit. The big thing that year was theft of scrap metal. Ben had a client who took the metal front stairs from one of the trailers the Fifth Police District was using as a post-storm headquarters. Because this was a Crime Against The Rebuilding, it was taken especially seriously. Unknown, and not worth knowing, whether drugs were involved. Ben didn't bother finding out. Nobody would have thought addiction was mitigating, anyhow, and treatment rather than jail wasn't an option because the prosecutors were savages and because there was no treatment to be had.

The public defender's office, too, had been emptied out and turned sideways. There were just a handful of lawyers, split between new public defenders like Ben and Boris who didn't know what they were doing and a cohort of older men—all men—some of whom, it was said mockingly, had wings named after them at the state penitentiary. That was more longevity than anything else though. You couldn't help but lose.

Now more of the houses were filling, and new restaurants were opening, and the crowds were getting bigger for music shows and art openings. The new lawyers who came into the public defender's office from all over the country were smart and they cared and they worked hard. New Orleans was a place to go if you were bright and ambitious and wanted to see and feel suffering and be part of it. They said the city was coming back. That wasn't quite right. Like a river: It's diverted, redirects, resumes its course to the sea, but not like before. It runs in a new bed. The city is here for itself, moves for itself, sustains itself. It finds its own level. And *coming back* implies some kind of endpoint: That the city will be what it was or what it never was. But here we are always between sundown and star rise on the sixth day, with creation always becoming, and decaying too.

Whatever had changed, Banks Street didn't look so different than it had right after the flood. A man came walking fast by him in long jean shorts, no shirt. Corded muscles on his arms. He went past like he didn't see Ben and through the doorless entry of a vacant house. When Ben walked by, he saw: The shirtless man stood on bare floorboards, his eyes dark and huge and empty like the house's windows. Every muscle on his arms flexed and held. He dropped his pipe on the ground and breathed out the blue smoke.

On the corner some kids were dealing. When Ben came up on them, they turned very casually and walked away extra slow to make sure he didn't think they were scared. "You should explain to them," an older woman said, from her front porch. "You should tell them what they're doing isn't going to do them any good." "Talk to my lawyer," one of them shouted over his shoulder. A second later a white Impala like the cops drive turned down the street, a block away, and the kids took off in different directions, the littlest of them running as fast as Ben had ever seen anyone move, holding his pants up while he ran.

On the next block there was McTell, sitting on the front steps of an abandoned house under the shade of linden trees.

Ben:

"I tried to visit you at Templeman."

"They cut me loose last night."

"You left an address with the bond clerk. Anybody can find you."

"I follow the rules."

"I guess you went to the grand jury."

"You taught me to be a good witness."

"You shouldn't have gone without me."

"You're not my lawyer. I don't have a case."

"You've stopped paying me now?"

"It's a conflict of interest."

"Fucking jailhouse lawyers."

"They promised they'd give him fifteen years."

"They can't give him anything. He's at Feliciana. He can't plead until he's competent again. You understand? You're not going to get anything for your testimony."

"I am, and so is Robert. A month after Eddie House gets convicted. They'll keep him up there until then. He'll be safe. The newspapers will forget about him."

"He's incompetent."

"They agreed to stipulate to competence. All you have to do is file your motion."

They agreed to stipulate to competence. So maybe the language wasn't special to Ben. He didn't have any secret understanding or knowledge, except the comforting and corrosive knowledge that nothing that happened would really touch him one way or another. A car, a Dodge Charger, made the corner a block away, and slowly turned toward them. The windows were down. Then Ben saw a woman with pink close-cut hair behind the wheel, listening to bounce music; two kids were in the back seat, car-dancing.

Ben can see how it will happen, though. A car—a minivan, or maybe a Monte Carlo, who knows—will make the corner at Roche-blave and turn lakebound toward Banks Street. Driving slow up the block, toward McTell sitting on the porch steps of an abandoned house, his forearms resting on his knees. It will stop easy, just run out of momentum, and a kid, eighteen or nineteen, will stand up out of the back seat. It could be happening in slow motion, like an old TV show. The ground will be wet after a mid-afternoon rain; tall grass along the roadside and the smell of the swamp. Or maybe it will be almost midnight, green and purple.

Does Ben know the child who will come to kill McTell? Maybe he'll be tall, squinting for lack of glasses, a kid who once played basketball for an audience of lawyers and social workers in a prison gym. Or short, muscled, nodding indignantly as his mother works herself into a high dudgeon with lies about his curfew observance. Quiet until you believe he's slow; quick and angry so that you won't notice he's slow; eleven years old, white T-shirt, body cantilevered way out the window of a stolen car as he drives along Louisiana Avenue trying to find his way home, right by the bookstore and a few blocks from the bar where the public defenders sometimes had duck fat fries and Belgian beer. It wasn't strange to Ben that children could kill. Killing wasn't such a special thing that it should be reserved to the grown or the wise. Anyone could do it.

McTell said:

"You're worried about something?"

"I'd rather be inside."

"I'd invite you in but they haven't delivered my furniture. Or my key. How do you feel about climbing through the window?"

"I'm not dressed for it. Let's go to my office."

"I like it here."

"We're less likely to get shot in my office."

"Don't tell me you don't want to be shot. It'll make you more like the common folk."

"That's what I thought the first time, but I remain stubbornly different."

McTell lit a new cigarette. Ben took a step over to the stairs like he wanted to sit, but McTell didn't move over. Ben kept standing. He took off his suit coat. He was sweating through his shirt. McTell:

"When did you see Robert?"

"Four days ago."

"How is he?"

"He's a good kid."

"How does he seem?"

"Tired."

"Your plan for him didn't work."

"It could have. But Robert had a different plan. Like father."

A little ways down, there was a circle of six or seven mismatched chairs on the sidewalk in front of a narrow red and yellow cottage. Folding chairs, an old cane number, a couple that looked like they might have been plundered from a shuttered school, with paint and ink on them. They were burdened by a few skinny women and a man with an irregularly trimmed beard. In the middle of the circle was a guy Ben recognized from court: A hollow-eyed con-artist lawyer who represented prostitutes and kids whose moms didn't know any better. He was always withdrawing from cases because he hadn't been paid. The public defender would take over the cases, since a defendant with no money to pay that guy had no money left at all. He was waving a book and preaching, words Ben was grateful he couldn't hear.

McTell leaned back against the steps and spread his arms out on the porch. Ben hadn't seen him before outside of a jail or a prison, with the little uncoiled graces of a free man. He looked for a second like he was at home, like a young man sure of his supper. McTell:

"He's got a hustle, too."

"Too?"

"Like you and me. He's got his own—what do you call it?"

"Shtick?

"What? Theory, right?"

"Theory. You need to get into witness protection. They need to move you. You can't stay here if you went to the grand jury."

"That's why I can stay. It doesn't matter what happens now. It's all recorded. I kept my end of the deal."

"You're sure they're going to keep theirs?"

"That's your job. You're going to do it?"

"I found someone who will. Your friend Barry."

Ben thought about McTell sitting by his silent son's bedside in a high room at a Memphis hospital, watching through smoked glass the aimless, unknown city. He remembered his own days during his father's mourning period: On a little wooden stool on the floor of their family room, the mirrors covered, his meager beard growing in a little bit on his cheeks and chin. His fatally sentimental father who read with him the prophets—Isaiah, Micah, Nehemiah's chronicle of the return—on a porch overlooking green hills, and told him that this too, justice and mercy, was part of his inheritance.

He thought: We are always in the boat with our fathers, at the moment when the good clear water rises up to meet them; they are always there with us, on top of the bridge. We are born needing from them and never give up needing. It's too much for anyone, all that needing. There was Boris's dad, Yevgeny Pasternak, or whatever he called himself now, somewhere in a desert town in California, sitting in a plastic chair with his feet in a plastic swimming pool, at liberty. Ben's own father, lungs filling; he was manumitted, too, by his own hand. They were disloyal, just like we are; they betrayed and abandoned and lied, just like we do; and fell short, again and again. How can we not understand that, in our time? Nobody ever promised us that we would be forever under their guardianship. They didn't, certainly. He thought: We can claim only what we're freely given. And the corollary to that: It's because nothing is holding us here, because we could abandon it and leave, that our loyalty means something. We're all carpetbaggers. A nation of carpetbaggers. It's because we're always wandering, because we were born wandering, that it means something when we make a home; and because we're always looking for a home that it hurts so much when it's time to leave.

He said, but he knew it wouldn't matter:

"You were right, of course. I lied about having kids. But I did have a father. I wish I still did. I wish you would go somewhere else and keep yourself safe."

"I have nowhere else to go."

"There's anywhere else to go."

McTell gestured at the crumbling house on the overgrown street.

"I've got everything I need right here."

Ben was beaten:

"You're a lucky man."

"What about you?"

"I'm lucky, too."

Freedom was the exception; the rule was concrete and iron, men stacked in tiers and boys in rows. Knowing this—knowing that his clients would lose—Ben was always supposed to be speaking not just to the judge and the jury but also to the court of appeals, the higher judges who could review the full record of mistakes and their consequences. Those two things—mistakes and consequences, error and prejudice—are different. The trial judge may make all kinds of errors, but unless they changed the outcome the defendant doesn't usually get a new trial. No harm, no foul. In court, Ben was always trying to make a record of what would have happened differently if the judge had done the right thing. Imagine you try to introduce evidence that the decedent shot first. The judge says you can't. So you make a proffer: Judge, if you'd ruled differently, this is what I would have been able to show the jury. Then the record will show the counterfactual. Something else might have been possible.

That hard gray courthouse, catty-corner from the public defender's office, where pain and love and sacrifice are measured only in years: How long until a childhood is over, until a man comes back to his children, until there's nothing left. Don't be deluded by the fiction of a better world nor the nobility of the profession nor the majesty of the law. There is no faraway future. Sometimes prisoners get released and

they hurt people again. Sometimes they themselves are killed. Ben
had seen mothers stand up and tell judges to hold their sons in jail,
where at least they would be safe. He'd seen mothers cry when their
sons were released, and seen those same mothers crying at funerals.
Still, what can you do? There's only preparation and practice, there's
only duty. There's only the choice in front of us: The forever law of
the sword and the neck. Will you stay your hand or let it fall. Justice
is only today. A woman is crying in your waiting room. A man asks
to go free. A boy faces the end of his life. Is that not something? It's
everything, and it's not enough.

Wildflowers and weeds on the sidewalk, the street layered in sand
and grit. It was said that Mid-City was still coming back after the
storm. In fact, the veneer of a neighborhood had been scratched away
and the land was growing back through. Ben offered McTell his hand.
McTell lifted his own hand off the stair and waved goodbye to him,
a little bit. Then Ben left and crawled back into his little gold car and
drove away, north.

Closing Argument

One more story, in the nature of an epilogue. A story that happened at the beginning, not long after Ben and Boris started as public defenders in New Orleans.

Back then there lived another child, Nehemiah James. He stayed down in the houses that had been built over the old St. Thomas Development. They called these new brightly painted houses the River Garden. Ben had heard that some people in the old St. Thomas, before the storm, used to board up their windows to keep out the bullets. It was better to live in the dark. Now the boards were everywhere, and sometimes it felt as though the dark hadn't let up either.

Nehemiah and his cousin went up to Magazine Street and met a dumb, hungry tourist drunk outside a bar. They offered him drugs and he followed them back into a lot with no lights, where they set on him. When he ran away onto the street, a car hit him and kept going. Nehemiah and the cousin robbed him while he lay there bleeding, with a shattered hip. Nehemiah was fifteen. Ben didn't know—he literally couldn't imagine—why a fifteen-year-old child would do that. That didn't make it either better or worse. Just beyond his ability to understand.

Nehemiah still had the victim's wallet on him when he was arrested, and the victim identified him from a photo array. Ben and Boris went and talked to the victim in a little apartment outside of

Mobile where he lived with his girlfriend and their little daughter. He worked at a gas station. He admitted he'd been trying to buy drugs, but he didn't seem to have any doubt about his identification. They waited to see if he'd show up at the trial. It was a long way to come for justice. When he did, though, Nehemiah pled guilty in exchange for the judge's promise that he'd be placed on probation. It was a good deal. Easier to keep him out of prison because he was charming, and did well in school, and had never been in trouble before. The problem, Ben explained, was exposure to the older cousin. Ben proposed a whole set of plans to keep Nehemiah on the straight and narrow.

Even though there wasn't going to be a trial, the victim asked if he might address the court. This was terrifying. The judge didn't know the full situation. She didn't know it was possible he'd never walk without limping again. The whole deal could have blown up. He came in—still walking on crutches, two months later—and took the witness stand in the tiny courtroom. He was probably ten feet from Nehemiah and looked right at him. Nehemiah in fear and shock. Imagine being confronted face-to-face with the worst thing you ever did.

"I just want to say that I used to be a teenage boy too. I'm still acting like one, too much. I did something stupid going to buy drugs. I have a little girl. I shouldn't have done that. You did something stupid too. I hope my baby forgives me. I forgive you. I don't want you to go to prison. We all have to grow up. We all just have to grow up better. I want you to be okay. I hope you're okay."

Here was something else Ben didn't understand. He had no questions that were small enough for the courtroom, and the prosecutor only ever had small questions. So the victim asked the judge if he could go. But when he was at the door, Nehemiah stood up.

"If it's alright," he said, "I want to say I'm sorry."

"That would be alright."

"Would you shake my hand?"

"That would be alright."

He handed his crutch to the bailiff, and Nehemiah shook his hand. "You're a good kid. You're gonna be okay." He was, for a while. Nehemiah did well on probation as far as Ben knew, which wasn't very far. Ben was on to the next case. He just knew that Nehemiah went to school every day, in the eleventh grade, and he never gave a positive urine test, and his teachers loved him. Boris, though, went to visit the kid every week. He met him after school and looked at his homework, talked to his social worker, smoothed things over with his basketball coach after Nehemiah skipped practice, got him a summer job. He called the kid at night to make sure he was home by curfew. Then four months later Nehemiah was shot right there on lower Magazine Street and he died at the scene. *Squad car responded to shots fired and discovered decedent, B/M, DOS. Fourteen casings in the street.* The report was as complete an obituary as Nehemiah would get.

There wouldn't ever be any suspects, either, because there wouldn't ever be any witnesses. Ben and Boris went door to door. Nobody would talk; nobody saw; none of Nehemiah's friends knew anything about it. Eventually Ben called the lead detective. *You want us to make an arrest, counselor? You'd be saying something different if we'd picked up one of your clients.* That was true. An arrest turned justice into a competition and Ben had picked a team. *Our sources tell us it's a gang thing.* Give me a break. New Orleans didn't really have gangs, just groups of kids who grew up on the same block with nothing to do and the same misery in all of them. *They say your client got into it with Eddie House.* Okay, so there was one real gangster, who everyone knew about but nobody ever testified against. Came up in the old St. Bernard Projects, and after the storm moved into Hollygrove. He was the bogeyman. Everyone put their murders on him. Give me a break, again. Eddie House killed Nehemiah? *I heard it was about your client's trips to Houston. He used to go to Houston with his big cousin to buy heroin. The DEA was following them. Did you know about that?* No, not about that.

When they walked into the church, Nehemiah's mother and sister came over and grabbed and held Boris and cried. The church was small and full. It had been left standing when they tore down the old projects all around it. The preacher asked: "How did you know Nehemiah?" Ben said: "I met him last year, when he was in tenth grade. He was an extraordinary young man." Ben was hoping to pass for a teacher, or social worker, or something. Better that than the child's lawyer from when he chased a kind man into traffic and robbed him while he lay on the ground screaming in pain.

Ben sat with Boris in the choir seats behind the preacher's podium, facing the audience. The preacher spent an hour on his text, the sixth chapter of Isaiah. Boris sat beside Ben, held the Bible in his hands, and read along halting and confounded and afraid like a man making his own translation from a spell book, a necromancer's guide, an ancient and cruel tongue. Ben knew it in the original Hebrew.

Ben thought a lot about Isaiah, the luckiest man in the ancient world. The only big-time prophet in the Hebrew Bible who did not himself experience devastation and captivity. He did everything he could to experience a personal tragedy, and he failed. The coddled cousin of the king, with a long life of prophecy extending across the reigns of some of the most righteous and prosperous Judean monarchs. He lived through the destruction and exile of Judah's sister-kingdom in the north, and even through the siege of Jerusalem, which he repeatedly prophesied would end in the city's doom. But it didn't—at the last minute, the Assyrian army was stricken by the plague of God—and Isaiah had to survive survival itself.

> In the death-year of King Uzziah:
> I saw the Lord sitting on a bench,
> high and supreme,
> and his robes seemed to fill the chamber.
> Seraphim standing above him
> Six wings—

Each one had six wings—
with two, he covered
his face and with two, he covered
his feet and with two he hovered.
And each called to the other, saying:
"Holy, holy, holy!
The Lord of Hosts!
The whole earth floods with his glory."
They shook the doorposts
with the sound of that call,
and the house filled with smoke.
So I said:
"Woe am I.
I am ruined."
For I am a man of unclean lips
and I live among people of unclean lips
but my eyes saw the King, the Lord of Hosts.
Then one of the seraphim flew to me
and in his hand was a coal
taken with tongs from the altar.
He touched it to my mouth:
"See, this has touched your mouth.
Your sin is removed, your offense is atoned."
Only then did I hear the voice of the Lord, saying:
"Who will I send?
And who will go for us?"
So I said:
"Here am I.
Send me."

The preacher didn't talk about the boy Nehemiah. He didn't mention the dead boy even once. So you can be present in your own story even if you are not named. So you can be absent even if it is your story, child. Nehemiah's sister screamed until she had to be half-carried from the room, and the words never stopped nor slowed.

You don't tell the story because you've done anything to deserve it, nor because you are skilled or virtuous. Only: When he chanced to look down from the throne, you chanced to be there with your eyes open, and so he touched fire to your lips. Now you do your best to find the words in whatever language is your patrimony, of law or love or loyalty. But what can you say? Death and miracles; a confusion of winged creatures; the great temple desecrated by his robes, this empty show of power dressed as justice. Those hollow trumpet blasts, flat repeating echoes back and forth. Holy, holy, holy. Wings beat like a rising of startled birds off the water. The whole place trembles like it will fall. What is burning on the altar, to give off that foul-smelling smoke? Children lie in state, dressed in their high-school colors. In the back of the room, boys in bunches in clean black and white T-shirts, tearless, paying respects, shifting on their feet, crossing their arms, impatient to be gone, waiting their turn. They call one to another without words: *Holy, holy, holy.*

Send anyone but me, he thought. What can I say? I am ruined. Something unseen and awful burns on the altar. The grief rises up like smoke, drains down like water, and fills every room in the house and the ground beneath it. The vision is sacred; to speak it is sacrilege. They are not my dead, and I do not have the words to be their witness, a man of impure lips. But I swear my eyes did see them, the fiery angels. Now the whole shallow earth is filled with their glory. It is a seed that someday will be born.

About the Author

Joshua Perry was a public defender in New Orleans for ten years, serving as head of the city's youth public defender and as General Counsel to the Orleans Public Defenders. Since then, his civil rights cases have included representing immigrant children separated from their parents at the Mexican border and suing the FDA to preserve access to abortion medication. As the State of Connecticut's Solicitor General, he leads a team representing the state in complex cases in federal and state appellate courts. He lives in New Haven, Connecticut with his wife and three daughters.